OF BOA CONSTRICTORS, ELEPHANTS AND IMAGINARY WHALES

CAUTIONARY TALES

NORMAN BEAUPRÉ

Dedicated to all those who suffer from the the lack of creative imagination in their lives and live to be wary of cautionary impulses... and for children who know the within of things and need not be cautioned about understanding hidden things. Readers, be child-like and live life fully and creatively.

La vie est faite pour créer tout comme l'a fait le Grand Créateur. C'est son oeuvre qui nous invite à être libre et d'être poussés par le vent d'une sagesse purifiée par l'amour du verbe et de l'espoir qu'un jour nous deviendrons vivace par l'entremise de la vérité viscérale qu'est la parole émise par l'âme en gestation. NRB *[Life is made to create just like the Grand Creator made it. It is his work that invites us to be free and pushed by the wind of a sense of wisdom purified by the love of the word and hope that one day we shall become full of life by means of the visceral truth that is emitted by the soul in gestation.]*

Other works by the same author:

1. *L'Enclume et le couteau, the life and works of Adelard Coté, Folk Artist,* photos by Stephen Muskie, NMDC, Manchester, N.H., 1982. Reprint by Llumina Press, Coral Springs, FL, 2007.
2. *Le Petit Mangeur de Fleurs,* Éd. JCL, Chicoutimi, Québec, 1999.
3. *Lumineau,* Éd. JCL, Chicoutimi, Québec, 2002.
4. *Marginal Enemies,* Llumina Press, Coral Springs, FL, 2002. 2nd ed. LitFire Pub., 2018
5. *Deux Femmes, Deux Rêves,* Llumina Press, Coral Springs, FL, 2005.
6. *La Souillonne, monologue sur scène,* Llumina Press, Coral Springs, FL, 2006.
7. *Before All Dignity Is Lost,* Llumina Press, Coral Springs, FL, 2006.
8. *Trails Within, Meditations on the Walking Trails at the Ghost Ranch in Abiquiu, New Mexico,* Llumina Press, Coral Springs, FL, 2007.
9. *La Souillonne deusse,* Llumina Press, Coral Springs, FL, 2008.
10. *The Boy With the Blue Cap----Van Gogh in Arles,* Llumina Press, Coral Springs, FL, 2007. 2nd ed. LitFire Publishing, Atlanta GA, 2017.
11. *Voix Francophones de chez nous---contes et histoires par Normand Beaupré et autres,* Llumina Press, Coral Springs, FL, 2009.
12. *La Souillonne, dramatic monologue,* translated from French by the author, Llumina Press, Coral Springs, FL, 2009.

13. *The Man with the Easel of Horn---the Life and Works of ÉMILE FRIANT,* Llumina Press, Coral Springs, FL, 2010.

14. *The Little Eater of Bleeding Hearts* translated from the French, *Le Petit Mangeur de Fleurs* by the author, Llumina Press, Coral Springs, FL, 2010. 2nd ed., LitFire Pub., 2018.

15. *Simplicity in the Life of the Gospels---Spiritual Reflections,* Llumina Press, Coral Springs, FL, 2011.

16. *Madame Athanase T. Brindamour, histoires et folleries,* Llumina Press, Coral Springs, FL, 2012,

17. *Cajetan, the Stargazer,* Llumina Press, Coral Springs, FL, 2012.

18. *L'Étranger Extraterrestre,* Llumina Press, Coral Springs, FL, 2013.

19. *Marie-Quat'e-Poches et Sarah Foshay, Dialogue à deux faces,* Llumina Press, Coral Springs, FL, 2013.

20. *The Fallen Divina----Maria Callas,* Llumina Press, Plantation, FL, 2015.

21. *Souvenances d'une Enfance Francophone Rêveuse,* Llumina Press, Plantation, FL, 2016.

22. *The Day the Horses Went to the Fair---Animal Lover and Painter, Rosa Bonheur,* LitFire Publishing, Atlanta, GA, 2017.

23. *Lucienne, la simple d'esprit,* LitFire Publishing, Atlanta, GA, 2017.

Contents

Just a word or two for those who need explanations:

As Antoine de Saint-Exupéry says in his tale **The Little Prince** regarding his very first drawing of a boa constrictor digesting an elephant when he was but a child, grown-ups always need explanations. He says that when adults are shown the drawing made by the young boy, Antoine, they see a hat That was drawing number 1, the closed boa. Next came drawing number 2, the opened one showing the elephant inside the boa's stomach. He tells the reader that adults just could not fathom drawing number 1. They only saw what they called a hat. You give them a drawing and rather than see with their internal eye, the eye of creativity and the imagination, they only see the outside of things. Grown-ups, he postulates at the very beginning of this tale, do not look deep enough nor do they hear the whispers of the inner spirit. Yet, the spirit of things lives bountifully in children who tend to look with their inner eye, the eye that serves them well in detecting the hidden meaning of things. Without explanations and without too many words, they see. It shows that children go beyond the dull, plain and rational practicality of things in their world of imagining and imaging. Children see things through the inner eye of innocence and candor. So sad when one loses this gift of seeing things with the inner eye.

In my book entitled, "Trails Within, Meditations on the Walking Trails at the Ghost Ranch in Abiquiu, New Mexico", I profess to see things such as trails, deadwood, rocks, and desert flowers in a different way by capturing the reality of things through the lens of a camera and deciphering the aesthetic, visceral, and spiritual dimensions of these things. Of course, I have a very active imagination and I attribute this to the fact that I never truly lost the gift of a childhood vision given to imagining things and seeing things as others did not always see them. I clung to this gift as if I did not want to lose a precious beneficial quality that had been given to me. It was not only part of my heart and my mind, but a genuine part of my soul. In this book, I try very hard to define inspiration, intuition and the harmony between creativity and soul-gathering. You see, I infer that creativity emanates from the soul and dwells in all of us as a spiritual power to capture things all around us and transfer them to our imagination where creativity does its work. The imagination is a tool that we have as human beings; it enhances the way we see things and projects them onto our everyday living. Otherwise, things would be ever so dull and uneventful. Children have imaginary friends, imaginary games and colors, imaginary words that they invent. It's an imaginary sense of living. Grown-ups try to rid them of this gift by attempting to instill in them what they call reality through reasoning so that growing up children may be able to better live in what adults call the real world. Oh, the practicality of it all. However, some do grow up to become poets, writers of fiction, dreamers and women and men of such imaginary skills that they change some people's lives by their influence. These grown-ups see reality from a different perspective. They have become fundamentally creative persons. Creativity helps all of us humans to decipher the Creator's work in all its splendor and vivacity, and thus imitate the way things are seen, heard and made in all of creation. That becomes the realm of childlike perception through the imagination. I infer with a sense of obvious truthfulness and confidence on my part that reality is not only found in the practical and sensual modes of perception, but it also belongs in the realm of the imagination at work.

As a teacher for over thirty years, I always tried to give my students the facts, the various levels of the meaning of history and the practical aspects of any given subject in whatever course I designed, but first and foremost, I tried very hard to offer them the opportunity of going through windows and doors of the creative self. Dare to penetrate these openings to see if you will discover things you never thought existed,

I would tell them. There was also the opportunity to add magical elements of words[*la magie des mots*] that can change mud into gold, as the poet Baudelaire said. Poetry can do that. A world map is just not an itinerary and geographical meandering, but it can be seen as an adventure to other lands and other places where the spirit lives and thrives. How? Through the lives and cultural diversity of the people that inhabit this earth. A painting is just not a canvas with colors and some designs, but it conveys an aesthetic power to stir the imagination and propel it to the stars, as Van Gogh did in his well-known **Starry Night,** *La Nuit Étoilée.*

So, inside the so-called hat that every grown-up sees in Saint-Exupéry's tale, there resides an astonishing phenomenon of an elephant being digested by a boa constrictor simply because the author, as a child of six, had read about boa constrictors swallowing their prey whole. He wanted to draw a sketch of what he saw with his delving inner eye. The eye of his imagination. Only he and the Little Prince could see it that way. It's amazing what a boa constrictor can swallow and digest of gigantic proportions. One can only perceive it through one's imagination at work, unless it's done with a scientific procedure best suited for persons of rational intentions and scientific propensities. With scalpel in hand, the scientist opens up the boa constrictor to discover the large prey being slowly digested. However, that is not the intent of the imaginative person such as the little Antoine de Saint-Exupéry. The grown man, Antoine, is a writer, not a scientist who delves into raw scientific facts. However, scientific facts can be imagined in literature, and that is what the Little Prince is all about. There are other planets out there and other beings like the rose being watered by a little alien who seeks adventure and is given a box to house his little lamb. His work has been to pluck up the baobabs that constantly invade his little planet. Now, he leaves the planet to find the secret of his young life, that of true friendship and the quality of love. Most of all, he learns of the secret that is given to him by the fox. That the essential is invisible to the eye and that one only sees clearly with the heart. The essential must be seen with the heart and it's only then that one discovers truth and the transparency of living things and consequential events such as the existence of a rose on asteroid B 612. The heart is linked to the imagination in this tale, and so the inner eye sees more clearly than the outer eye. It's a lovely and haunting tale written by an aviator in exile in New York during World War II, as everyone knows.

As for the imaginary whale, I'm thinking of the whale and Jonah in the Bible. Some versions have it as a large fish while others call it a whale. There's even a song in French entitled *"Jonas dans la baleine."* Be it a large fish or whale, the story tells of how the prophet spent three days in the belly of the beast. He was then spewed out onto dry land. How is this story linked to that of the Little Prince, you might ask. Well, the Little Prince tells us about an elephant inside a boa constrictor, while the Bible story tells us about Jonah inside the whale. One is being digested while the other only spends a short time in the belly of the beast. Both are stories that address the inside properties and possibilities of a given animal. As for the Jonah story, some believe the story because it is a Bible story and, for them, it's a matter of faith. Is it a factual story or a myth, one might ask. Taking myth as an explanation of a phenomenon, we can take the story as a different kind of truth, a creative truth, and not a lie. Some claim that the Jonah story is real because Christ refers to it in the New Testament. He compares it to his spending time in the "belly" of the grave only to rise on the third day. Be it as it may, the Old Testament story tells us about a prophet being swallowed by a big fish. The reader is open to imagine the story the way he or she wants to, but the fact is that it's a phenomenon and the method or angle of the myth suits it very well. One can easily put rationality aside and see this story as a phenomenon and thus believe it as a cautionary tale. The warning being do not oppose God's interests and his commands. Do not be so vain as to dismiss God's bidding when he calls. Don't be an incredulous, fearful and passive Jonah. In Saint-Exupéry's tale, do not belie what the imagination of a child can or cannot do.

Speaking of whales, one might indicate to me that one of the most well-known whales in literary history is the great white whale, Moby Dick. Well, it's not my intent nor my interest to go through literary history and explore all of the whales that have become part of world literature. I'm only interested in those that have captured the world 's imagination by their relationship with creative and spiritual dimensions of human endeavors. **Moby Dick** is such a classic that it would be dishonest on my part to eliminate it and it's huge creature from my explanatory preface. At the very least, the mention of it as a cautionary tale. Ahab, the ardent avenger and eternal hunter of whales, particularly the great sperm-whale that is called Moby Dick, is consumed by his determination to avenge the loss of his leg by the beast that hounds him ever so blatantly constant. The whale that is Moby Dick is thus the haunting figure of a huge beast that serves as a cautionary example of man against beast. Ahab, you see, is the man who is driven not only by revenge, but by some inner drive to hunt and to kill what has become his passion for mastering strength over beast. Ahab will not leave well enough alone. He's devoured by the thought of conquest and the mastery of the great seas, the vast and sought after subliminal territory of the soul in torment. That's what the seas are, vast areas of yet to be conquered unknowns quite often mysterious and alluring. Will Ahab ever really know what he is doing or will the great white whale of the seas devour his very existence as a sea captain. It's more than a cautionary adventure; it's a tale that puts fear in people's hearts and souls. Deep and unimaginable fear that gnaws at one' mind and deep-seated entrails. It's visceral, to say the least. I know, for some, it's just a story.

Furthermore, on another level, adding to the myth of elephants, when we come back to it, there is the parable of the blind men and the elephant originating in the Indian subcontinent. It's the story of a group of blind men who have never come across an elephant before. They learn and conceptualize what the elephant is like by touching it. Each blind man feels a different part of the elephant's body, but only a single part. They then describe the elephant based on their partial experience, and their descriptions are in complete disagreement on what an elephant is. The moral of this parable is that humans have a tendency to project their partial experiences as the whole truth and ignore what other people's partial experiences can provide to fit and complete the whole. One should consider that one may be only partially right and may have partial information and not the entire truth. There are various versions of this parable such as the one about blindfolded men on a dark night touching a large statue and relating their experiencing their versions of touching. The 19th century American poet, John Godfrey Saxe, retold the parable, and thus introduced the story to a Western audience. The story of the "blind men and the elephant" has been published in many books for adults and children. It's a cautionary tale in some fashion since it shows us how misunderstandings occur when partial truths are woven together to make the entire truth misrepresented or twisted. Imagining is not always factual and may present us with convoluted or twisted facts if we are not careful how we interpret them. Whatever the case, imagining is a gift from the gods, one might say, and it is an instrument of being able to peer into the innermost recesses of things and ideas that stimulate the creative processes of the heart and soul. We human beings are able to imagine things only if we have the power of creativity at our disposal. Those who create are those who have an open mind and a sensitive soul. Some of the most creative people are topnotch scientists such as Albert Einstein, Leo Szilard, Andrei Sakharov, Rachel Carson and Carl Sagan among many others, who have the knowledge of scientific facts while remaining humanistic and imaginative in their research and scientific ventures. They have the power to fuse the sciences with the humanities so as to form a healthy alliance between facts and creative fiction. Fiction does not mean untruth, but a different kind of truth, not unlike myth. Added to their strengths as human beings they know well enough to enjoy and even create what is so very important in the fine arts, music, poetry, and all creative effort that goes to form a holistic mind and heart. For them education is ever the formation of the mind that leads to not only the love of knowledge, but the passion of both knowledge and creativity. It has been proven that the best scientists and the most productive ones are those who deeply invoke and relish the humanities. Not only relish but feel passionate about it. Blah, blah, blah, and so forth, you might say. The intended explanations stop here, for I do not want to bore you to death with them.

Now, cautionary tales are stories couched in folklore and preserved in our collective memory to insure that nothing is lost, not even tales and stories. We may not remember every detail of them, but they are there waiting to be recovered, if we so choose. They are part of our human heritage since we human beings are, from the very beginning of times, storytellers. We love stories, we tell them, invent them, and keep them locked in our cache of memories. Of course, there are all kinds of stories and tales. Some entertain, some instruct, some caution us, some even scare us into having nightmares. So cautionary tales are warnings of danger, danger of an action, location or thing. The narrative usually tells of someone disregarding a particular danger and performing the forbidden act or seeking a forbidden location and whatever else it may be. The results are that the violator comes to an unpleasant fate. A cautionary tale may also deal with moral issues and for that reason are often told to children to teach them a lesson about conforming to a rule or for their own safety. Some see cautionary tales as the rigid adherence to conformity. Others use cautionary tales to satirize the intent and taboos surrounding them. Some writers such as Hilaire Belloc, Lewis Carroll and Eugene Field choose to twist the intent of cautionary tales and make them targets of irony and perverse tight-fisted ethics.

My cautionary tales do not revile nor make fun of the traditional intended purpose, that of warning readers about some impending danger of wayward behavior that does not conform to normality or sound ethical behavior. This author is not a moralizer nor is he a preacher of the fire and brimstone kind. It is my intent to weave a yarn out of my imagination that will produce the desired effect of cautioning readers about not seeing things with the inner eye. Seeing with the inner eye means to see with the soul and not exclusively with the rational self. It's perfectly alright to think and to judge rationally. However, sometimes rationality shortchanges the full awareness of things and situations. One must learn to scrutinize things and situations with a holistic perspective. That means mind, heart and soul. Soul has the power to set straight a moral compass that will guide human actions and thoughts according to what is the Creator's intent in fashioning and molding the human spirit. The human spirit is that spark that reflects the divine presence in our lives. If one deviates from the intended purpose of being human with all its potential and strengths, then trouble sets in and one is led down the garden path of misfortune and painful confusion. I fully realize that I am not reaching my full human potential when I deviate and go astray from my moral and ethical compasses. We all know that there is a distinction between right and wrong. Between good and bad behavior. Some call it rules while I prefer to call it guidelines. How does one choose or how does one select the right moves is the big question. Some want to avoid moral relativism by centering on a set of rules that are permanent and solidly based on higher constructs. Is there a higher being that hands out these rules. Some will say yes to this. Others will say no, while still others do not know what to say. I decided a long time ago to base my guidelines on Christ of the gospels and his message of love(Some may interpret this as romanticizing). I certainly do not expect everyone to do the same. I do, however, expect everyone to follow some rules or guidelines that will bolster the moral and ethical behavior of any human being. I realize that I am now in the thick of it with morality and ethics. I do no want to start measuring up the quality and integrity of anyone's moral values. I leave that up to one's conscience. We all have one although some have sublimated it in one way or another. I am reminded of Jiminy Cricket in the Disney film about Pinocchio. He is seen here as the conscience of the wooden puppet turned live as a little boy for whom Geppetto, the creator and wood-carver, has deep affection. And speaking of the story of Pinocchio, there is a scene where both Geppetto and Pinocchio are in the belly of the Terrible Dogfish or in Disney's film, the whale Monstro. There is always a monster when good fights evil, it seems. Are we given a tale that is cautionary and preachy in Pinocchio? For some it is just that. For others it's simply a tale of delight and entertainment.

What I want to do with my tales is to reveal what happens to a particular person or a group of people in a particular circumstance how his or her actions cause one to come to grips with what is good or bad without full realization on their part until the danger comes to a head, like pus coming out of a sore or bad pimple. My cautionary tales are meant to be gentle warnings of what happens when...Well enough of explanations. Here are the tales. Enjoy and be advised of what may happen if...

1.

The Boy Who Ate Pumpkin Seeds

There once was a boy named Thomas-Peter McClarey Thomlinson who had a double first and last name because his mother wanted him to have two first names rather than just one. She also added her own family name to her married name, just to make sure her son would have a full-bodied identification. The first part of the double last name came from her side of the family, the McClareys, while the second part was from her husband's side, the Thomlinsons of Thomasborough, England. Most people thought that the whole thing was very cumbersome, if not ridiculous. The other boys had only one first name and one last name. She wanted Thomas-Peter to be different from the other boys. From birth, she wanted him to be different and carry his differences in his heart and in his presentation of self. And so, she started the whole thing by having him baptized with two first names, and later on, added to his being seen as different. She even made him wear pink and other colors rather the traditional blue-for-boys. Her neighbors laughed at the boy when he wore pink, but she persisted in dressing Thomas-Peter that way while protesting their behavior toward the boy. The boy knew nothing about wearing particular colors, especially those reserved for girls. He grew up thinking that pink was for every child, boy or girl. Sometimes, his mother chose the color yellow or light green for her son, but never blue. Blue was for other little boys, she said. Then, there were the games that Thomas-Peter played and the toys his mother bought him. She did buy him a toy train and a cowboy hat, but she also bought him paper dolls and frilly things that girls like. She did not care what people said. She did as her mind told her to. She did not like to please people who felt indifferent or were totally ensconced in rules and regulations. That's why she disliked the way some people acted when faced with what they called the problem of facing rules with indignant sensitivities. That meant that they did not subscribe to rules that did not please them or rules that went contrary to their officious determination.

The boy's mother, a complicated woman and a multidimensional one at that, was called Mrs. Edwina McClarey-Thomlinson by those who did not know her. Edna-Fay was the name her friends and relatives called her simply because they did not recognize a name given to her by a distant relative at her baptism. So they called her Edna-Fay after her great-grandmother whom they revered. She was a true McClarey, they said. Her husband called her "Hey you" for lack of spontaneous affection. She didn't mind, for she told herself that as long as he provided for the family and did not frequent too often barrooms and pool halls, she could easily tolerate any thing that was of little or no consequence. Her husband, Pearly, was an affable man with a dry sense of humor, but he could, now and then, make people laugh with his corny jokes and his wry smile. He loved Peter as he called him, as he avoided at all costs subscribing to his wife's blandishment of double names. That's how he saw it, a cajoling and enticing way of taking a hold of someone. Of course, Thomas-Peter did not know the difference between being taken a hold of or any device his mother contracted to take over the simple life of her son. It started with names then proceeded with clothing, then toys, and on to other manipulative devices that ensconced the poor son in a marked and decisive way. It was like rubber stamping him like a piece of merchandise and making it her very own. The way she liked it and the way she wanted it to be. The boy grew up that way, the mother's way without knowing what other ways there were. The mother's way. That's what the boy was taught. The father never intruded in the sequence of instruction by the mother. He stayed away rather than become part of the process of educating his child. Not that he was a cold fish or a bland appetizer-kind-of-dad, but he just did not get involved. The son Thomas-Peter had very little attachment with his dad. The father-son relationship was practically non-existent. So, Thomas-Peter continued to wear pink clothes as a child, he continued to play with paper dolls, and he persisted in being attached to his mother who was, after all, his direct line to communication and feelings.

The McClarey-Thomlinsons had no relatives. None that paid them a visit now and then. If they had some, they lived far away. The mother never talked about having relatives on either side. So mother, father and son lived practically in isolation. The neighbors were there in the neighborhood(what would a neighborhood be without neighbors), but the mother avoided them, and the father stayed away from talking to anyone he did not know. So, Thomas-Peter had no neighborhood friends. No friends at all. The mother compensated for that by buying her son lots of toys and lots of paper dolls. She played with her son when she took time to do so, outside of her cleaning and cooking and baking. She never read to him, never spoke of things happening in the neighborhood, in the village, the country or even the world. She never told him tales and stories. She had never nurtured the culture of telling tales. Never. The child that grew up as Thomas-Peter never developed as a boy of culture and delight. Delight of being a boy with a creative imagination and a background of historical facts and cultural enrichment.

One day, the mother received an anonymous note telling her that she was breeding a sissy and that it was a poor thing indeed for the boy to have such a mother. It wasn't signed and had no return address. The mother was angry. She threw the note away, but the message remained in her head for a very long time. Who would want to write a thing like that, she asked herself. The boy, her son, was not a sissy. Sure, he played with paper dolls, had frilly things, and wore pink clothes even at the age of six, but what did that have to do with his identity and disposition as a boy, she asked herself. They were wrong. People who wrote notes like that were wrong, she told herself.

The mother forbade her son to eat any nuts since she thought that nuts were unwholesome if not malicious things to have as part of one's diet. She had heard that all variety of nuts were harmful and that given the nature of harmful things, she refrained from serving any food that had nuts in it such as pecan pie, date nut bread, peanut butter, almond joys, and so many things that she deemed harmful for the boy. The father thought that his wife had lost her sense of reason if not her ability to manage a household and raise a son. He felt that she was too gullible in accepting all prescriptive notions that she came across be it in writing or by word of mouth. He thought that she had become overly watchful of their son since she watched him like a hawk.

Edna-Fay decided to home school the boy because she did not want him growing up with ideas generated by others and taught by mean-spirited teachers. She had had a very bad experience in school while she was under the tutorship of a Miss Constanshiply who tried awfully hard to make her think and learn proverbs. She hated proverbs and hated her teacher for trying to make her learn silly lines of so-called wisdom such as, "The early bird catches the worm", "A penny earned is a penny saved," and "Look with your eyes and not with your nose." Furthermore, Edna-Fay hated the arts since they did not teach her anything about palpable reality, she said. She did not like reading poetry simply because she could not relate to it. It made her squirm in her seat. "Why should we learn poetry when we don't speak that language," she had asked her mother. "We learn it because it's nice and beautiful," had answered the mother. That had not persuaded Edwina. When Miss Constanshiply tried to make her see things in a different way she was used to, like seeing a butterfly or a moth as beauty in flight after a metamorphosis in a dark cell, she only saw them as nasty little creatures that wore down her patience. She did not like cats, dogs, hamsters, or any other pets. She thought they were all pests and demanded too much of one's time. She did, however, like to go to the zoo and look at tigers and monkeys. She did not like elephants, since they ate peanuts and sprayed themselves with a burst of water. She did not mind animals, as long as they were kept in a cage. Her father had brought her to a circus once, but she told him never to bring her there again. She thought that the barker and the trapeze artists were too loud, and they frightened her with their loud voices. Besides, she did not like the lion tamer to strike his lions with a whip. She never would have thought to bring her son to a circus, not even a parade. People in a parade did not impress her. They were too loud and the band music was never good enough for her. She was never satisfied with things and with people. Nothing and no one could satisfy her. The only thing that satisfied her was bringing up her son, Thomas-Peter. The way she wanted to. She was going to mold him into the kind of man that fits into her mold, an extraordinary creature of male subservience. She did not like male dominance, and she was going to do something about that. Her son would not be a pumpkin-head like so many other men in the world who lord it over everyone especially women. That's how she called them, pumpkin-heads because that's what they were, vegetable heads that cannot think or act right. That's how she felt and how she thought.

In the process of bringing up her son, Edna-Fay did not realize that Thomas-Peter had taken a very strong liking to pumpkin seeds. He did not get them at home. No, Edna-Fay would never have provided them. She hated nuts and seeds. The boy got them from his friend at school once he was allowed to go to school with motherly supervision. Later on, he would steal money from his mother's purse and buy pumpkin seeds at Charlie's corner store. The clerk never asked him what he wanted. He simply reached for a bag of pumpkin seeds and gave it to Thomas-Peter who gave him the twenty-nine cents.

One day, Edna-Fay discovered pumpkin seed shells under her son's bed. At first, she thought nothing of it, although she was a bit suspicious until she found bags and bags of pumpkin seeds in one of her son's drawers. You see, Thomas-Peter had nothing to do, no reading, no creative arts in his young life, no storytelling, nothing. That was because his mother never opened him up to such things. He was hungry for those things, and so he found that pumpkin seeds satisfied his hunger for things that had been missing in his young life, but never satisfied. Pumpkin seeds became the equalizer in the limited experiences of his life.

Every day, Thomas-Peter ate bags and bags of pumpkin seeds, and was never completely satisfied. His mother never realized that her son had become a pumpkin seed fanatic. She did not see things that she did not want to see. Day after day, the mother did realize that her son's facial colors were changing. They changed from rosy-pink to a soft yellow. Then, the tint of orange took over his face. The mother started worrying. She thought of bringing Thomas-Peter to the doctor, but she decided against it fearing the doctor would tell her that she was not taking good care of her son. She started giving her son vitamins, vitamin A, vitamin B, vitamin C and then multivitamins just to make sure that her son would have the necessary vitamins to bolster his natural complexion that he used to have. She spent a lot of money on vitamins. She even bought a special cream at the pharmacy that insured users of a healthy glow to their skin. Nothing seemed to work. In the meantime, the son continued to eat pumpkin seeds and grow bigger and bigger in the face. His entire head was bloated, it seems. He started looking like a big squash or a huge vegetable, so that he refused to go out in the daytime. He only went out at nighttime accompanied by his mother who started being ashamed of her son. And, he never stopped eating pumpkin seeds. The mother tried to make him stop his exacerbated hunger for pumpkin seeds. She gave up trying to discipline her child and turn him into a well-polished, obedient young man. She left him alone. Her husband tried to tell her that she could not see what was happening to their son, but she refused to listen to him. She told him that he did not understand what a mother understood. She saw everything with the eyes of a mother who could tell what was happening, she told her husband. "You only see the outside," he told her, "but you don't see the inside." "I see everything," she answered him. "Yes, everything you want to see and that's all," replied the husband.

And so, the boy continued to eat pumpkin seeds voraciously. His skin color was turning orangy and the texture was slowly becoming rough-like and somewhat bumpy like a strange gourd. The mother started to believe that no matter what she did or thought, she was on the right path as far as her son growing up. She would not change a thing, she told herself. Not a single thing. Her eyes saw things as they should be, she said, and her vision sharp and clear. She saw things as clearly as a hawk sees things from a distance. No need to change things just because some minor things changed. She was adamant about that. She left Thomas-Peter to himself and persisted in giving him all kinds of vitamins, even though he fought her insistence on forcing him to swallow them. After a while, he just spitted them out telling her she was wasting her time with vitamins. Weeks passed into months, and nothing had really changed except Thomas-Peter's facial texture and colors. He looked more like a strange gourd than ever before, so that his mother refused to take him outside in the fresh air. The son continued eating pumpkin seeds and throwing the shells in the wastebasket beside his bed. Every morning it was emptied and replaced with a disinfected one. The mother insisted on that. She really believed that things would eventually change. They had to, she insisted.

After a while, Edna-Fay began to have nightmares about her son turning into something other than what she had ever expected. She did not speak about it to anyone, not even her husband. He would not have listened to her anyway. He would have told her that she was making up all kinds of stories just to get his goat. The household began to be more and more glum and colorless. Nothing consequential was happening except that Thomas-Peter was getting more and more glum and less and less talkative. He had a very hard time forming words with his tongue that had become practically numb and formless. Words just swam around the inside of his mouth like eels or un-swallowed food. Fortunately for him, he could still eat pumpkin seeds. There came a time, however, that he could not swallow them anymore, so he spitted everything out into the wastebasket. The mother did not like that at all. She thought that this was very unsanitary. She decided to take away the wastebasket from his room. The situation got worse when the son began to spit pumpkin seeds and shells on the floor. Edna-Fay became angry and told her son that he was living in pig sty, and that she was no longer going to clean his room. "Pigs live like pigs," she told him. "I'm not going to stand for that," she said. "I do not have a son anymore," she added. "He's changed." she told him, and the son simply smiled at her with a very large grin from ear to ear. That exasperated her.

One bright sunny April day, Edna-Fay walked into Thomas-Peter's room only to discover that her son had turned into a giant pumpkin. A big, orange-colored pumpkin with a huge dried-out stem sticking out of the top of the head. Pumpkin seeds splattered the floor. Silence pervaded, and not one word spoken about the boy who ate pumpkin seeds. The mother refused to accept this and never walked into the boy's room after that. Her face remained colorless and glum from then on. The father was the one who fed his son pumpkin seeds. He never abandoned him although he was very unhappy about the situation that his wife had created, he murmured to himself. It had become a very sad situation indeed. The father was the one who had seen coming the dangers of creating a lifeless person who would, one day, turn into a pumpkin. But there was nothing he could do about it, so complacent was he about things and people. He had cautioned his wife about not giving enough freedom to their son, but Edna-Fay refused to listen to him. She had done everything her way, and now she suffered from the lack of acknowledging her failures. The pumpkin boy was certainly one of them. A son turned into a gigantic vegetable. Too many pumpkin seeds can be dangerous, but not enough can make a child listless and cranky for lack of some necessary food. What's a mother to do?

2.

Mister Butterscotch, the Candy Man

He was called Mister Butterscotch because he handed out butterscotch candies wrapped in yellow cellophane twisted at both ends. The kids loved them and asked for more whenever Mister Butterscotch went around distributing them for free. He was a short and fat little man with whiskers that went down well below his chin. His smile was both tantalizing and contagious. He always had bagfuls and bagfuls of butterscotch candies that he took out of his extra large pant pockets. His pants were baggy and were worn below his protruding fat belly. They were clean, but full of creases and wrinkles as if they had never been ironed. He wore an old red woolen hat with a big tassel on his head, and it made him look like a perpetual Santa Claus. Some people said that he had simply appeared in the neighborhood one day and never left. The kids loved him, but some grown-ups were very suspicious of him. Simply because they were afraid of him, afraid that he might do some harm to the kids by some means or other. They did not know how or when, but they were afraid. He was too friendly, they said. Too inviting by his smile and gentle voice. He was too smooth just like his butterscotch candies. Smooth and sugary, they said. Nobody knew his real name, except kids started calling him Mister Butterscotch. He wasn't young and he wasn't old, just about the middle of aging. Where he lived and where he had come from, nobody knew. He simply was a gentle and generous soul who loved kids and loved to spread joy and merriment around him. Yet, most grown-ups wee suspicious of him in spite of his generous soul and his merry presence among them.

One day, people discovered him taking butterscotch candies from the nearby candy store and putting them in his pockets without paying for them. They called it stealing. They reported it to the owner but the owner, Mister Plentiful, told them that he had given Mister Butterscotch permission to take as many as he wanted. People were flabbergasted at such gestures on the part of both men. They could not understand why this was allowed to happen. How could the shop owner take this in stride without saying one word, they said. Mister Plentiful just looked at them and smiled. His teeth flashed white and his lips were bright red. His eyes lit up every time someone asked him about Mister Butterscotch. Who were these two men, people wondered. They certainly were strange, but with a different kind of strangeness about them, they said. No one knew how they had come to their village, why they were there and what they were planning to do. Perhaps they were plotting some kind of scheme. Perhaps they were out to get them some way, somehow. Suspicion, that was the situation that existed with Mister Butterscotch and Mister Plentiful. The villagers became more and more suspicious as the days wore on. One of the villagers, a Mister Padorevsky, people called him the immigrant-stranger because he came from Poland and had not been with them for more than fifteen years, he proposed that someone look into the matter. He himself volunteered.

Most of the villagers were of old stock, four, five and even seven generations of belonging. They all knew one another and all kept to themselves. They rarely went outside the confines of the village. Ramroonden it was called. Ancestry ran deep in that part of the world. As new generations evolved, the young rarely stayed in the village. They would rather explore the outside world where adventure and new experiences awaited them. Besides, there was no work to be found in Ramroonden, only trades like the bread maker and the barber that had been handed down from father to son, if there was a son to take over. Nothing seemed to move too fast in this village. It was as if time had slowed down so much that one could hear the ticking of the clocks minute by minute and hour by hour. The pace of living was truly very slow and no one tried to hasten it. It would have been inconceivable to change things around. There was a time to live, a time to work, a time to grow and a time to die. And so, the pace of living was very precise and measured by the ticking of the clock. TIME was written on the villagers' faces and no one went against time and commonplace gestures such as doing things the old-fashioned way. It was as if time had stood still since the very beginning of the village. Modernization was not known, nor was it sought. Modernization would only change things and make people strangers to themselves and to others. Furthermore, technology was a strange word for them as well as a strange concept not to be learned. It was safer to live in a place where things did not change. The good old days, it was called.

Even though the villagers accepted Mister Plentiful and Mister Butterscotch in their midst, they could not bring themselves to make them their own as villagers. They were by far strangers. That's what they all said. Except the kids who could care less about the subject. All they were interested in were the butterscotch candies wrapped in yellow cellophane and twisted at both ends.

It was a beautiful fall day when the leaves started to change color that little Robbie McDermott happened to go to the village store to get some sugar for his mother. He was home-schooled by his mother so that he could do errands for her even during week days. His mother was baking cookies, those that he liked, the ever popular peanut butter crisps, and she needed some sugar. Errands could very well be integrated with the schooling, she said. Besides, the mother told herself that she kept Robbie at home fearing the outbreak of the flu season. She did not want her son to catch the "bug", as she called it, from the other children. She was very protective of her Robbie. When Robbie did not get back from his errand, Mrs. McDermott started to get worried. She left her kitchen, locked the front door and went to see if she could find Robbie. On her way to the grocery store, she noticed that Mister Plentiful's store was closed. There were no lights inside, and the blinds had been closed. There was no activity there. She shrugged her shoulders thinking that Mister Plentiful had the flu and stayed home for the day. However, Mister Plunkett, the owner of the corner grocery store, was there in his store stocking the shelves with canned goods. He told her that Robbie had been there to pick up a pound of white granulated sugar, and had left right away. She then thought that Robbie might have wandered on Main street in search of Mister Butterscotch for a few candies. But, Mister Butterscotch was nowhere to be found. Strange, she told herself. Main street was completely vacant. No dogs, no cats and no people, and no Mister the policeman, Tom-Rob Farley. It was eerie, she told herself. She started worrying. What might have happened to her son, Robbie. He couldn't have gotten lost, she thought. She looked and looked everywhere she could, but could not find Robbie. Where in the world could he be. Maybe he had been kidnapped. Kidnapped! That was a terrifying thought for her. Kidnapping never happened in Ramroonden. Never! Ramroonden was a village where everyone knew everyone. There were no real strangers in town. Except Mister Plentiful and Mister Butterscotch. They were still considered strangers even to this day. Terrible things can happen with strangers, she told herself. Why Mister Butterscotch could very well be the pied piper who used his candies to lure the children just like the Pied Piper of Hamelin who had used his magic pipe music to seek revenge from the villagers. Terrible things can happen if children are left at the mercy of kidnappers, she said to herself.

Mrs. MacDermott rushed to her friend's house, Miss Pandernagel, a spinster with no children but loved them as her own. Her mother had taught her to be wary of strangers and not to accept immigrants from foreign lands. The spinster lived alone and hardly went anywhere except the local neighborhood. Mrs. MacDermott told Livinia, that was the spinster's first name, how her little boy had disappeared on an errand to the grocer's. She was devastated, she told her. How could he disappear like that without leaving a trace, she added. Someone must have kidnapped him and taken him away from the village, was her theory. She could not think of any other reason for her son's disappearance. Miss Pandernagel tried to convince her that the boy had not disappeared, but had been distracted by some event or by someone telling him tales in the nearby woods. The mother would not accept such an answer. She told her friend that she could not and would not buy such an answer to her query. She would do her very best to find her son and bring him home.

In the meantime, the grocer finished stocking his shelves and bringing the produce from outside where they were displayed for all to see. He went on working as if nothing had happened. The disappearance of Robbie had no influence on him, and he continued to do what he always did early afternoon. However, he started wondering why no one came to his store, and why even Main street was deserted. He told himself that there was nothing wrong. People would start coming out of their homes and looking around as they always did. After a couple of hours, nothing happened. Nothing. Where were they?, he asked himself. Where were his everyday clients? Now, he was really worried that something had happened, and it was truly bad. Nothing like that had happened before. Nothing. All of a sudden, the policeman's wife, Mrs. Farley, came rushing into the grocery store. She was all excited and flushed. She could hardly talk. She blurted out with cut syllables: "Some-thing bad, hap-pened, some-thing real-ly bad." "What is it?, Mrs. Farley," asked the grocer. "Let m-m-e cat-ch my-my breath," she replied and she sat down on the little keg in the middle of the floor. "What's wrong, Mrs. Farley? You look so pale and drawn. I'd swear you were going to have a heart attack." "Don't tell me that, Mr. Plunkett. I think I'm going to faint." "Let me get you a glass of water. Please don't faint on me in my store. I wouldn't know what to do." The grocer rushed to get a glass of water from the back of his store where there was a faucet and some glasses, and he hurried back to give it to her. She gulped down the water and finally retrieved her good sense of clarity and calm. She told the grocer that her husband heard that there was a dead body in the brook in the nearby woods. He had hurried to see what was going on and take a look at the body, if there was one. There was no body in the brook. No crime, no dead body. He went back to the house to tell his wife that there was no body in the brook and that someone had been lying to him. However, as he got closer to town, he remarked that Mister Plentiful's store had been broken into and the lights were on all over the place. He thought that was strange since he knew that the store was totally dark before. He did not know what to make of it. He went inside the store and saw no one there. He looked around and found a child crouched down behind the counter trembling like a leaf. He began trying to lift him up but the child would not let go of his crouching. He was as rigid as block of marble. Finally, he opened his mouth to tell the officer that he was scared because something had happened that he could not fathom. Mister Butterscotch and his candies wrapped in yellow cellophane twisted at both ends were missing. He could not find him anywhere. He tried to warn Mister Plentiful, but he himself had disappeared. He ran back into the woods where he thought he had seen some candies sprinkled on the ground as if someone had thrown them away. But no Mister Butterscotch. He went to the brook only to find a strange creature who looked like an old man, craggy-face, stooped shoulders, eyes burning with fright, and limping along with difficulty. This creature was ugly and worn by fatigue. He just was not one of the villagers. Who was he?

He ran and ran until he reached Mister Plentiful's store and decided to go in since the lights were now on and the door wide open. He thought he would meet Mister Plentiful there and tell him about the missing Mister Butterscotch. But there was no one there. He began to be afraid, so much so that his shoulders trembled and his knees shook. He hid behind the counter not knowing what to do until Mister Policeman arrived and spotted him there.

Where were Mister Butterscotch and Mister Plentiful? It was a real mystery. Something strange had happened. Really strange. Almost weird. Enough to make one think that weird things were happening all at one, said Mister Farley, the police officer. Finally everybody, well almost all villagers, gathered in the village square and began to chatter away until Mister Farley quieted them down and asked each one of them if they knew what had happened to Mister Butterscotch and Mister Plentiful, and why was the village in such a commotion. No one knew anything. Then someone in the crowd said,

----I know what happened to them.

----What? replied Officer Farley.

----Well, I think, no I know that both of them were in collusion with a gang of strangers that hover around here in the village. They seek to separate all of us and to render us enemies.

----Enemies? someone said with a bold surprise.

----Yes, enemies, I tell you. Enemies are what separate people from people, friends from friends, and families from families. Until we learn to recognize evil in our midst, we shall remain vulnerable and prone to evil ways of strangers.

----How do you know that? replied Officer Farley.

----I know because I know. I'm the true discoverer of things and of people.

----That's a lie, answered a man with a hat holding on to a cane standing in the background.

----You, Magritte-la patte, shut up and don't tell lies to these good people here.

----You know very well, replied the man with the hat, that I know you and I know that you yourself tell lies. You're a liar.

-----Shut up, answered Magritte-la-patte. Just you shut up.

Office Farley intervened and quieted the two men quarreling. Other people tried to speak up but no one had an answer to Officer Farley's question as to where were Mister Butterscotch and Mister Plentiful.

-----Good riddance, shouted Magritte-la-patte.

----Don't say that, said a young woman in the front row. They're both good men.

-----No, they're both strangers to all of us.

----No, shouted an elderly woman who wore red woolen gloves. They're both one of us and not strangers. They've been with us over a dozen years. One gives butterscotch candies wrapped in yellow cellophane twisted at both ends while the other runs a little store where we all go to get some supplies and gather bits and pieces of news. Mister Plentiful is always kind to us and the children. Never a bad word crosses his lips. Never.

---- You people don't you know how to differentiate good from evil? asked Magritte-la-patte.

----Officer Farley interjected by saying, Let's not get into a long argument about this. All I want to know are the whereabouts of both men. Does anyone know? For god sakes, please speak up.

The voice of a young boy came hovering over the heads of them all. It was the voice of young Robbie McDermott.

----I know where they are.

----Then tell us. Tell us now so that we may end our search. It's been a great mystery for us all. They disappeared and no one knew their whereabouts.

----I'm not going to tell you where they are because you will hunt them down and put them in jail. They just don't belong there.

-----Who's going to put them in jail, my boy?

----You, sir, Mister Policeman.

-----Only if I find they committed a crime.

----What crime?

----Any crime that's against the law.

----What law?

----Stop being so inquisitive and irresponsible, boy.

----I'm not irresponsible. I'm inquisitive because it's good to ask questions, as my mother says.

----You're irresponsible because you do not mind your elders, that's all.

----I always mind my elders. That's probably why you all think I'm not responsible for my words and actions.

Robbie's mother stood next to him holding a bag of sugar.

----Leave the poor boy alone, shouted an old man in the back of the crowd. He hasn't done anyone any harm.

----Shut up, you scoundrel, shouted Mister Farley. You're nothing but a good-for-nothing dressed the way you are. All in rags and tatters.

----That's not my fault. No one takes care of me and feeds me. I have to wear my rags because I have nothing else and nobody cares, anyhow.

There was great commotion in the crowd what with everyone talking out loud and nobody listening to a single word uttered. Finally, a gentleman by the name of Mister Wodzchek addressed the crowd with these words,

----My friends. I have been with you for over nine years and I have been well received by you all. No one has yet uttered a single ugly word against me. Probably because I have money and I'm always dressed like a gentleman. I am a gentleman and I do have money in the bank. I pay my bills all the time as well as my taxes. I give money to charity and I tolerate everyone be they insiders or outsiders. Now, for the question of Mister Butterscotch and Mister Plentiful. They're safe and sound. Mister Butterscotch is awaiting outside the village ready to dispense his butterscotch candies wrapped in yellow cellophane and twisted at both ends. That's his trademark as a giver and not a taker. As for Mister Plentiful, well, he's a bit exhausted for having run after Mister Butterscotch. But, he's alright now.

----But why did they run away? asked an old man dressed in coveralls with a plaid bandanna around his neck.

----Because they were afraid of this old man who was chasing them. He was a terrible sight to see, I tell you. Thanks to this boy here, he ran and ran while the ugly old man kept chasing him.

----What happened to this ugly old man? someone shouted from the back..

----Nobody knows, said the man from the back of the crowd.

----That old ugly man was not playing by the rules, said Mister Farley. I know because I'm the policeman here.

----What rules, someone shouted.

----The rules of the game.

----What game?

----The game of life, dear people.

----The game of life? That's silly, sir, shouted a young man dressed in clothes too big for him.

----Well, I'll tell you young man. I'll tell all of you. Life and living it is a game, a great big game. We all have to take chances in life. That's the way life is. Some of us are lucky and some of us are not so lucky. Luck is never stable. It's devious many times. Luck is luck and it's never the same for anybody. Some are favored by it while others have to bear the brunt of its capriciousness.

----I'm never lucky, shouted an old woman who wore a purple coat and a mangy feather hat.

----Thank your good chances that you are still alive, lady, shouted someone in the back of the crowd.

----Let the gentleman speak, said a young man to the right of the lady with the purple coat.

----Yeah, shouted several voices.

----Well, my good people, as I said already, luck is fickle and does not spare anyone of its wayward wanderings. It's never on the side of justice and always on the side of happenstance. You have to take what life gives you, good or bad. Now take for example, the two gentlemen you have among you, Mister Butterscotch and Mister Plentiful. They're fine gentlemen but you have not yet discovered their good qualities, their God-given attributes.

----Yes, we have, shouted a middle-aged man dressed in uniform with an emblem on his right-breasted pocket. The emblem consisted of a seagull, a rock and a blue sky. Below the design were stitched the words, "Seagulls fly, rocks sink." It represented the outfit known as the Safety Mariners. They were the ones who made sure that seagulls were well taken care of and never abused by those who threw rocks at them. These people were the ones who never tolerated outsiders be they birds or people. However, birds came from all over the place and never nested at the same place all the time. Some did, but most of them never did since they did not feel wanted by the people of the village called, Ramroonden. .

----But we do want birds in our village, shouted Mrs. Vanderburen, a woman of some character and spite. She was always picky about people who wandered in and out of what she called "her" village. She only wanted good, solid, and permanent inhabitants. No outsiders who brought distress with them. No poor and miserable souls, no beggars, no social outcasts and no one to disagree with her. For after all, she was the oldest citizen and the one to whom people had to bow when greeting her first thing in the morning. She was a lady, she'll have you know. A lady of class and *savoir-faire*, she would tell people day in and day out. She did not want strangers whoever they were or where they came from. Nothing foreign and nothing alien. Why would a community accept vagabonds and strangers in its midst, she pontificated all the time.

----But we all come from somewhere, and we were all strangers at one time or another, shouted a middle-aged man who wore shirt and tie, and who had the most mellifluous voice one could ever wish to hear.

----But we the citizens of this village right here and now are definitely not strangers, said Mrs. Vanderburen.

----However, you all come from somewhere else or at least your ancestors came from elsewhere at one time or another.

----Yes, and we can trace our ancestry as far back as two centuries ago, said Herr Schnerr who could trace his ancestors back to Rhineland.

----Not always clean and bright with illustrious deeds. Some of them were pirates and robbers, like you, Herr Schnerr. I know better. I'm the voice of all your consciences, you who hide behind fake ancestries. Do documented ancestries make one better than another? Well, do they?

----At least they put a stamp of authenticity on people like us who have them, said a man dressed with a skullcap..

----How about those who don't have them?

----They aspire to have them but cannot afford to pay for them. That's all.

----That's all?

----Yes, that's all.

----Show me the ones who claim to have such papers and I'll show you liars and cheats. Hypocrites!

One by one, several people started to walk away. Some even ran as fast their legs allowed them to scurry on. Then, an old man, craggy-faced and dressed in ugly rags, wearing his hair all disheveled started to speak to all of them,

----People of Rumroonden, I'm the long-lost relative of both Mister Plentiful and Mister Butterscotch. I'm their uncle who raised them when they were left to die by an old oak tree in the forest. I took care of them and nursed them the best I could. They grew up to be fine young men. One day, they decided to look for a place to stay and live among people who would give them generosity and a sense of identity. I could not continue to take care of them since I was very poor and practically destitute. They wanted to stay on with me, but I told them they had to search for their own fortune elsewhere. That was some ten to twelve years ago. I did not chase them away nor did I choose to keep them beside me. All I told them was to be generous with all people and live in harmony with whomever. Then they found you.

----Why did they come here of all places? asked an old woman with a yellow coat and purple gloves.

----Because they found that the children here were among the nicest children they had ever met. They did not find the adults too generous with their acceptance of strangers, but they decided to stay on and hope that their own generosity would melt away the unkindness of their hearts. They never found out if it ever melted away since the adults kept being unkind to them.

----But we are not unkind, shouted an old man in front of the crowd.

----Yes, you are, sir, for you have not learned to spread kindness throughout your village . You consider strangers as enemies and you never allow anyone to become an integral part of your community. You have to be born here to fit in. As much butterscotch candies handed out freely over the years, there was nothing that sweetened your minds and souls here in Ramroonden. The children ate them and as they grew up they wandered away from this community to find work and hospitality. So you have become a community of old curmudgeons and cantankerous sticks in the mud.

----How dare you insult us like that, shouted an old man wearing a tall hat.

----I dare to because I loaned you my two adopted sons, Mister Plentiful and Mister Butterscotch, and gave them all the money I had to buy butterscotch candies for you miserable creatures, and you haven't yet accepted them as your own. Yes, I was destitute but I had saved enough money over the years to grant enough to my two young men on a venture of identity and generosity.. I'm taking them away from you.

----You cannot do that, shouted Robbie McDermott. You just cannot do that.

----Not I, but the good Lord above who looks down on all of you his created beings and sees your good deeds as well as your failures. You have been found wanting, people of Ramroonden. I, the Lord in rags and disheveled hair, I am here in disguise warning you that my two angels will no longer dispense butterscotch candies to your village. You have not changed your manners nor your intolerance for strangers among you. Why, I was almost assaulted by your Mister Policeman. He thought I was an old unwanted creature hanging around. I was not wanted here, he said to me. So, you have kept your distance and I will now keep mine.

----You can do whatever you want, but please do not take away Mister Butterscotch, said Robbie McDermott.

----On account of the butterscotch candies or the man himself? asked the old stranger.

----On account of Mister Butterscotch, sir. He's such a good person, a kind one.

----Well, I'll see what I can do. Mister Butterscotch has another mission to accomplish, but I'll tell you what I will do. I will allow him to dispense his butterscotch candies in the yellow cellophane paper twisted at both ends to remain with you wherever you see them in candy stores for free. If and when you render kind services to anyone, especially strangers, they will be there. But it at any time your services become corrupted with unkindness, they shall be taken away from you. So, to this day Ramroonden is known for its butterscotch candies wrapped in yellow cellophane and tied at both ends. They're so delicious, people say. Just like the Hershey kisses that have become a trademark of that town in Pennsylvania, an angelic gift from Mister Hershey. As for the butterscotch candies wrapped in yellow cellophane twisted at both ends,well, they still exist in Ramroonden for it seems evident to all that unkindness with strangers has not grown but has slowly and gratefully been diminished by those who love the sweetness of butterscotch candies wrapped in yellow cellophane and twisted at both ends. A gift from heaven, some say.

3.

Raggedy Ann meets Winnie the Pooh

There is a story about Raggedy Ann and Winnie the Pooh that keeps circulating around but never quite resolved, that is, the story of how the raggedy doll and the Pooh Bear met once upon a time. Raggedy Ann first came unto the world stage in the last century and has been very popular with children, especially little girls who love dolls. As its name implies, it's a doll made of cloth and is very flexible and easy to handle, soft like a bunch of rags put together by any given doll-maker. This doll can be tossed around, slept in bed with the owner, it can be swung around up and down, and it can be easily left here and there only to be found afterwards. It has red yarn for hair and a triangular nose. It has dark button eyes and wears a perpetual smile on its face. It can be dragged around anywhere; if it gets dirty then the mother can just throw it in the washing machine, then the dryer. The doll usually has a heart printed on its chest. Yes, it has a heart just like humans do, but it's outside and not inside. Little girls and little boys can see that very easily. It can come alive if the owner makes it do so by good use of the imagination, the gracious gift of many children. Raggedy Ann has a fellow doll, Raggedy Andy, but she's the one that most people prefer, especially little girls. Little boys do not usually play with dolls. They are not accustomed to do such a thing by virtue of the many signs of manly behavior around them such as football, baseball and so many other sports activities. Men and little boys much prefer wearing the "Patriots" sweatshirt with Tom Brady's signature on it, if possible.

Of course, some women and girls also like to wear such memorabilia, but little girls love the Raggedy Ann doll. Raggedy Ann is simply the very best doll a child can have. It's a testimony of the past and the future when every toy will be reduced to non-technical or non-digitized forms of toys. Imagine a world transformed by the simplicity of the art of entertainment for a child without all those deliriously exaggerated and supersaturated values of technology at work. Don't get me wrong. I love technology and its power to shape human efforts and our world in transformation, but I dread the day when all will be transformed by technology gone wild. But, we are straying from our cautionary tale.

As for Winnie the Pooh, he was born, or should I say conceived by A.A. Milne who based the character of Winnie after a teddy bear owned by his son, Christopher. Mr. Milne also created several other characters such as, Piglet and Kanga that enter his many stories. Everyone knows that the name Winnie comes from a Canadian black bear that the son often saw at the London Zoo. Pooh comes from a swan the father and the son had met while on a holiday. As for Winnie the Pooh, the author explains that the toy bear is often called simply the Pooh because his arms were so stiff that they stood up in the air for weeks so that the poor thing could not even get a fly off his nose. He had to blow it away, and thus came the simple name of Pooh. So much for names.

Winnie the Pooh is naive and slow-witted, but he is friendly, thoughtful and steadfast. He is often considered to have no brains although he has, once in a while, some clever ideas. Such as riding in Christopher Robin's umbrella to rescue Piglet from a flood. Winnie the Pooh is also creative and has a talent for poetry. His stories are often punctuated by short poems of his "hums." Pooh is also very fond of food especially honey. He is very social and loves to have other characters around him. And so begins our tale of how Raggedy Ann met Winnie the Pooh

Raggedy Ann met Winnie the Pooh one day in the springtime when everything seemed to be in complete harmony and nothing awry in the world of the imagination. Except it was a cloudy day with intermittent rain and the mists of springtime had already spoiled the early morning hours. So that the outdoors were too soggy to play and too forbidding as far as enjoying long walks. It was a day to stay indoors. However, indoors meant staying alone all by oneself and wondering what to do. Aunt Millie kept suggesting ideas about keeping busy, but none of them merited any auspicious care on the part of Raggedy Ann who wanted some fun and excitement. She especially wanted company around her, someone to play with. She had no one and no one was coming to see her. What a miserable plight to be all alone and wondering if someone out there will come and relieve the misery of loneliness. Raggedy Ann felt her heart beating fast while it remained heavy at times. It was a stamped heart on her breast, but it moved and she could feel the pressure of interior movement. Of course, we all know that she had a triangular nose, button eyes, floppy arms and legs, and she was a lovable thing. Yes, she was indeed a thing, but children who held her in their arms or dragged her along as they walked, or especially the little girls who slept with their Raggedy Ann dolls, they thought of her as a living creature. She was indeed alive in their imagination that spun all kinds of things to entertain children. You see, children have a very lively imagination and they can perceive as many things as they so desire. All that a child has to say while playing games with other children, it's night and the darkness of night prevails, or it's morning, and the sun is already up shining bright and early. Or they can say close your eyes and suggest things to the other kids, and there it is a wish come true or a command materialized. All by the power of an active imagination. Is Raggedy Ann an imaginary person? The doll isn't, but the creature that she is by the glory of the vivid imagination of a child is definitely real. Real in the sense that reality is seen through the eyes of a child. It is not the reality of grown-ups, but the reality of one who lives in the world of dreams and the suggestive madness of words and purposeful ideas. In Baudelairean terms, its the suggestive magic of words that weaves tales, poetry and any fabrication of the mind. The body may be at rest, but the mind is ever spinning and spinning thoughts and ideas. So, back to Raggedy Ann, she, or should I say it, can enliven anyone's heart and mind if you let her. However, it takes more than the imagination. It takes the liveliness of one's soul. Now, that's quite another level of being and thinking. It belongs in the realm of creativity. I maintain that the creative powers that are in us lie at the core of the soul. It's a spiritual thing. The spirit moves us and we get the power to create things and ideas through the power of the Great Spirit, the Creator and Great Maker. Now some of you may consider that a little too spiritual and maybe moralistic, but I'm a firm believer in the powers of the Great Spirit much like the original Native dwellers of this planet do and still do today through their descendants. But that's yet another thought to be considered. Raggedy Ann is a toy, a doll and not necessarily a spiritual being. Although she could be if a single soul so wished it and thought of it that way. Spirituality exists want to or not . It's up to anyone of us to hitch one's star to it and soar beyond our wildest dreams.

However, I'm not here to discuss spirituality and the conception of otherworldly things or ideas. I'm here to relate to you the meeting between Raggedy Ann and Winnie-the-Pooh. How did it happen and what happened when they met. You see, I'm going to use my imagination. There's nothing like the imagination at work. "Who are you?" you might ask. I could answer, "I'm the author or I'm the narrator. Whatever works." "Whatever works means what?" you might answer back. Now we're in a quandary. What is a quandary? you might ask. Well a quandary is a perplexing situation or position. It could even be a dilemma. What has quandary to do with Raggedy Ann meeting Winnie-the-Pooh? Well, nothing. We got off track. That's all. Where are we going with this tale? you might ask. Nowhere. Then, let's get on with it.

Raggedy Ann loved to be alive and doing things. She loved the company of children. They enlivened her heart. She didn't think she was pretty, what with her strands of red yarn hair, her painted eyes and her added smile, but she was what she was, a doll made of rags and paint. But what rags! She may have been floppy, soft and easy to manage, light to the touch, and above all, raggedy, as people said. However, she was her own self and nobody could tell her that she was ugly. She was not ugly. She was pretty much what her creator had wanted, a raggedy doll with feelings and filled with friendship and delight for children to handle and enjoy as much as they wanted to. Although she loved children to play with her, she simply adored having the company of other toys and playthings. It was her charm and delight.

Now, one day the doorbell rang and it was a woman with a bear in tow. A plush bear with a smiling face, but with eyes that seemed despondent The woman introduced herself as Wanda and explained to Milly that the toy bear was feeling despondent because he was all alone and helpless. He had no one to talk to or play with. He had told Wanda so. How did Wanda get to know the feelings of a toy bear, and how did she get to understand his words was quite a mystery in themselves. Be it as it may, she understood every thing about this bear that she called Winnie the Pooh. Communication between them was perfectly clear and simple. It was all part of the mystery of the imagination at work. Some humans can understand these things while others do not and cannot take it in. There is no clear sense of intercommunication between a human character and figurative character. I mean, one that isn't flesh and blood.

Enough said. When the two ladies went to the kitchen and left the two playthings in the living room, well things began to happen. The Raggedy Ann doll and the Winnie the Pooh bear started to talk to one another. After introductions that were brief and sort of meaningless, the two toy creatures began to ask each other questions.

----What do you like? asked the doll.

----I like most everything, answered the stuffed bear.

----But what do you like most?

----I like everything. I told you.

----But there must be something that you much prefer over others.

----I don't know.

----What do you mean, you don't know. Are you stupid?

----Don't you call me that. Others do all the time. They think I'm stupid. I may not have much of a brain, but I'm not stupid.

----I didn't say you were stupid. I just wondered why you couldn't tell me what you liked best. That's all.

----It's hard for me to choose one over the other. Like, I like honey very, very much. I also like cookies too. I just like to eat them when humans give them to me. They don't often do that Only in stories.

----Stories?

----Yes, stories people like my Mr. Milne tells about me.

----Oh, yes, those stories. I have some too, but I don't know who writes or tells them.

----I don't suppose my Mr. Milne tells your stories. I don't think he knows you.

----Well, do you like honey best, then?

----I suppose so.

----You suppose so? You suppose so? Don't you know? That's a stupid answer.

-----Don't you go calling me stupid.

----I don't call you stupid. I called your answer stupid.

-----That's just like calling me stupid. Don't you know?

----Yes, I know. I know the difference between calling someone stupid and calling his answers stupid. There's a difference.

----I don't see it. If you call someone's answers stupid, then you infer that's he's stupid.

----No, I don't mean that, and I didn't say that.

----Well, what exactly did you mean and infer?

----Let's stop being philosophical about things. Infer, refer, and all that isn't quite in my vocabulary.

Both of them stopped talking for a while.

----Pooh, what is it that you like best in the whole world? That's all I want to know.

----Why?

----Why? Because I want to know what you prefer in all things and above all things.

----Does it matter what I prefer or not?

-----For me it does. It tells me how you grade things and evaluate things.

----I'm not a professor who doles our grades.

----I know that. You never graduated from school. You never went to school far from graduating with a degree and teaching as a prof.

----I never said I was educated like humans are. I'm just a stuffed bear called the Pooh.

----I'm not educated either, but I have common sense and I know a few things or two. And, I'm not stupid.

-----You're the one who called me stupid.

----I never called you that. I said your answers were stupid, not you.

----That's the same thing. One infers the other.

----Stop using infer as if you were a philosopher.

----You know what a philosopher is. I heard the answer one day while sitting on a park bench and heard two English teachers talking about philosophers. One said that philosophers were somewhat strange and that they always talked in terms one couldn't understand The other gave a definition of his own. He said that a philosopher is like a blind man in a dark room going in circles and talking nonsense. No one notices him and no one wants to hear what he is saying.

And, they both laughed.

----Are you a philosopher, Pooh?

----Of course not. I'm a common sense Pooh. I blow off any fly that sits on my nose and I don't worry about things anymore than I worry about flies on my nose. I pooh them away just like I pooh away silly or stupid questions.

----Don't you like philosophers?

----I do not know any of them. How can I like them or not like them?

----How did we get on this silly question of philosophers, anyways?

----I don't know, Raggedy Ann. I was just wondering how come we get into such a deep and confusing subject the first time we meet. That's all. I like things simple and plain.

----All I was asking was what was your favorite thing in life.

----Here we go again. I don't know.

----You don't know? That's a silly thing.

----Now, don't get started on stupid, Raggedy Ann.

----I didn't say stupid. I said silly.

----That's almost like it.

----Words, words and more words. Why did human beings invent them?

----To communicate with one another. Sometimes they're of no good use. They confuse and mix things up.

----But they're necessary. We all need them to communicate.

----I think we're going round and round without coming to a solution.

----Why do we need a solution? We have no problem before us.

----I don't know, Pooh. The problem seems to be that of not knowing what one prefers over other things.

----Is that a problem for you?

----It's a problem when one does not get the right answer to one's question.

----Is there a right answer to everything?

----Oh, let it go. You'll never answer my simple question of what you like best.

----I like honey. I like cookies, I like Piglet. I like many things. I like them all the same way. No preferences. That's all.

----That's stupid, Pooh.

----Here you go again. There's nothing stupid about liking everything the same way. You're the one who is stupid because you keep insisting that there has to be preferences in the world of ours. Preference make for stupidities and doubts. Well, I have none of that.

----You just do not understand, Pooh. Your mind goes blank and refuses to admit to preferences.

----I do not have preferences, Raggedy Ann. I just don't.

----Well, you're just not like the others. I mean the rest of us playthings.

I know that. It's just a cautionary thing that I exercise here with you. Its doesn't pay to have preferences. Honey is honey, Piglet is Piglet and all things are the same when it comes to being and serving as things of characters you like. I love all things and I love all characters that come across my path. It's that simple.

----I don't understand you, Pooh. I don't understand how you can complicate things. I just don't.

----It's not complicated, Raggedy Ann. It's a matter of not

succumbing to likes and dislikes. Then everything is smooth, just like honey going down your throat.

----So you do like honey more than other things in your bear life.

----I didn't say that. I said that honey is smooth when it goes down. Try it sometimes. You'll see.

----I don't like honey.

The two ladies came out of the kitchen and walked over to the two toys. Millie picked up Raggedy Ann while Wanda picked up Winnie the Pooh. Wanda went out the door holding the Pooh by the arm. As they were going along on the sidewalk, the Pooh whispered to her " I don't understand women. I mean girls like Raggedy Ann." "Why?" "Because they're stupid broads. Stupid redheaded, raggedy, and heartless dolls." Wanda saw the Pooh smile changing to a smirk. A sad and doleful sign of his displeasure. She tried to sew back a smile on Pooh's face but did not succeed in doing so. Pooh remained with a smirk on his face until he realized that he could not spend the rest of his life like that. Raggedy Ann was not going to change what he thought of her and he was not going to spoil his good intentions on the entire matter. No. He was going to smile once again thinking of honey pots, Piglet and so many other things that brought on a smile to his face. He realized that smirks only brought displeasure, countermeasures, and harm to good intentions and good fun. Pooh would not be Pooh without a smile. Throw cautions to the wind and live, he kept telling himself. However, he never forgot the broad with the red yarn hair, the button eyes, and the smile painted on her flat face. She never lost that smile, Pooh told himself. Why not imitate her then and be happy even though he, Pooh, did not always want to. That's when he resorted to his honey pot with pure delight and exquisite flavor and smooth swallowing.

The meeting of Raggedy Ann and Winnie the Pooh had good results since both of them are still very popular to this day. They both have a smile on their face. I like them both. What is your preference, reader? Or don't you have any? I caution you to be true to your thoughts and tell the truth in any event. Oh, why can't I just shut up and write. After all, Raggedy Ann and Winnie-the-Pooh are playthings, not human beings. They can be manipulated like playthings and made to say things that are simply imagined. That's up to the creativity of the writer. Writers can be sane or...hummm...stupid, at times. What exactly is stupidity? Ask Raggedy Ann or even Winnie-the-Pooh. Stupid is what stupid is... oh, alright, that's enough.

4.

The Summer of Clam Digging in the Back Bay

Have you ever gone clam digging? I mean digging with boots on, in the mushy, wet mud of the back bay at Hills Beach? The back bay at Hills Beach used to be where clam diggers went to get the very best of small, mouth watering, freshly dug and shucked clams. If you went there to earn some money selling shucked clams, then you could make yourself some big money out of a day's work. From early morning until sunset. We had a neighbor at Hills Beach who had a large family and needed extra money to live on, and so he spent hours upon hours in the back bay digging clams, and selling the shucked ones to a company that paid good money for them. Bent over like a digger in all seriousness of endeavor, and not daring to lose any time stopping to get a breather, well, the clam digger of the back bay could very easily earn enough money to buy what he or the little woman wanted. I used to go along simply because my mother dragged us, me and my two sisters, to go clam digging early in the morning in the summertime. We lived right there on the banks of the bay. We could smell the bay's low tide mud and the raw fishy smell mixed with the strident sounds of the squawking seagulls. There came a time when, unfortunately, the back bay was closed to all clam diggers for reasons unbeknownst to us. It was unofficially announced that the back bay had become contaminated with something or other. Some called it the red tide. Nobody could explain what it was. The clam diggers all suffered from a lack of being able to go clam digging in a territory that was so familiar to them. Rumors had it that it was the big canning company, the big S that had used its political power and finagling around to prevent little people like us to infringe on their territory and their means of making a profit. Besides, the fishermen and lobster-men of the area were in collusion with the bigwigs to prevent us the non-Yankees, the old residents dating from several generations back, to use the back bay as a clam digging flat. We never knew the real reason behind it. Be it as it may, clam digging was done in hiding, and in very early hours of the morning when the authorities were not there to supervise and catch the culprits. Some people spied on them and reported them to the authorities only to have them pay a fine for so-called illegal clam digging in a flat where it had been forbidden to dig clams.

My mother was devastated upon hearing the news, and was caught digging clams when she thought nobody was looking. She suspected a neighbor named Chauncey whom she had not befriended on account of his unfriendly way with people. He was a mean, cantankerous, old buzzard who liked to laugh at people who could not speak English well. Like my mother whose tongue twisted around each time she tried to pronounce words with a -th, "de tird floor," for example. She did alright in French, but could not get the hang of the English sounds and pronunciation. She tried hard, but could not duplicate the correct verbalization of the English language. She hated it and she despised Mister Chauncey for laughing at her and making fun of her awkward if not deficient pronunciation. He, on his part, did not like people like my mother who did not belong, as he often said in public.

One day, Mr. Chauncey went fishing and caught nothing. He returned to his home and started wondering why the catch had been so bad. Was his bait contaminated? Was his rod and reel no longer good? Did he lose the way of fishing and the skills for a good catch? He wondered out loud until his best friend, Mister Quatramain, came to see him and talk about fishing.

----Did you have a good catch today? asked Mister Quatramain.

----No, not at all, Sid. His name was Sidney.

----How come?

----I don't really know. Someone must have put a curse on me.

----That's not possible. Who could have done that?

----Anyone. But, I know of one who does not like me and my fishing, and is always spying on me.

----Who's that?

----That woman who bastardizes the English language.

----Who's that, Ed? His first name was Edwin.

----Well, you know, the woman with five kids who lives across the way in the brown cottage.

---- You mean the talkative one.

----Yes, and moreover, she's a damn liar.

----What do you mean she's a damn liar?

----Well, she tells tales about people and lies about them.

----Are you sure?

----You can be damn sure about her lies and her way of dealing with people.

----I think you have it in for her. I don't think she's that bad.

----You don't think, well I know so.

---- How come?

----She lies like a drunken sailor, that 's all.

----Now, that's going a bit too far.

----I don't care. I hate the son-of-a-bitch.

----But, she's not a man to call her that. Shame on you, Ed.

----I didn't mean that. I'm so angry about my empty catch this morning and my inability to get to the bottom of it. It makes my stomach turn real bad.

-----But don't blame it on Mrs. Palardy. She's not the kind of woman to put curses on people.

----I didn't mean that she put a curse on me and my fishing. All I meant was she was a busybody and a woman who had a hard time speaking our language. She's been here in the States for such a long time, and yet she can't speak English well. I don't get it. Did you ever hear her say, "Me, I don't know me if he lives on the tird floor or not." Real canuck, as they say.

----She came here twenty years ago with her family, got married and had children. She belongs here. Her trouble with her speaking English is not her fault. Some people simply cannot learn how to maneuver the tongue in order to pronounce words correctly. That doesn't mean they're vicious or bad. They're people like you and me. She speaks both French and English. Can you do that? Speak two tongues?

----I have one and that 's enough. Don't get me going on the subject of languages.

----You started it, my friend.

----I know. I wish I had a civil tongue in my mouth and stop mouthing bad things about people. It's my Yankee stubborn streak and hard-headed way of seeing things, I guess.

----Now, don't get started on vilifying our roots.

----Vilifying?

-----Yes, saying bad things about things and people.

----Why can't I keep my mouth shut once in a while?

----That's because you're as stubborn as a mule and as hard-headed as an ass.

They both started to laugh and guffaw out loud.

----You know Sid, I'm just going to bring some of my clams that I dug up yesterday to Mrs. Palardy as a peace offering..

----But, I thought that the Back Bay had been closed to clam digging for quite a while now.

----Shhhh. I know a way around it.

Now, I do not know if this is a true cautionary tale, but it will do as far as keeping your mouth shut when the urge comes to utter false accusations and plain lies. It's like clam digging. Better to leave the clams in the mud of the Back Bay than to sling the mud, I say.

Aunt Stella's White Furry Cat

My aunt Stella had a very fluffy white cat whose fur was so white and so fluffy to the touch that you could have sworn that the poor cat was only fur and bones. My aunt Stella loved her white furry cat. But, oh, she was a disgruntled and even malicious cat. She would not allow any of us children to pick her up and pet her. She always kept her distance from people, sometimes even my aunt Stella. My aunt called her, "Ma Minoune" which is an endearing term in French for a female cat. Other cats had names like "Penney", "Princess" or "Tabatha." My aunt's cat was simply and affectionately called "Ma Minoune." That cat had thunder and lightening in her eyes. Her eyes would glisten with some inner fury every time you looked at her. If you dared approach her, she would backtrack a bit, pull out her claws and warn you not to get too close to her. I don't know why. My aunt Stella's cat was simply unapproachable.

We lived in Hills Beach in aunt Stella's and uncle Fred's cottage by the back bay. My aunt and uncle lived downstairs and we lived upstairs. My aunt and uncle both worked at a local shoe shop. He was a last operator while she was a top-stitcher. Their cat stayed mostly at home and very seldom went outside. She had a tendency to hide under some soft cushions or behind the bureau in the bedroom. She only came out for feeding time which was somewhere around two o'clock in the afternoon. My aunt prepared her cat food in a special dish and always left it in the same spot in the kitchen where the fluffy and furry white cat found her daily nourishment. She was a cat with a daily routine. She slept a lot, ate when she was hungry and went to the litter box(cat box my aunt called it) for her daily animal needs. Once in a great while, aunt Stella let her out of the house when the cat scratched at the door. The cat would always return after a very short period of time. She would wander a bit around the yard, sometimes go for a stroll on the edge of the bay, and then return home to the luxuriating comfort of her hideaway.

We had a dog named Trixie and Trixie was a lively dog, a Cocker spaniel given to us as a puppy by my uncle Bill who lived in Springvale. He would banter around, play outdoors and was fond of the attention that was eagerly given to him. We loved Trixie. We raised him and spent quite a bit of time and energy on him. We would bring him to the beach and for walks along the banks of the back bay, or out in the yard to play with him and have fun. He loved fun. He loved to explore things and new adventures like the bees buzzing around the tall grasses or the sight of another dog coming into view. He was fun to love and fun to watch, especially fun to show him tricks and games. My mother got to love him, and he was a good companion when we were in school while my father was at work. My mother used to tell us that the dog knew when the time had come for our arrival home after school. He would put his nose on the window in the parlor exactly at 4:25 in the afternoon and wait for our arrival. School ended at 3:25 but it took an hour by bus to get home, some seven miles away from school. There were so many stops, and we were the last ones to get off the bus. Trixie would jump up and down and wag his tail furiously as soon as he saw one of us put a foot into the house. He would calm down after he had greeted all three of us children. He was a good dog, a kind and gracious dog who had a lot of love in him. He was our first dog, and we lavished him with our love. He had a tan and brown coat, button eyes and always a wet nose that he would jut into your hand as soon as you began to pet him. We loved him, my parents loved him and my aunt and uncle loved him, not as much as we children did, but they tolerated him with some affection.

One day, "Minoune" the cat did not return home for quite a while, enough so that my aunt started to worry about her. "Where was she?" she started asking. "She never stayed out so long before. Something must have happened to her. I know." My mother tried to comfort her by saying that sometimes cats like to wander around, and they do not have a sense of time. "At least cats don't," she said. My aunt to insist that her cat had a good sense of time, and she knew when to get back home. "Alright, if you say so," replied my mother.

It so happened that our dog Trixie came home that afternoon, belly full almost dragging on the ground with white furry things and feathers around his mouth. We couldn't believe our eyes. What had he been up to, we wondered, especially my mother. We all wondered what he had eaten that filled up his paunch to an extreme of gluttony. He simply walked very slowly into the house and parked himself on a rug where he stayed throughout the entire day and night. We tried to talk to him and to ease his discomfort of being so full, but he would not respond to our words nor to our gestures. When my aunt Stella saw Trixie in such a terrible stance, belly full and protruding like a giant melon with white furry things and feathers around his mouth, she shouted in disbelief that she knew Trixie had eaten her white cat, la Minoune. She felt horrified at such a thought and told my mother that she now understood why her white cat had been gone for so long. It was a shame, she said, a terrible shame. My mother cautioned her not to jump to such conclusions for she was sure Trixie had not eaten the white cat. How could he? Although Trixie was not too friendly with the cat, for she had not been at all friendly with him even repulsing him when he tried to get close to her, he would never harm her. Aunt Stella refused to accept my mother's caution. She insisted that Trixie had eaten her precious cat what with the white residue around his mouth. Caution did not prevail and she continued insisting that Trixie was the culprit of her cat's disappearance. Why, aunt Stella even stopped talking to my mother. She pouted like a hurt child.

Two days afterwards, my aunt Stella's cat came walking in through the opened door with nonchalance, and with her head uplifted as if to announce that she had returned home. We were all surprised. My aunt Stella was even more surprised. She ran and caught the cat in her arms saying, "My poor Minoune, where have you been? I'm not ever going to let you out again." My mother stood there amused. She looked at Trixie on the floor and cautioned herself in saying anything about the incident of the lost cat and the jumping to an odd and spurious conclusion on my aunt Stella's part. Dogs do not eat cats. By the way, we found out later that, noticing the remains of a seagull on the edge of the back bay, Trixie must have found the poor bird either in distress or in some bad physical shape and had eaten the poor thing. That was our conclusion. Of course, poor Trixie could not tell us about it He simply had the evidence in his paunch digesting it for days. La Minoune remained the haughty and independent animal that she was while claiming dominance over the dog Trixie. She passed by him giving him her haughty look and flirtatious eye. The dog let her be. He had had enough of her and her ways of flaunting her fluffy and furry white coat as if she were a diva or a star. She was no star to us kids; she was just a skinny, furry white cat with her nose up in the air. She knew how to live supreme in my aunt Stella's house on the Back Bay at Hills Beach, Maine. Minoune seemed to say, throw caution to the wind, for here I am, and here I will stay regardless of any circumstance. We thought she was a haughty cat and a naughty one at that. My aunt Stella continued to lavish praise and small delights on her fluffy and furry white cat. I always thought that she was losing her time and patience on this dumb broad of a cat.

6.

The Winter Of Our Content

Children are often glad to see winter coming, especially when it brings them the joyous season of Christmas what with the colorful toy catalog from Sears and Roebuck we had at our disposal. We children at our house would gather in the warm and cozy living room early evenings before the holidays to ponder the choices we had at our fingertips at every glossy and marvelous page of this special holiday catalog. It usually arrived at our house right before Thanksgiving. Sometimes friends would join us in our delight of looking at such a treasure of toys offered to boys and girls. Of course, we were all old enough not to believe in Santa Claus anymore, and we all knew that our parents could not even think of buying us things they could not afford, especially things like bicycles, doll carriages, true-to-life dolls with eyes that opened and closed, Gene Autry outfits, and expensive things like that. But, at least, we could enjoy them with our eyes glued to every page that was turned with delight and anticipation. Our parents always cautioned us not to count on getting any of these things for Santa would definitely not bring them in his sleigh for any of us. We just smiled at the thought of a sleigh-riding Santa Claus since he was but a dream to those who believed the stories about him. Of course, there would be candy, a full stocking by the fire, and some toys. The anticipation of Christmas was ever in our minds and restless hearts. Christmas anticipation was like expecting all of the joys and delights that surrounded us around Christmastime. It was indeed a very special time of year. What was truly important in our lives as children was the intimate presence of both mother and father in our midst. They loved us and we loved them to pieces, as we say. We were three children in our household, and we counted on our mother and father being there. Father kept on working at the mill while mother continued her washing, the cleaning of the house and, of course, baking special treats for us like molasses popcorn balls, chocolate fudge, cookies shaped like a star with sprinkles on top, jams and jellies made from berries that had been culled in early September and stored away in a very cool place, and, of course, pork pies. On top of it all, mother would spend every evening cutting patterns for my sisters' new dresses out of printed cotton fabric gotten from feed bags or specially-priced remnants from Mrs. Therrien's mercantile store on Main Street. She also got to work on a pair of pants for me taken from my father's old Sunday pair of pants, old but still fresh enough on the reverse side to make a pair of pants for the little boy that I was. She was a busy woman, my mom was.

It so happened one Christmas when I was but eight years old and my sisters were seven and five and a half that my mother had to be operated on for her goiter. The operation was to take place in Boston, some ninety miles or so away...at Christmas time besides. My mother did not talk too much about it except that she would be gone for a couple of weeks and would miss spending Christmas with us. She could not help it, she said, because it had to be done, and the dates could not be changed. Her throat was much enlarged and she suffered from pain and discomfort. She looked like a puffed up turkey. It wasn't funny, but sometimes we simply had to laugh a bit.

On a Monday morning three days before Christmas, she, dad and aunt Stella, boarded the train for Boston, and we were left in the capable hands of a dear neighbor named Mrs. Lebel. She told us to pray for our mother and pray hard so that mother would be home soon after the operation. Well, mother was gone for three and a half weeks. In the meantime, father took care of us the best he could.

We three children wondered how Christmas would be with mother gone and my father left in charge. He was a good dad, but a not-too-resourceful man. He lacked the qualities of a gifted individual who could come up with good results. Not like my mother, for sure. But, he was a good man, a kind soul and a generous man who loved his children, and he loved Christmas. The three of us wondered how the gifts and the food would turn out. Without mom there would certainly be things turned upside down or completely forgotten like the Christmas stocking. Dad knew nothing about food preparation, and he was gauche with the handling of things such as washing the dishes, washing our clothes and all of the ordinary things a mother would do around the house. We were surprised at his maneuvers and his awkward moves at times, but he managed very well with the help of Mrs. Lebel to guide him.

One thing I remember so very well about that Christmas that year were the stockings hung behind the stove. We did not have a fireplace. That was for the well-to-do. He had taken three of our long cotton beige stockings that we wore every day, since boys and girls wore them then. He had hung them behind the kitchen stove with oil burners that were heating the house, and hung them there Christmas eve. Well, little did he know that the contents of our stockings would be heated to a point where everything would melt such as the wrapped chocolates, the bubble gum, the hard candies and the tiny candied hot dogs that had sort of bubbled up and stuck on each orange that he had placed inside the stockings. Oranges were scarce then and too expensive for everyday purchases. They were usually given at Christmastime, if the family could afford it.. When we each looked inside our stocking, we found everything in a sticky mess. However, we were not saddened nor disappointed by this. We enjoyed whatever we could put into our mouths and praised our dad for thinking of us at Christmas. Of course, we had toys under the Christmas tree that we opened with enthusiasm and glee.

Mother returned home on a Tuesday afternoon, four weeks after her operation. She told us all about the operation, the string of small metal clamps around her throat, the ward she was in and the good friends she had made. She especially liked one woman by the name of Mrs. Wellerby who came from Ashton, Massachusetts and sympathized with my mother being so far away from home at Christmas time, especially far away from us kids. She promised my mother that she would send us a surprise through the mail. We lived in silent expectation for two weeks until a package was delivered at our house, and mother opened it to find a large metal box of scrumptious cookies. It was a Christmas cookie box, a fancy one with Santa in his sleigh and the reindeer streaming through the air. We were ever so delighted since we had never received anything through he mail before. It proved to be a winter of contentment and merry thoughts in spite of the loss of our mother's presence at a very special time when children love to have both their parents with them. Mother had cautioned us before she left for the big city that things would go right and things would arrange themselves just so according to the maneuvers of the holy angels ever watching over us. "Trust in your angels, my dears," she had said, "and things will not go wrong." Why would they? Throw caution to the wind, my grandmother had said. The wind blew, the snow came and Christmas went by without any hitch except for the unexpected, sticky surprising mess in our Christmas stockings. My father never talked about this incident after that. The sticky mess inside our cotton stockings remains hidden in our memories never to be divulged...except now.

7.

Booby-Boo's Great Adventure

ooby-Boo was a strange little fellow and a wild one at that. He was named Booby-Boo because his mother had given him this name for all of the stupid and funny things he did. He went around the house shouting Boo, "Booby says boo." His real name was Bobby but he kept saying Booby, so he was called Booby-Boo.

Booby-Boo was a lad of six; he had just stepped into the adopted fringes of the age of reason which was seven years old. That's what people traditionally accepted as the age of reason. However, some young people like Bobby clearly reached the level of being rational and intellectually sharp much before the so-called age of reason. Sometimes, they were called precocious. Not that Booby-Boo was precocious, but he was certainly smart and ahead of his years. He knew he was smart, and he dared to show his ability to plunge right into the possibilities of the age of reason. He loved to explore his own little world, a world of plants, animals and things in general. He especially loved insects, ants that crawled fast and furious on the floor and on the sandy soil next to his room. He would look outside his window and spot a whole army of ants marching towards the foundation of the house. Off he would run outside to meet the tiny creatures and pick some up with a straw and watch them crawl in and out of his sleeve. He never wished them harm; he liked them and protected them from other bad boys who would slap them and brush them away. He found the ants to be amusing and entertaining by the way they just hurried along. Booby-Boo especially liked the way they built their small ant hills out of sand. Then, he would crouch down and watch them for hours on end building a pile of sand that was their very own pyramids. That's what Booby-Boo called them. He had seen pyramids built in Egypt in a magazine, and had wondered how people at that time had carried so many stones and placed them one by one to form what we now call pyramids. He would have loved to be with these people building such a marvelous structure. They were so huge and strong that they had lasted for years and years. To think that just with the swipe of a foot, the poor ant hills could be wiped away in an instant. That's what some bad boys did. They didn't like these ant hills, so they swooshed them with the brutal swipe of their foot and sent the sand scattering all over with the ants running amok like wild creatures whose habitat had been crushed by the cruel foot of a lad boisterously chanting the war song of an enemy of wild things.

Besides ants and ant hills, Booby-Boo liked nothing more than to find a hidden bird's nest on a limb in one of the trees in his back yard, and watch over it for hours at a time. He did not get too close to it for fear of hurting them and, of course, mindful that the mother was ever watchful in protecting her brood. He never ever touched an egg and never thought of robbing the nest of its eggs either. He simply watched. One day, he thought that a mother bird had abandoned its nest and its two little blue eggs. It was a mother robin, and she never returned to the nest. Booby-Boo ran home to tell his mother about it and she told him that there was nothing he could do about such a thing. He wanted to bring them home with him and take care of the eggs. "Forget it," his mother told him. She recognized the fact that the eggs were abandoned and done for. They would just perish with time. Booby-Boo cried over this episode and convinced himself never to abandon a single egg, insect, or any other animal that came his way in the future.

Booby-Boo was ever on the search for an adventure of some kind or other. He was searching for that special adventure that he would consider great. Great meant for him of considerable magnitude or considerable importance like meeting the man in charge of all the areas in the community, the big boss, the mayor. That, he considered great. He was too young to get involved in politics, but he recognized the fact that politicians were important in the running of affairs locally and outside the community. Politicians were the bigwigs. People voted for the ones they trusted and confided their priorities to them by their vote. Booby-Boo did not understand fully the workings of city hall and all that mattered in the running of any particular office such as that of the mayor. He was too young to vote anyway. He often asked questions about this and that to his mom. That was a clear sign of curiosity and intelligence, said his mother. She welcomed that. Booby-Boo was indeed curious and intelligent.

One day, Booby-Boo happened to come across a geography book, a large one with glossy pages filled with maps and pictures of important cities and countless rivers and even the oceans. He had never explored such a vast array of information before. He immediately fell in love with this huge geography book. He had found it in the attic of grandmother's house. You see, Booby-Boo loved attics where treasures could be found, treasures that had been hidden away for years. There were antiques of sorts, old glassware and dishes, old clothing, old hats, and very old shoes and, of course, old books with beautiful leather covers that had been layered with dust for years and years. Each layer represented one year upon another year. One only had to blow hard on them to dispel the dust and uncover the layers of dust and reveal their true identity as masterful examples of the craft of books. Books were the deposits of history, of geography, of philosophy, of theology and, of course, stories. Yes, stories, the essence of the product of the creative imagination. Booby-Boo loved stories. He loved storytelling as read by his mother in the early evening hours before going to bed. He very much loved the storytelling pauses of his beloved grandmother when she had the time to do so. She was a busy lady and oftentimes could not find time to tell stories. However, there were occasions when she simply sat down with her grandson and spent several hours telling tales and most engrossing stories. She had a way of rolling her eyes and cracking her voice when she told mysterious stories. She could also smack her lips and tug at her left ear lobe when telling about the gingerbread houses decorated with delicious icing when recounting the tale of "The Gingerbread Man and the Forest People." She had a special and precious way of telling stories, that lady of infinite charm.

It was on a late afternoon in November when the wind was howling outside and the dead leaves swirled around like *un tourbillon de feuilles mortes*, like little whirlwinds of dead leaves that grandmother started to tell Booby-Boo about the cautionary tale of the mouse, the rat and the chipmunk.

All three animals lived in the woods filled with all kinds of creatures, big and small. The mouse lived in a small tree trunk where the bark had been peeled away to make room for the mouse family. The rat lived under some rocks piled high under the branches of an old fir tree, and the chipmunk dwelt under some old branches where the chipmunk family had burrowed to make themselves a comfortable place to live. All three, the mouse, the rat and the chipmunk came out of their dwelling holes to play in and around the neighborhood. They always had fun running and scooting away from one another, only to find each other in the same circle after a short time. They all loved each others company. The mouse was called Rooney, the rat, Pompinut, and the chipmunk, Floopsy. Rooney loved teasing both Pompinut and Floopsy because he had a streak of benign maliciousness in him. He was never outright bad or downright mean. Pompinut was a little rat with a streak of innocent ignorance about him while Floopsy was always scurrying to gather something or other, and so they called him Gather-Gooroo.

One day, the three little animals sat there wondering what to do next since they had exhausted the possibilities of play along with fun and games that they usually devised and then executed with creative imagination. Rooney's mother always cautioned him not to go where the big animals lived, and not to tease any of them for he could get eaten up. Pompinut's mother did not care too much about his wanderings, and never cautioned him about anything except to stay close to home. Floopsy's mother was always after him to clean up around their dwelling place and not bring too much junk that he loved accumulating. Rooney came up with the idea of asking Mother Hubbard who lived right down the road to see if she had any ideas to give them, Floopsy told him that the old lady did not care about other animals, for she had her dog and took good care of him. She not only cared for him but treated him with every delight that came to her mind and he grew to become a spoiled brat. Other animals said that about him. People wrote nursery rhymes about Mother Hubbard and her dog. Some even sang songs about both of them. Floopsy and Gather-Gooroo both wondered what was in Mother Hubbard's cupboard. Rumor had it that she kept all kinds of things in there, like stuffed animals, yoyos and tops that spin, beautiful and colorful pinwheels that spin colors when you blow on them, popcorn balls made of sugar and spice, red candied apples, and everything else that the imagination could devise. Nobody really knew for sure. It was said that the one thing she did keep under lock and key was her recipes for games, and how to mold a gigantic clay figure that spoke words and sang songs. It seemed that everything was left to the imagination of those who squandered their talents in imagining things. All this was enough to make the three friends think about exploring Mother Hubbard' s cupboard. But how?

The three mothers had warned their offspring not to go even near Mother's cupboard for it invited trouble, they said. They had heard about the trouble caused by some strange power in the cupboard to inquisitive eyes and hands. Some grew blind while others had their hands cut off by some mysterious force that hovered over the cupboard. The mothers even mentioned the malicious doings of the old farmer's wife who cut off the tails of the three blind mice. They said that they were mischievous mice, and that's why they had their tails cut off. "Stay out of mischief", the mothers told them. All three mothers told each one of them not to cause mischief and not to be mischievous for they would lose their tails. The mouse, the rat and the chipmunk did not want that at all. A mouse without a tail, a rat without a tail and a chipmunk tailless even though it's a very tiny one?

In spite of the maternal warnings, the three adventurous rodents devised a plan to escape from their mothers' clutches and run away to Mother Hubbard's cupboard. They did not know how far it was, but they thought they could easily get there and come back with some loot.

Early one morning in September when the sun was still high enough in the sky and the foliage was still green, and the spirit was shining upon the three friends, that is the spirit of the hills named Spiritoo by all, the three little rodent friends took off to find Mother Hubbard's place. They thought that it must be higher up in the hills for they could see the top of the chimney from afar. Animals did not have chimneys, but people did.

As the three musketeers approached the house after an hour's trek, they came upon a pond that prevented them from reaching their destination. You see all three of them could not swim. Then came along a duck swimming in the pond. The duck asked them what they were doing there. They answered they were going to see Mother Hubbard on top of the hill, over there.

----Why? asked the duck.

----Because we want to ask her about her cupboard, answered the mouse.

----What do you want with the cupboard?

----We want to see inside it, answered the chipmunk.

----Nobody goes inside Mother Hubbard's cupboard, it's forbidden territory, said the duck.

----But we only want to peek inside, that's all, replied the rat.

----I'll tell you what, replied the duck, if you happen to get to see what's inside, I want you to tell me what's in there. I've been wanting to know for a very long time.

----But we can't get there like this. We'll drown if we try to cross the pond.

And so, the duck made the three of them climb on his back and he paddled them to their destination. It was a big duck with a very strong back.

----Be careful, the duck warned them, don't try to get something that's not yours, and don't try to offend Mother Hubbard by being too sneaky. She won't like that.

----We'll ask her permission first, said the little mouse. Mom always cautioned me to ask permission of anyone in charge and be polite and kind.

----But, be careful and don't be afraid to come back without having looked inside the cupboard, for you might not be able to get permission from the old lady. And, be on the lookout for the dog. He's mean. A mean old dog.

----How do you know? asked the mouse.

----I know because I've been chased by that dog.

----What's the dog's name? asked the chipmunk.

----He has no name. Just dog. That's all.

----Didn't the old lady give him a name? asked the rat.

----I don't think so.

----That's silly not giving your pet a name, said the mouse.

----All I know, the dog has no name.

----How can you call him if he has no name? asked the mouse.

----How am I supposed to know that?

----Everyone has a name, don't you know that? replied the rat.

----Yeah, what's your name, asked the chipmunk.

----Donald, replied the duck.

----Naaah, said they, you can't be Donald Duck,

----Of course not. I'm Donald the drake.

----The drake? asked the mouse.

----Of course, a drake is a male duck. Don't you know that?

----Well, we learn something new every day said the mouse.

After the goodbyes, the three little rodents ambled heir way up the hill to Mother Hubbard's house. They found the house to be a bit dilapidated but livable for an old woman and her dog. All three of them managed to sneak into the old house having found enough holes in the foundation. They ran as fast as they could, their little legs racing the best way they could carry them. The three of them met on the first floor of the house. They started exploring going here and there where they thought the cupboard would be. It was easy to find it since it was a very big cupboard and could be seen easily. Now, how to get inside the cupboard was the main question. They looked and looked to find some entry. They were too small to open the cupboard doors and had to find some way of penetrating inside this huge thing called a cupboard. They had never seen one like that. It was a big one, a tall and square one with four doors. Its must hold many, many things, thought the mouse. The cupboard must be full of stuff, thought the rat. What a big storage place, said the chipmunk to himself. All agreed that it was practically impossible to penetrate inside this giant piece of furniture. The three of them kept going round and round the cupboard until they heard the barking of a dog, the dog. They got scared and wished they had never gone inside Mother Hubbard's old house. As the dog got closer to them, they hurried to try and hide somewhere, but the dog sniffed them out. All at once, they saw an old woman dressed in an old-fashioned cotton dress with a huge apron over it. She had white hair turned into a big bun at the back. She wore glasses, the kind old grannies wear. She looked mad. All of a sudden, she took out her broom and decided to give the intruders a whack in order to get rid of the marauders, as she called them. She did not like rodents. She reached for a carving knife and ran after all three them. She wanted to cut their tails off. Did she do it or not. Did old Mother Hubbard cut off the tails of Rooney, Floopsy and Pompinut? Without a tail these three rodents would not be able to navigate around. Well, that's the end of this cautionary tale, or should I say cautionary tail...that's just a bit of "pun" humor.

Be cautious now and don't go sneaking into somebody's house and furniture for you might get your tail, oh, I mean your hand or fingers cut off, unless you are a rodent of some kind. Do rodents read? Remember, knives are sharp and dangerous in the wrong hands. Curiosity did not kill the cat but landed three rodents in a dangerous spot. I wonder if they ever got home...well.

8.

My Daddy's Gun

I had often seen my daddy's gun in the bedroom closet where my mother insisted it be kept away from the children. She was deathly afraid of the gun, any gun. For her, it was an instrument of death and killing. A means of killing beasts and humans. Although my father had it for hunting purposes, she still did not like it in the house. My father insisted that it be kept where he could easily retrieve it for his hunting days in November. He would drive up to Augusta where my uncle Danny lived with his wife Mina(short for Hermina), my mother's sister. Even she accompanied her husband in their hunting expedition for deer. My mother sometimes joined them just to enjoy the great outdoors and to spend some time with her sister. They would go to Dead River into the wild woods to hunt. Very often my father would return home without his fallen deer. It was a matter of the hunt for him and not of killing a poor animal. My mother did not like venison or deer meat as she called it. It had a wild taste to it, she said. She found that it was a lot of trouble going through the entire processes of deer hunting. First there was the license, followed by the pertinent information about opened hunting areas in Maine, finding the proper lodging, bringing the food needed for the hunting expedition which was a lot of cooking and baking before leaving home, then came the hunt itself. If you were lucky, you would bag a deer, a big buck with giant antlers or a doe. What with killing the deer, processing it through the warden's registering stops, having the carcass with the head and antlers lying and strapped onto the roof of the car, and taking the whole thing home to have the meat processed by a skilled butcher, it was all a dang-bang job, said my mother. Very often, the meat was given away to some neighbor or relative who loved deer meat.

My name is Norman, but I was called Nomie by my family and friends. I was but eight years old when I was able to accompany my father and mother to Dead River during the hunting season. That was back in 1946. I had gotten special permission from school to be absent for an entire week. That was a special treat for me since I did not particularly like school. I did not like books, assignments and particularly report cards that showed the parents the mediocre or poor grades that some students got. My parents did not look so much at the grades as the good conduct grade. I wasn't afraid of that since I was a shy and timid boy who obeyed every rule and regulation, including the teacher's directives. I always got an A- or B+ on that score. They were always glad to see that I was a student with a good conduct grade, and that I never proved to be trouble for my teachers. I wasn't trouble for anyone, not my teachers, not my parents, not my aunts and uncles, not my grandparents. No one. I was an obedient and mindful child. I obeyed everyone and anyone in charge. I was afraid of being punished for infractions that I had not even committed. They called at times, a scaredy cat.

Dead River was a large forested region with many rivers and lakes in the Northern Appalachian Mountains. As I read about Dead River in an almanac my father had, Dead River played a role in the American Revolution. In the fall of 1775, then the newly commissioned Colonel Benedict Arnold led a force of over 1000 men on a grueling trip through Maine as part of the invasion of Canada. I then got interested in this part of Maine history and started to do research on this expedition. Apparently this was a most difficult military expedition for both its leader and his men. They met many a challenge along the way like some losing their way, others losing their boats in the white choppy waters, and still others losing their lives before getting to the Chaudière River. General Washington had great confidence in Benedict Arnold and had confided this expedition to him. But, it proved to be a disaster. The affair with Major André and Benedict Arnold's treachery is very much complicated so that some historians do not believe he was a traitor. However, the label of traitor sticks to Benedict Arnold's reputation even today. He's considered to be one of the most renowned if not infamous traitors in American history. I just found the entire story of Benedict Arnold and his exploits during the American Revolution extraordinary, exciting and somewhat mysterious. What has this to do with hunting and my father's gun? Well, it hinges on the right to bear arms in this country and the right to hunt. Bear arms to defend oneself is fine and constitutional, but killing human beings is an act of violence and it's wrong in my book. Owning guns for hunting is alright as long as the huntsman does it according to regulations and the law. All in deference to the humanity of it all. Human lives are sacred and must be protected; animal lives are also sacred in their own way as God's creatures. Guns kill and guns must not override the tenets of sacredness and humanity. There, I've said it. Now, back to my cautionary tale.

Once we arrived at the Dead River campsite, we started to unpack and took everything out of the cars and placed every article that we brought along, as well as uncle Danny's and aunt Mina's belongings and provisions inside the house camp. It had an unfinished interior with plain wooden studs and beams with unvarnished planks on the floor. It had the rustic look that one anticipates when going camping in the wilderness. All I could think of was that we were so very far away from home. In the wilderness. Although, I appreciated the surroundings and the hunt as an adventure. I was going to go out there and explore. I was going to seek the adventure of a young boy in search of the wild. No such thing, said my mother as a caution against the danger lurking out there in the wilderness. "But, 'ma," I said, "there's no real danger in the wild. No one to harm us. It's just wild animals, and they're as friendly as I've seen in books dealing with animals that look so friendly and tame." "Yes, wild animals like bears and mangy wild cats." And so I had to stay indoors or close to camp.

At night, sitting before the fire, I could overhear the adults talking about hunting and the deer they were going to get. Even my aunt Mina was excited about the hunt. She had the guts and the determination of a man, that one. She was a strong woman. My mother was too, but she did not have the guts that aunt Mina had. Aunt Mina even dressed like a man which was very infrequent for a woman then. She put on red and black plaid woolen pants, a woolen shirt and a matching woolen jacket. She even wore a matching cap with visor. She had to dress up warmly because it was very cold in late fall in the wilderness of Maine. Of course, she had her gun and she knew how to use it. She was quite a gal my aunt Mina. She was the best of cooks. Why she could turn out the best of devil food cakes with white marshmallowy icing, a splendid roast pork with good browned potatoes, homemade bread, and pickling that she herself had done the previous season. She was an exceptional household cleaner and everyone marveled at her ability to iron white starched shirts, cotton dresses and aprons. She had been raised on a farm in old Quebec, and so she was trained to do many chores and excel in them. She married my uncle Danny and both of them raised a family of six children. One son, Robert, became an excellent hunter and butcher. He's the one who would cut and prepare the deer meat, if and when a deer or two were shot. I don't remember my father ever shooting one. That was fine with him because all he truly enjoyed was the hunt and the wilderness.

As part of the adult conversation, there were stories about this man or that one who had shot a huge deer with antlers so big and so wide that Norbert, a neighbor, could not fit the dead animal on top of the roof of his car. That was his name, Norbert. I never got to know his last name. There was another tale of two guys who went hunting at nighttime. That was against the law. They were caught by the warden and brought before the judge. They paid a very high fine for their offense, as far as I could hear. "Shame," they all said. Shame because these two men knew the law and broke it. There was plenty of deer around, they said. They didn't have to go out at night and break the law, they said in whispers. Then there was this episode of one man relieving himself, "crapping" they said, in the woods and a big buck happened to come along and the poor hunter missed his chance to get his deer. They all laughed as if the poor hunter was right there with them. Another tale, was the one about the hunter who was caught stealing the registry tags from another hunter, so that he could bag two deer. Some people are greedy and will do what they can to get what they want. I remember reading about Native Americans whose strict ethical policies included hunting and killing deer or buffalo only for their nourishment needs and not for exploitation. These animals were given to them by the Great Manitou to feed themselves and their families, and not to fill their greedy mouths with surplus food. Take from nature what is explicitly needed and don't go grabbing everything you don't need was their policy. They were wise to act that way, wise in their way of living and thinking.

Well, the tale I want to tell you is the one about a hunting expedition of three men as told to me by my father. One man was called Harvey, the second one, Gilbert and the third one, Stanley, the fart. Yes, the fart because he had a lot of wind to dispose of. Not only that, but he had a lot of wind he had to dispose not only from his behind but from his mouth. He was a talker, that one, my father said. He could talk you ears and your mouth off so much of a windbag was he. He blabbed all the time giving no one a chance to cut into his dry tales. Why he even interrupted everyone and did not allow them to finish what they had to say. The conversation was lost with him. It wasn't a conversation, but a one-sided exclamation of self-indulgence or plain and simply a show-offishness unmet and unwanted by all who knew him.. Everybody liked Stanley, but they could not stand his farts and his big mouth.

The tale goes like this. One day, the three men went hunting. They went hunting with bow and arrow. There are special dates established by a particular state government for such hunting. In Maine it's between the months of September and October unless it's during the expanded season of September and December. The deer must be legally transported and registered when caught. The archery season allows for multiple permits for antler-less deer. The three men obtained all the permits they needed for their hunt. They were going to bag as many as they could, they said. They chose Islesboro in Waldo County open to deer hunting with bow and arrow during the archery season. All three of them enjoyed the environment and sought refuge from spying wardens, they said. There were fewer wardens around, they maintained. So off they went bows and arrows, food supply and all enough to provide for at least two weeks. They even brought bottles and bottles of beer hiding them, in the trunk of the car under piles and piles of blankets, pillows and sundry items.

Stanley insisted on getting a couple of bottles of whiskey, but the two other guys said no. It would be better that way, they said. That way, it would guarantee that no one would get drunk easily. Unbeknownst to Harvey and Gilbert, Stanley had hidden a bottle of whiskey in his personal possessions. That way he could have his refreshment, he told himself. Stanley just couldn't be without his whiskey. He liked the way whiskey ran down his throat smooth and mellow, he said. But, he especially liked the way it clouded his mind, so that he was not responsible for the foul language he so often used. He simply shrugged it off. Why the other two guys befriended him, people did not know. Two rational guys with common sense and a feel for courtesy being friends with someone who farted, belched, and talked like a stewed drunk was not the kind of guy that Gilbert and Harvey wanted as friends, but Stanley had money and he paid all of the expenses of their hunting trips as well as all the provisions they brought with them. He was a flush guy, people said of Stanley. Flush with his money and flush with his words.

So what happened on their last hunting trip, you might ask. Well, this is a cautionary tale because of its character and moral lesson to be had. Do not go hunting with a guy whose brain and good common sense is obfuscated by liquor. One evening after a good meal and a few too many swallows of beer topped off by Stanley's bottle of whiskey, Harvey had to go outdoors to get some fresh air, he told Gilbert and Stanley. In the meantime, Stanley decided to go hunting and took his bow and arrows with him, although Gilbert warned him about hunting at dusk. It might be dangerous he told him. "There's enough light outside for me to see the deer," he told his friend. "Wait until tomorrow morning when the sun is out and you'll be able to see straight...and to think straight." "You mean, I'm drunk?" said Stanley. "Close to it," replied Gilbert. However, Stanley was stubborn enough not to listen to Gilbert. He is so drunk, thought Gilbert, that he won't be able to shoot anything visible. Off went Stanley, bow and arrows on his back. After a few moments Stanley thought he saw a deer in the bushes and started to prepare for the aim and the shot. He trembled, at first, putting the arrow on his bow ready to aim and fire. All of a sudden he heard a loud scream and Harvey running out of the bushes with an arrow stuck in his bottom. He had been crouching to better see a squirrel that he perceived. The arrow hit him where it hurt the most in his buttocks. He shouted at Stanley and accused him of being stupid and a very poor hunter. "First of all" Harvey said, "you don't go out at night to go hunting. It's against the law, Stanley." "But it's not night, there's still some light." "Not enough to see clearly, Stanley. You son-of-a-bitch." Stanley helped Harvey to get back to the cabin and he and Gilbert drove the poor innocent victim of poor hunting to a doctor down the road. After the doctor had gingerly pulled the arrow out of Harvey's buttocks and bandaged the wound, the three men decided it was time to go back home and quit hunting once and for all. Better to hunt deer with a rifle, they said. The gun may be a better way of hunting deer but guns kill and do not simply hit their target with just a shaft wound. Stanley didn't want to get a gun. He was awfully scared of guns. He much preferred bows and arrows. Bows and arrows are fun, he used to say. Are guns fun though? My daddy's gun is still hidden in the closet never to be used again because my daddy fears hunting now. Too many accidents, he said. Like being shot in the butt, my mother said.

9.

The Man Who Stole Easter Eggs

Did you ever go on an Easter hunt. I mean an egg hunt. Brightly painted eggs strewn or hidden in and around the yard. It's an egg hunt for children who have nothing to do but get after their mothers to find them something to do for excitement. After all, children need to be active and stay active. That takes time and imagination on the part of parents; children do it almost instinctively. Time because time it's precious and needs to be carefully managed. Imagination because the need to be creative lies in the domain of the imaginings. How does one entertain kids? Easter hunt seems to be a good thing when the time tells you it's the appropriate moment, and the eggs are ready to be painted the colors of springtime. Of course, they have to be boiled first, otherwise they would be subject to accidental breakage and the yolks and egg whites would splatter all over the one who paints them. There is nothing more gooey than the inside of a raw egg. Boiled eggs are firm and easy to handle. Of course, they have to cool first. Hot boiled eggs are too hot to handle. I know.

When Easter rolled around when I was young, I was not accustomed to the Easter egg hunt since my parents did not believe in spoiling or wasting eggs for the simple pleasure of rolling them on the green, and picking them up and placing them in a basket. Rather, they would buy me a well-stocked Easter basket at Woolworth wrapped in yellow cellophane. There was, of course, a chocolate Easter bunny as tall as my uncle Edouard's hand, some yellow peeps, jellybeans strewn here and here, tiny chicks made out of soft chewy candy, and small chocolate eggs all lying on top of imitation green grass. Lest I forget, there was, at times, a chocolate cross also. It has since then become more and more absent from Easter displays. In our days, chocolate Easter crosses were considered religious;y inspired. After all, it was Easter celebrating Christ's Resurrection from the dead. The chocolate crosses were even eaten by non-Christians, such as some of the Jews that I knew who lived next door to the Nolettes. It did not matter for everyone enjoyed chocolate in any shape or form. As a matter of fact, Easter is and was considered more the bunny day than the celebration of the Resurrection. Who would have thought that the bunny would replace Jesus as a day of celebratory eating. All children received an Easter basket. It was an expected item on our list of Easter anticipations. We had a heck of a time choosing first what we would eat, ending with the chocolate Easter bunny. Pamela, my cousin, ate the bunny first; she loved chocolate. But, there was no Easter egg hunt.

Easter egg hunts were in the domain of other children whose parents and relatives knew about them. It had been part of their traditional activities. An Easter basket full of candy and chocolate delightfully packaged was one of the great treats of our childhood days. I never experienced the egg hunt. I didn't know anything about it. Besides, it would have been a loss or waste of hard boiled eggs, my mother used to say when she heard about egg hunts. Different traditions merit different ways of doing things, I suppose. Of course, I do think that the other kids, I mean the egg hunt kids, were also susceptible of earning a big Easter basket from Woolworth or Fishman. It would have been unimaginable not to get one. After all, children love candy, especially chocolate Easter bunnies.

As for my cautionary tale about Easter eggs and the man who took a liking to them, and in the process stole them, it begins like this. Once in a small town where people gathered every Sunday for religious services to hear the pastor speaking to them about God and his commandments, there was one man who constantly denied that he was an atheist when confronted by someone who accused him of atheism. Although an unbeliever, he never said that he did not believe in God. Of course, he rejected everything that had to do with religious cult like prayers and hymns sung at church, Eucharistic services and communion and everything else that was associated with religion and cult. He just did not believe in all of this hocus-pocus, as he called it. He did not deny there was a God, but the idea was not for him since he did not believe in such a being. It was a matter of reason over faith-filled garbage, as he called it. As far as he was concerned, he thought that everything connected to religion was a fabrication of faith-filled men and their imagination. They imagined things; they made up stories and filled the minds of people with them. That's what he thought with absolute certainty. Black and white evidence, he called it, that the reason could never produce any such things as religion and its machinations. Why, it was as plain as the nose on your face, he said. He asserted that he wasn't an atheist since atheists were classified as non-believers, and he said that he was a believer, but not in an almighty God of Creation. He believed in things that did not require prayers, kneeling, declaration of faith, Sunday services, and many other things that demand adherence to a proclamation of faithful service to God and neighbor. He was a strict adherent to freedom and reason, he said. He did not even believe in hell, angels and all those ideas that send chills up the spine for those who think of the otherworldly features of belief. Robotson was the man's name, and he was of strict doubt and reason. He doubted everything and rationalized everything. Was he a doubting Thomas? No, for he did not believe in the gospels. Why spoil good reasoning thoughts on superstitions, he used to say. One thing he did believe in was Easter eggs. Colorful, hard chocolaty, crispy, caramely, fudgy, nutty, chocolate eggs of whatever blend or texture were his delight. They were real, palpable, deliciously tempting, and easily affordable through theft. Yes, theft that unmistakably forbidden word for those who cringe at its mere mention. Without any sense of moral values and guidelines, the man could easily allow himself to steal whatever he wanted, especially Easter eggs. Why Easter eggs since he did not believe in Easter? Because, he marveled at them and wanted them so bad that he would do anything to get some. His appetite and his avarice were such that he considered them with esteem and honor to his pride of being able to covet them without any remorse. Except, he did not realize that his actions were building up within him a huge cauldron of self-indulgent and dishonest calculations that, some day, he would not be able to extinguish. The cauldron of lies not only to others but to himself. How could he not realize that? The voice that is within the soul is sometimes nearly extinguished by reason of stupidity and pride. However, it never dies; it can never be completely extinguished. Faint whispers can be heard if the person involved bothers to pay heed to it when they surface now and then. Some believe and some do not believe in the existence of the conscience. It's a matter of belief of disbelief, I suppose. Nevertheless, the man called Robotson, did not hear those whispers even though they were there. He had turned a deaf ear to them even when he was a teenager. His heart had turned cold, his head had turned hard and obstinate, his soul smothered like a breath smothered by a pillow and held there constantly. His soul could not breathe. Robotson had turned to stone. But, his desire for Easter eggs was deeply alive and morbidly haunting. He could not refrain from this deep and haunting voice that brought him to a level of desperation so intense was this malicious desire. He could not help himself. His willpower had dwindled to a mere shadow of strength within him. He was certainly stubborn, deliberate in his choices, and resolute in his actions, but that did not stem from his will, but his inclination to do whatever filled him with pleasure and intense satisfaction. Robotson was a man of pure self-satisfaction. Egocentric to the core and stubborn like a mule, he would not and could not budge from his own human decimation. Had he lost his willpower to choose right from wrong? Some people wondered. Strange as it may seem, Robotson didn't even like the colorfully painted Easter eggs. He would not eat them; he was never tempted to crack one open and eat the inside content. He simply was fascinated by them, attracted to them for their colors and intricate designs. One day, while Robotson was deep in silence meditating on the ways of getting as much as he could out of the next egg hunt, he thought of Mister Rightly's abundance of Easter eggs. Not only did he want to capture all the colored eggs to add to his collection, but this time he also wanted to get all of the chocolate eggs he could in Mister Rightly's candy store. Mister Rightly had the very best of chocolate eggs, bunnies and crosses for the coming Easter season. Robotson did not have the money to buy any of them, so he had to figure out how to get a hold of as many of the chocolate Easter delicacies he could from Mister Rightly's candy store. How? There was only one way. Wait until the store was closed and then steal his way inside the store. He did not want to vandalize nor ruin anything in the store since Robotson still had a grain of good sense inside of him, enough to prevent him from doing harm. After all, he was not a violent person.

This is the way he planned his caper. He would wait until Sunday night when the store closed early, wait for the store owner to leave the premises when no one was around, no neighbors, no watchmen, no policemen on duty, no one on surveillance. Absolutely, no one around to mind the downtown area. Everyone would be home enjoying their Sunday evening meal. Even the youngsters would not be outside playing in the streets. Only cats and dogs wandering around. No watchdogs either since no one owned one. Perfectly quiet and dark enough to steal without anyone noticing it. No chance of being caught. That was a comforting thought for Robotson. But, what about alarms? Well, Mr. Rightly did not believe in alarms in his store. He trusted everyone and anyone just because it was a small town and everybody knew one another. He even trusted Robotson in spite of his reputation for being an avid chocolate eater which he was not. He was a collector of precious cargo. Besides, he had never been caught stealing. He was a bit odd and strange in his demeanor, but no one suspected him of stealing. Besides, there were few robberies in the town called Edenbrook. Robotson was simply a man with a tendency to be on the fringes of society, people said of him. He was not anti social, simply not a social being. He didn't go to church, but that was alright with the townspeople. He did not practice warmth and politeness in his greetings, but people understood his penchant for being a cool cucumber of a man. That's how they considered him, cool and dry and even as cold as a fish sometimes. He showed very little emotion and feelings. People wondered if he had any. People did not bother with him. They just let him do his thing and left him alone. He did no harm to anyone; he did not bother with anyone.

Some people in town suspected that Robotson had a craving for chocolate especially chocolate eggs although he also liked Easter colored eggs. That they knew since he was always there when the egg hunt was on. They saw him gallivanting around and spying on every child chasing and picking up the eggs on the grassy knoll of town. People did not see him picking up any, but they did not know that he had already taken some much before the egg hunt got started.. One woman startled him picking up an egg, but she refrained from stopping him. She did not even scream at him for fear of frightening the children who would soon arrive. She told herself that the egg hunt sponsors could easily spare one egg on this poor fellow who had fear in his eyes, and who most probably had never gotten a colorful egg as a child.

Robotson started collecting Easter eggs when he was but eleven years old. His parents had never brought him to an egg hunt, nor was he ever permitted to step out of the house to join those who participated in the annual egg hunt on the green. His parents knew that he craved for chocolate eggs and Easter candy, and they thought that one chocolate Easter egg was sufficient to satisfy his appetite. They only offered him one once a year. After a while, he started looking elsewhere to find chocolate Easter eggs. He took them from Easter baskets unattended. Stole some from Mister Rightly's candy store when he wasn't looking, and became quite adapt at pilfering in broad daylight. He did not steal large items like the very large solid chocolate Easter bunny on display at Mister Rightly's. He stole some jelly beans and later on small eggs wrapped in foil. He would simply slide them into his pants pocket without anyone noticing it. The customers buying candies were many, and no one was interested in Robotson maneuvers. Besides, Mister Rightly had, oh, so many candies in his store especially around Easter-time. He wasn't going to miss a few candies, the young lad told himself. If his mother caught him eating stolen candy, his mother would ask him where he had gotten it. His response was that Mister Rightly had given it to him out of the kindness of his heart. His mother would always tell him not to go and bother the good Mister Rightly.

Robotson grew up agile and adept at what he wanted, no matter the circumstances, no matter the time of day. He would steal a cookie from the cookie jar even though his mother had told him not to take one on his own. Then, there was the trinket from the neighbor's house even though he did not really need it. He also took a thimble from old Mrs. Tarrington just because he wanted to have it. He stole some sea shells from Lyla Doolittle's collection. He did not have any shells, and he wanted to start his own collection. He had asked her for some shells but Lyla had refused him. So he took some anyway when she wasn't looking. But, his very favorite thing, the desired item that he wanted so desperately, the item par excellence was Mister Fabrice's marvelous and richly designed Fabergé egg that was displayed in a locked glass cabinet in his living room. That was a most desirable thing for a young lad who loved beautiful things especially the most lovely egg he had ever seen in his life. He had seen it when he had made an errand for Mister Fabrice, and the owner had showed him the jeweled egg out of pride and personal *joie de choses acquéries,* possessions. That egg, Robotson knew that he could never steal. He could not eat it anyway. Mister Fabrice had told the boy that he had gotten the Fabergé egg from a friend who had an entire collection of the jeweled eggs patterned after the Russian renowned Imperial eggs commissioned for Easter gifts by both Czar Alexander III and Czar Nicholas's II. They were the original Fabergé eggs and had delighted all those who had seen them He was so proud of his egg, said Mister Fabrice to young Robotson, that he would never separate himself from it, not even if it meant starving. Robotson was indeed startled by this admission so that he always retained in his heart the great desire to possess things especially enviable and costly things. Never in his life would he ever be able to possess an egg like that So, Robotson trained his eye on colorful Easter eggs and, of course, Easter chocolate eggs. However, Robotson discovered that less and less was he attracted to and craved for chocolate eggs. His taste buds had deteriorated to a point of finding chocolate less appealing. He even hated it now that he could not enjoy its pleasure. However, he still craved for the looting of chocolate eggs. Just for the fun of it and the delight of stealing them, he told himself. So, he continued in his pursuit of robbing them as much as he could and stashing them in his cache. He reveled in the thought of having so many chocolate eggs. Strange that nobody noticed his robbery, not even his mother. His mother rarely went to his bedroom and never cleaned it. It was left to the disposal of her son who was not a clean-nick. Robotson thought of giving away some his cache, but the thought of separating himself from his eggs made him cringe with apprehension, not from shame. He knew no shame. He had never felt shame for his conscience had been silenced years much before puberty. What is shame anyhow if not the result of knowing and acknowledging something that goes against probity and the right thing to do? Why should a fellow like Robotson worry about it and even justify his motives and actions? He had no motives; he only acted on his penchants and immediate desires. He became an automaton of feeling, motives, and ethical behavior. It seemed nothing fazed him. Nothing but the loss of possible chances to collect chocolate and colored eggs. Theft was his great, or should we say, lowest construct as an automaton. Some wondered if he was truly human. His mother did not like remarks like that about her son. "Of course, he's human," she would say to Mrs. Faucher, "it's just that he's not like other human beings." "He's more of a deadpan or a *nature morte,* the other woman would say, "nothing really alive in him, just the appearances of a human being, is as much as I can say about him. *Vraiment une nature morte et sans vraie vie....*like a still life but without the true life behind it At least the artist painted true life though lifeless. " It was then that Robotson's mother would start raging against her and pronounce every swear word that she knew or could know like *une déchaînée,* as we say in French, a loose woman loosening her invectives that had simmered in her soul for a very long time.. Her son was not that bad, she would say, a little off-key but not bad. "He's just a bad apple in a barrel of lies and treachery," would answer the other woman. Later on, the two women would find peace between them and continue to knit together sweaters and socks for the downtrodden of the parish.

Robotson had tried as much as he could to refrain from ever thinking about stealing, but it was stronger in his inner being than he could conceive and much louder than the voice of a conscience allowed to speak up. His had been silenced for years. Who was to blame? The elements, the Creator or the social determinants? There was enough blame to go all around. Robotson did not allow blame to stir him to accept it whatever people blamed him for, not even think about it. It was, for him, a non issue. So he pursued his life s work, that of planning and executing his petty thefts. After a while, he decided to really steal something valuable like Mister Fabrice s Fabergé s egg. He was tired of collecting eggs that he did not eat His mother had died and he was now living alone in a dingy apartment. If only he could get his hands on the Fabergé egg. That would give him the possibility of getting some money in his hands and probably enough of it to get himself a new place to live.

He resolved to map out a plan to steal the desired egg. When he had it all done, he was about ready to execute it when he heard that Mister Fabrice had died. Perfect, he said, "I'm now free to do what I've been wanting to do." When the time came, he carefully entered into Mister Fabrice's house thinking no one was there, and he went to the curio cabinet to get his hands on the Fabergé egg. It was gone. What a disaster, he thought, what a terrible disappointment. As he was getting ready to leave the premises he heard a knock at the door. A policeman! The neighbor had called the cops having heard noise inside Mister Fabrice's house. Robotson was caught red-handed, but with no booty. The officer led him to the station where they booked him for breaking and entering, for they found on him a chocolate egg that he had taken from Mister Fabrice's table. He had not been able to control his infamous desire for chocolate eggs. So, he was sent to jail. In the meantime, Mister Fabrice's will was read and it was found that the Fabergé egg had been willed to a man called Robotson with the attached note, "For my friend, Valjean Robotson, who always was honest with me, did my errands and loved my Fabergé egg. So I bequeath it to him with pride an honor." I need not caution you about stealing something that is already yours.

10.

Of Boas and Boa Constrictors

Melody Rancourt had the very best of things that her father provided since he was a rich businessman and loved to lavish nice things on his daughter. She had everything from slippers made in Italy, dresses imported from France, purses made in Romania, and jewels made of gold and splendid silver. She had a locket that cost her father three thousand dollars. Inside the locket was the picture of a movie star that Melody adored. It was Indiana Jones in the snake pit. She loved his bravery and his daring as an adventurer. Not that she admired the actor who played the part, Harrison Ford, although she found him good-looking, but she simply loved the character he played so well in the film. She saw the movie thirteen times and never got tired of looking at it. She especially liked the scene where the hero drops into a snake pit and how he manages to walk away free from the snakes. However, he walks right into another "snake pit", that of the Nazis who are also looking for the Ark of the Covenant. She enjoyed the suspense, the drama, and especially the way the hero prevailed upon his fate as a hero to march out of the perils of the adventurous search and emerging as a hero. Only in movies could one see that, she thought. She knew that the whole story was made up by some Hollywood screenwriters for some producer and talented director, but she dismissed the fact that it was Hollywood glitz. To her, the whole thing was captivating. She was glad that they had created this hero-character for she enjoyed every minute of the entire movie. Hollywood was a dream-maker and a dream-whisperer, she told herself. Of course, there were other film-makers outside of Hollywood, but this tinsel-town was the very epitome of film-making. It had been for years. She also liked films such as, "The Nun's Story" set in Belgium and Africa and she loved Audrey Hepburn as an actress. She loved all of her films including "Roman Holiday" Melody would have liked being Audrey Hepburn. She asked her father to take her to Rome and explore the spots that Audrey had been in the film, but her father told her he didn't have time to travel. So, he bought her a guidebook. Besides these films, she also relished the French films, "Jean de Florette" and Manon des Sources." She had learned enough French to follow the screen dialogues. She loved the hunchback papa, Jean de Florette. She thought he was a most charming and valiant character. She sympathized with the character and felt that Dépardieu had played the role so very well. Also, she enjoyed "The King and I" and thought Deborah Kerr deserved an Oscar for her brilliant acting. Why did Yul Brynner get one and his co-star didn't? she asked herself. Added to this list, were two films not so well known, "The Way" with Martin Sheen and "Monsieur Ibrahim" with Omar Sharif and a talented young man by the name of François Dupeyron. She really loved this young man and she thought he was the one she would someday marry if her father let her and paid a tremendous dowry in the process. It was all a dream. She knew that. But dreams are real and they can come true if one truly puts her mind to it. So, she thought and thought. She dreamed and dreamed. The reality of it all was that none of it came to full realization. She also knew that money did not buy dreams and turned them into full-blown reality. Money bought things and influence, but not dreams. Dreams had to be woven like a colorful cloth be it jacquard, interwoven silk threads, or so many other precious threads woven by the dreamer. The fabric of dreams was made of the hours spent imagining things and characters, she told herself. So she spent hours upon hours weaving dreams, be they actual nighttime dreams or daydreaming. She let her creative imagination do its work. She had a daring and colorful imagination. Her father often accused her of spending too much time dreaming all kinds of things. She told him that she could not do otherwise since she was nailed to her wheelchair. You see, Melody was a cripple. Since birth.

Melody had a terrible disease when she was born. It was called muscular dystrophy. A rare form in Melody's case. She could not walk like other children, and she could hardly move a muscle without feeling some pain. She could not even move a single muscle without some agonizing discomfort. She was destined to spend her life, whatever length it would be, in a wheelchair. Her father bought her an electric one. She moved about without too much difficulty as long as she was able to use spaces for the disabled. Her mother had abandoned her of sorts. Not that she had left her out in the streets, but it was almost like that. One day, she just left never to return. Melody used to tell people that she was a half-orphan. No mother.

Melody turned out to be a lovely child, beautiful round face with deep dark eyes and creamy complexion. She knew she was lovely simply by looking at herself in a mirror. Besides, people told her she was lovely. With time and the many movies she watched, she grew to behave adoringly by adopting the ways of movie stars. Melody loved dressing up, that is, she loved beautiful clothes that her father was able to buy for her. She knew exactly what she wanted like cream-colored shawls, fancy hats with ostrich feathers, dresses made of silk and finely woven cotton, as well as purses made of real calf's leather. She very seldom used purses, but she wanted them anyway. She would pretend she was in Hollywood with the stars, and that she was bound to get a star in the Star Walk. She just had to, she told herself. Why, she dreamed of getting an honorary Oscar just for the fact of loving movies as much as she did. Dream on, she told herself. She had a favorite movie where she could envision herself to be a young Marlene Dietrich, or was it Gloria Swanson, playing the eternal movie star. What did it matter if it was Marlene or Gloria, they were both film-queens weren't they? "My close-up, Mister DeMille," she would repeat to herself over and over again. One day, she insisted that she had seen Nora Desmond with an elegant boa, a boa made of exotic feathers. Of course, she could not see the color since the film was black and white, but she could see that the boa was a very nice and elegant one.

She wasn't sure she was dreaming that but she could easily see in her mind's eye, a fashionable boa around Nora Desmond's neck coming down her smooth shoulders right down to her wrists. Oh, it was splendid. That's when she urged her father to get her a boa. One that was as nice and elegant as the one she had seen in "Sunset Boulevard." Her father told her that she was too young for such costumes, and that she should wait until she grew up to bother with such extravagant things. That's when she would tell her father that she didn't have that much time. Her disease would not allow her to pass thirty. Her father would then reply that he was sorry, and that he would get her what she wanted in spite of her tender sixteen years.

"Where does one find an elegant boa?" the father asked his secretary. "A what?" "A boa. You know a boa that a woman wears around her neck just like Nora Desmond." "Who's Nora Desmond?" "Nora Desmond, Nora Desmond of 'Sunset Boulevard,' "Is Sunset Boulevard in Hollywood?" "Not exactly. 'Sunset Boulevard' the movie." "I never watch movies, I watch TV."

And so, the father asked around and finally found an elegant boa at an antique store off Main Street. It was feathery, fluffy and cream-colored with black tail feathers here and there. He was sure that Melody would love it. She had better or else I'm not running around for a boa, he told himself.

When Melody saw the boa, she shouted, "Oh, Daddy, it's perfect Just what I wanted. My very own boa." She wore her boa at breakfast, for lunch and dinner, and if she had listened to her inner voice, she would have worn it to bed. However, she did not want to squish and render it lifeless like a dead snake, so she laid it gently beside her bed. If she happened to wake up, she would pull on it and put it around her neck until she fell asleep. Often enough, she would be found with her boa around her waist in the morning when her father woke her. The maid would take it off her and gently lay it on the bureau in the bedroom. Melody would willfully follow the transfer of her boa with eyes that were peeled on it persistently. She would not let it out of her sight so much was she attached to her cream-colored boa with black tail feathers here and there.

One night, Melody dreamed that her boa had grown into a large boa constrictor and had swallowed an elephant. Just like the drawing in her favorite little book, "The Little Prince." It looked like a hat to the adults that saw it, but in reality it was a boa constrictor who had swallowed an elephant Adults could only see the exterior of things, so said the author of "The Little Prince." Melody wanted to imitate the young lad who had drawn the boa who had swallowed the elephant. She set herself to work and started drawing boa constrictors who had swallowed large objects and other animals like a lion, a bear, or even a crocodile. After all, she followed in the steps of Saint-Exupéry and believed what this author had read in 'Living Stories' about the virgin forest and its animals. "She read in her book, "*Les serpents boas avalent leur proie toute entière, sans la mâcher. Ensuite ils ne peuvent plus bouger et ils dorment pendant les six mois de leur digestion.*" Yes, boas swallowed their prey whole without munching it and then they cannot move a muscle and sleep during the entire six months of the digestion. That's what she read and believed it. She knew she could not go to the virgin forest to ascertain the existence of boas swallowing their prey whole, but she could imagine one doing just that. Her boa would serve as an image of reality in the wild.

Melody kept dreaming and dreaming of her cream-colored boa with black tail feathers here and there metamorphosing into a live boa constrictor until she could not distinguish her own boa with the real live one. Both seemed too real for her. While awake during the daytime hours, she had let her imagination run wild so that at nighttime during her sleeping hours her daylight imaginings became the transformation of her dream, that of a boa constrictor swallowing its prey whole. Every night it would be a different prey. She even dreamed one night that the boa constrictor had swallowed her father whole. She woke up suddenly in fear and started to shake all over. She started yelling until her maid came in to calm her down. Melody told the maid all about her bad dream. Little did Melody know that the father had in reality been swallowed up into a large sinkhole that very night driving home. There had been a terrible storm and the river had eroded part of the road and created a large sink hole. Be careful of what you dream, my children. Sink holes like large boa constrictors swallow their prey or victim whole...and they are not hats in the eyes of grown-ups visualizing the after effects in their restricted and not very creative imagination.

11.

Why the Hare Lost the Race

I'm sure that most of you have read Aesop's fable, "The Hare and the Tortoise." It's a delightful tale with a moral to it. It tells of a hare and a tortoise involved in a race, and who would win such an competitive attempt. The hare was positively sure that he would win the race because of his swift capabilities and the speed with which he was endowed by the Creator of all living things. He would laugh again at the tortoise's inability to gain speed with his ineffable slowness caused by his heavy shell. After all, he, the hare, was the swiftest of all minor animals in the forest, he told himself. Some call it pride, others call it presumption. Whatever you may call it, it was a feeling of assurance and positiveness. The hare knew in his inner being that he would beat the tortoise. Why? Because it was written in the stars. "Written in the stars?" asked the other animals who were watching. "Yes, written in the stars because that's what I see at night," said the hare, "it's magic and magic works." The tortoise started laughing. "What are you laughing at?" "I'm laughing at you because you're always laughing at me. You don't even look at the stars because you're always looking at yourself." The hare did not respond immediately. One of these days he would find the right words to reply to this insult, he told himself. "I'm not vain and neither am I full of myself as this tortoise thinks," he whispered to himself.

And so, the race got on the way with the hare standing erect and proud of his competence. The tortoise waited crouched down with his heavy shell on his back. Nothing he could do about it; he had been created that way. All animals were given a particular endowment, and his was a heavy one. The Creator had told him that it was for his protection, but the tortoise did not always see it that way. He thanked the Lord for having given him that special gift, but did it have to be so heavy, he wondered. The hare looked at his legs and his ears and just smiled for he knew that he was well endowed by the Creator. He could hear very well and run as swiftly as any animal his size could. As for protection, well, his legs provided that for him. He ran fast and could easily outrun any predator. So he thought.

So, the race began around noontime because it had taken a long time for the tortoise to rise, open his eyes and get ready for the morning sun. Besides, he was in no hurry to get around and find his friends in the forest. Today, he had said, was the day he would just amble away and take it easy for he had no trouble or concerns awaiting him. Until, he met the hare and the hare started taunting him about his shell and his slow pace. "Hah, hah, hah," said the hare, "you're nothing but a slow-ass, a no-competitor with your heavy shell slowing you down." The tortoise started going away from his friends standing all around him, but one of them, a red fox told him to stand up to the hare and run the race anyway. The race was worth running, he told him. It would be a sign of proud daunting and a mark of persuasive determination, a feather in your cap, he added. "A feather in my cap?" asked the tortoise. "Yes, that's what everyone says." "But what does it mean?" asked the tortoise. "In one culture it means the custom of a warrior adding a new feather to his headgear for every enemy slain." "Also," interrupted the partridge, "it symbolizes the hunter as being the first one to bag a game bird and pluck a feather and place it in the hat band. I know something about that since I'm a game bird myself." They all laughed.

And so, the hare and the tortoise were ready for the race, if not of the century, the race of the week. The hare was ready stomping his feet on the ground, a bit anxious to get going. He knew he was going to win. As for the tortoise, he moved slowly up to the starting line inching his way until the hare cried out to him, "Hurry on up, you slow-ass, you tub of hard lard, you creepy-crawly hard-shell end-product of creation." The tortoise said nothing. He simply stared ahead and moved up to the starting line. He was a bit frustrated at his inability to move any faster and somewhat humiliated to show his slowness in front of all his friends. But, that's the way he was; he could not change things. He only wished that somehow he could wind up winning this race. Could he? He didn't know for sure. All he could do was do his very best. He would keep a steady pace and not deviate from it. He would not fool around. He would not fall into the clutches of despair, and he would certainly not let the exterior elements get the best of him, like the heat of the sun, the mugginess and the lack of breathable air get to him. He would be steady in his pace and persevere in his aim to conquer the negative factors of being too slow to win any race. He was slow but quick to assess any situation. He would not be flighty and scurrilous like the hare. The hare had a penchant for being fickle at times and lose sight of the aim of whatever was in question. The tortoise knew that if he was going to win, he would have to outmaneuver his opponent. But how?

The race started and the two animals of the forest racing towards an established goal looked at each other and quickly lost sight of each other after only a couple of minutes. The hare was out front some five yards ahead of the slow-paced tortoise. The hare knew that he was going to win; the tortoise knew that he had to work very hard to outpace the hare and win this race. After but fifteen minutes, or was it ten, the hare was slowing down to get a little rest from running so hard. He didn't want to become breathless and fall into some kind of dehydrated moments. After all, he could not throw this race. He just couldn't. What would he do if all of a sudden he fell into the trap of missing the aim of winning just by some accident of nature like going suddenly blind or losing his breath due to exhaustion or even through some miscalculation that endangered his energy level. It had happened once in a race with the partridge. The partridge had flown over the bushes and landed right on top of him, and he had hit his head on a rock. He had miscalculated that the partridge could fly and he couldn't. Whatever the possibilities of losing might be, the hare was sure he was going to win no matter the circumstances, no matter some possible twist of fate. Fate had nothing to do with it, he told himself. Fate only mattered for other creatures, for he was protected against fate since only men were susceptible to it. They were not assured of any protection against it. He had learned from his ancestors that hares were inured towards fate and protected against its devastation. That was their destiny and their gift from the Creator. He believed it. Be it fact, fiction or myth, he believed in what his ancestors had said. It was part of his heritage as a hare of the virgin forest.

As for the tortoise, he had no such guarantee. He believed in the forces of fate and fatality. He had been brought up believing that everything created, water, sand, rocks, mountains, sky and especially living creatures were subject to fate. It was written in the vast firmament of planets and stars. All you had to do said the ancestors, was to glance and study the paths of the stellar and planetary elements to find out how the universe is moved and influenced by fate. Science was only part of it. Science tried to explain it, but fate had its mighty hand in it. Science could try as hard as it could for science had the tools at its disposition in logic and mathematics. But, science could never solve all of the problems and calculations of the universe. That's what his ancestors had told him. So, the tortoise believed in fate and in its strong inevitable forces. Nobody, but no one, not even the hares could refute fate and its influence in the universe. Especially in the virgin forest where the animals lived. That gave the tortoise faith in himself and in the forces of the planets and the stars. He believed in it so much that he deliberately thought that chances of winning this race were good and they would get better. No doubt about that.

After the race had gotten into a full fifteen minutes, the hare decided to stop a while and lollygag around, just to keep himself amused. He did that so that the other animals would think he was assured of his win. He stomped and hippety-hopped around until he got tired of it. He then sat down on the soft grass and fell asleep. In the meantime, the tortoise went his slow but regular pace without stopping. He had in his mind the picture of victory over the fickle one. Besides, he had talent that very few had noticed. Talent for speed in perseverance and steadfastness. Speed to the tortoise was not necessarily fast and furious, but deliberate and well- timed. It was all in the hands of fate, he thought. If fate decides to crown you with glory and winning, then nothing can go wrong. The victory was at hand, so thought the tortoise. No matter what. No matter what anyone could do or think. Everything was driven by fate, so thought the tortoise. And he was convinced of it. It had been like that for centuries if not eons of time. It was all in the stars, he told himself. It was part of his own heritage and history.

At a certain point in the race, the hare suspected that something was wrong since he saw the tortoise going along at his constant pace while the hare just stood there daydreaming. What was happening, he thought. Things were not supposed to be like that. So he scrambled to hop to it and pass his opponent as fast as he could not losing any time. In a matter of seconds, he had passed the tortoise. Now, he was sure he was going to win the race. Nothing in the world would make him lose. Nothing. How could he not win with a slow-paced animal with a solidly heavy back like the tortoise, he told himself. The shell must have weighed more that the body of the tortoise, and it had to be carried around like a huge anchor or a heavy load of rocks. Always dragging the poor animal wherever he was going. These are the thoughts that swam in the hare's mind as he pursued the glory of victory that day.

All of a sudden, the hare crashed to the ground on which he was running. Something had hit his right leg. A broken branch from a huge pine tree perhaps, a rock that happened to hit him, or some mysterious thing that prevented him from running fast or running at all. He could barely walk. Forget the running. What was he to do with this mysterious happening. He looked downtrodden and totally beguiled by this strange thing that happened just as he was about to conquer his opponent. He tried and tried to finish the race with a semblance of rapidity but nothing doing. He just limped towards the goal, the end of the race which loomed some distance away. He could see it. Meanwhile the tortoise simply trudged along and passed the crestfallen hare. Slowly but steadily did the tortoise manage to keep on going with deliberate steps towards the prize of victory. It was his, not the hare. He could sense that in his head and in his guts. Victory would be his. "Whatever had happened to the hare?" he said to himself. It had to be some mysterious thing that he could not explain except to name it fate. Yes, that mysterious force in the universe upon which every creature came to exercise its destiny. It was indeed a force to reckon with. The tortoise knew then that his ancestors had been right all along. Perhaps the hare did not believe in fate, but now he was the victim of it. Fate had decreed that the hare would lose the race, and that the tortoise would overcome its lack of speed. Some observers and readers of the tale would adamantly proclaim that there was a moral to the tale and that good natural abilities are ruined by idleness, and that sobriety and perseverance can prevail over indolence. So said the Classical voices. The motto being 'hasten slowly,' while another interpretation was 'the more haste, the worse speed.' Still another was in the so-called true story that the hare realizes the stupidity of the challenge and refuses to proceed thus giving up the race while the obstinate tortoise continues to the finishing line and wins the race. Yet, another is applied to the biblical observation that 'the race is not won by the swift...[and]for a time of calamity comes to all alike'(9:11). Calamity or fate, things happen that are not always perceived or anticipated. Some scientific minds contend that the only satisfactory refutation has been mathematical, and since then the fable has been applied to the function of Zeno's paradox that movement is impossible to define satisfactorily. In mathematics and computer science, the tortoise and the hare algorithm is an alternative name for Floyd's cycle-finding algorithm. Whatever the interpretation or the moral of the tale may be, the true realization of this tale, as seen here, is that fate rules predominantly, and fate alone is the great prescriptive agent and decider of deeds and actions in the universe.

If you don't believe that fate is at work in the lives of all creatures great and small, just ask Charles Bovary.

12.

Why Roosters Have Coxcombs

Did you ever ask yourself why roosters have coxcombs and hens have not? For hens it is called combs, but for roosters it's coxcombs. Both have their own particular significance. That's a very intriguing question as far as I'm concerned. One that challenges if not defies research and trained observation. But there is a reasonable answer to this, and even a scientific explanation, as we shall see. To every question there is an answer and an explanation of sorts.

Coxcombs on roosters have a particular significance and function in that the coxcomb provides aesthetic qualities and it indicates the health condition of the rooster. A healthy rooster has a bright and shiny one. There is also the wattle which lies under the chin of the rooster, and it is of the same shiny color as the coxcomb. Moreover, roosters use their coxcombs for sexual attraction. Although both roosters and hens have combs and wattles, the combs of the hen are much less predominant. The rooster makes full attraction use of his. The hens go for the male who has the biggest and brightest coxcomb and wattles. We also learn that the combs regulate the heat in both the rooster and the hen since the blood flows in them. So much for the information about coxcombs for roosters and combs for chickens. But that's not the true importance and meaning of our tale. There is more to it than that.

At the first instance of creation, the good Lord created everything in the universe including roosters and chickens. Of course, they were not the first beings created by the powerful hand of God. Genesis only mentions them as part of the "all kinds of living creatures." The writer of Genesis did not have time and space to list all creatures, I'm sure. But roosters and hens were certainly created with the rest of the animals, the cattle, the crawling creatures and the wild animals. Of course, the roosters and the hens were domesticated later on in the history of the world. I do not think that Adam and Eve did the domestication of all animals. I'm not even sure they ate eggs. Be it as it may, our tale begins much later around the Middle Ages when things began to be organized in the kingdom of men. There were fiefs, lords, warriors going off to fight the infidel and peasants who took care of the many lands that belonged to the lords. These lords were too busy fighting and traveling here and there, around and afar. So they put their lands in the capable hands of the serfs who worked so hard tilling the land, taking care of the animals and reaping the crops each year. That was besides all the extra work they had to do like building huts, houses, barns and sties as well as other structures such as majestic cathedrals. But cathedrals were the responsibility of the craftsmen, the apprentices, the journeymen and the masters. They were part of guilds, bands of men and women who worked together and shared their expertise, either merchants or craftsmen. Enough of this.

Our tale begins in the latter part of the thirteenth century. There was once a man who had a large fief and who enjoyed parceling it out to his serfs for he was a generous man. He was lord and master, but he did not act like one. He did not show an inordinate pride and greed that most lords had at the time. They wanted to secure their lordship's rights and privileges, so they took advantage of the needy poor people by treating them like slaves more than human beings in need. There was compassion and trust in this man they called Henri-le-Maître-de-Vaillancourt. He had received his privileges and rights from his uncle who had no children to pass them on to. Henri was raised by a mother who was a simple and honest woman. She had showed him the way to a flourishing life full of pleasant memories and honest friendships. His father had died a pauper, and left his family with hardly anything. However, his mother's brother had been knighted by the king for his bravery in battle. He had fought with the crusaders and returned home a valiant and beloved man of bravery and honest deeds for which he was rewarded with a fief in the lower valley of Commerstant-de-la-vallée. That's how the fief was called. It was a large portion of arable land and the reaping of its crops were enviable. When he happened to die with a malicious malady associated with the plague, he left his fief to his nephew since he had no other heir. His sister was surprised and grateful for the great gift her brother had granted her son, called Emmanuel-de-Dieu. That's the name she had given him at baptism.

Now, Emmanuel-de-Dieu had two roosters and several hens that he took care of on a small plot of land that was part of the fief his uncle owned. He had taken care of his small menagerie and had shared the eggs with other serfs after he had paid his tribute to the lord of the manor, his uncle, Henri-le-Maître-de-Vaillancourt. His uncle had recognized his nephew's generosity and rewarded him with a few gold coins that the nephew stored away for the future. He wanted to join the craftsmen guild and become a master carver of stone. He had been awed by the building of Gothic cathedrals ever since he had seen the one in Chartres. He had traveled many leagues to get to Chartres, and he never minded the long journey from his village to Chartres just to be able to look at the rising structure that was the cathedral of Chartres dedicated to our Lady, the Virgin Mary. The cathedral stayed in his mind and imagination ever since he had witnessed its beauty, design, and its startling stained glass windows. They were of the bluest of blues to a point that glaziers called it the Chartres blue. The façade windows, the lancets of the Tree of Jesse, the Nativity, and the Passion were of an extraordinary blue and reflected the glaziers' skill in producing some of the loveliest and most cherished stained glass ever done. Emmanuel could not get over the magnificence of the cathedral and especially the exquisite windows. He returned home telling his mother that he wanted to grow up becoming a maker of stained glass windows. He had changed his mind about becoming a carver of stone.

Now, one day as Emmanuel-de-Dieu surveyed his domain now that he was master and lord of the land, although not knighted by the Duke of Alacrie, his lord and master, he wanted to stretch out his hand to help his serfs in their lot as servants and slaves to the land. Emmanuel did not want his domain to be a slave quarter. He wanted his fief to become a domain where even the poorest of men had a parcel of land they could call their own. The Duke of Alacrie told him that could not be done for land belonged to lords and masters and not to serfs. That was the law of the land, the law directly from the king. No one could change that except the king himself. It could not be done.

Emmanuel thought of a scheme in order to accomplish his wishes that the poor of his land could enjoy fully the fruits of their labor. He would tell stories and fables to the court of the Duke of Alacrie and cajole each one of them with his charm and wit so that he would fall into the good graces of the Duke. He knew the Duke, but the Duke did not know him well enough to grant him favors. Emmanuel was going to try and seduce the Duke to give him one privilege, that of granting him the right to parcel out his land to his serfs. That was not done at that time. Emmanuel would at least try to get that right. There is nothing that works as well as entertainment, he told himself, and he would certainly try to soften the ears of the court ladies so that they would plead for him at court. That way, the Duke would listen to them and reward them by granting Emmanuel's request. That was Emmanuel's scheme. Would it work?

After many attempts, the court was opened to Emmanuel and he was able to intermingle with the ladies whose husbands were off fighting for the king in order to earn royal merits. The poor ladies were so often lonely waiting for their sires, and quite often would entertain the presence of anyone would tell them tales and romantic stories called "romances.".

Emmanuel did not have romantic stories to tell, but he did have many tales in his marvelous memory that dealt with animals and other subject matter. He had learned this lore from his uncle, as well as the court jester who was a great friend of Henri-le Maître-de-Vailancourt. He also had a cache of fabliaux at his disposal since he had learned them from the serfs at his command. The ladies thrived on the romances of Chrétien de Troyes, but he wasn't always there to entertain them himself. In the intervals of time when the ladies got bored and wished for lively stories, since they were opened to anyone who would entertain them with whatever stories would be told. That is how Emmanuel was able to enter the duke's court He loved the ladies at court especially one called "La Belle aux Cheveux d'Or," the golden-haired one.

He first started by telling them the fabliau of Reynart and Chantecler, the sly fox and the gullible cockerel, the rooster. The tale went as such. The rooster then called a cockerel was named Chantecler because he could sing loud and clear, thus his name of Chante-cler. His ladies, he had four wives, were so very fond of his voice in the early hours of the morning. It would wake up every fowls and animals of the area including the people living around neighborhood. It was known as Chantecler's morning chant Its got to be so popular that the king of the forest decided one day to reward Chantecler and give him something very special, a crown. But the crown would not be of gold or silver, but of soft and bright fleshy growth on top of its head. Up to now, the rooster had nothing to designate him as a superior being in the barnyard. He was not a distinguished fowl; he was simply an ordinary two-legged animal with ordinary plumage. The hens so often did not even notice him, only his morning chant. They were not attracted to him and quite often would refused his attempts to copulate with him. No eggs therefore. The farmers and the serfs would get angry at the hens. They told their masters that it wasn't their fault if they did not find the rooster attractive. He was dull and unattractive that was all.

The lion then decided to reward the rooster by the power of his kingly privilege given to him by the Creator. So the lion gathered the animals of the forest as well as the domesticated ones and proclaimed a day of celebration in honor of the rooster, Chantecler. The lion's court had decreed this and so had the duke's court They all wanted to proclaim Chantecler, the rooster, the champion, of the barnyard. It was then that the coxcomb, that bright fleshy crown on Chantecler's head started growing into a glorious fixture that resembled an upright crown. From now on, he would reign as king of his own court, the barnyard with all of the farm animals. Everyone was happy and everyone rejoiced in this brave animal that became the chant-giver of the morning with a bright crown on his head. The ladies applauded Emmanuel and they told him that they would use their influence on the Duke to grant Emmanuel his wish.

It was thus granted to the honest master of the domain of Emmanuel-de-Dieu-le-Grand-Seigneur that he would be able to grant each of his serfs a parcel of land which they could till and reap fine results of their own. These serfs were the envy of all serfs. In turn they would eventually become the model of the bourgeois and their role in society. And this is how the rooster got his coxcomb. At least that's the way it was told through the magic of tales and legends that has delighted so many throughout the years. A cautionary tale or not? I leave it up to you, dear readers. Try to think of the caution of being wise and generous when you are tempted to go astray in your devious endeavors and your conceits. The coxcomb tale will serve you as an example of crowning interest and sexual attraction for those who so choose. Caution! It may serve you the way it was not intended... greed and perhaps lust. One never knows.

13.

The Tale of the Hummingbird Extravaganza

Do you know what an extravaganza is? I do not really and fully know myself, but I know a little about it. The dictionary gives us the definition of "a literary, musical or dramatic composition characterized by a loose structure, farce, or fantastic plot development; now, any spectacular and elaborate theatrical production, as certain musical shows." Since I work both in English and in French, I looked the word up in my French/English dictionary and discovered that there is no such word in French, just certain other words such as *histoire extravagante or invraisemblable.* I can understand the connotation of extravagant story but as to the qualifier of unlikely and improbable, I do not accept these as being true to the word extravaganza. Yes, we are dealing here with the word "fantasy" but even fantasy does not necessarily mean unlikely or even improbable. Fantasy to me means imaginative, created by the imagination and that's not unlikely and improbable. I may be wrong, but I stick to my thought on this. Be it as it may, an extravaganza to me means a spectacular show or presentation that is meant to be out of this world. It does not fall in the category of improbability, rather it falls in the category of creative madness perhaps and certainly in the realm of fantasy, and of head and soul harmonizing in a collaborative exercise of outstanding imaginings or imaging so that the whole splendor of whatever is being imagined becomes spectacular or as one may say extravagant as an extravaganza.

Have I gotten you confused? Stick with me, reader, for I will produce for you an extravaganza of sorts, one dealing with hummingbirds. Enough said of definitions and explanations. They're oftentimes boring aren't they?

Hummingbirds are ever so tiny and light, almost like huge insects rather than birds. They hover like little whirlwinds in the air. Their wings are like small robotized airlifts that propel them wherever they want to go. They do not stop to alight on anything. They simply remain in motion all the time while feeding and sucking up the sugary liquid that is offered to them. Of course, they do reach down the calyx of a flower to get the much desired nectar. It's always a marvelous sight for me to watch hummingbirds flutter, hover and spin in the air. Some of them are bejeweled and look like the jewels of the Creator sent to startle us and give us an extravagant sight of beauty and delight. Now, for the extravaganza and the hummingbirds.

It all began a long time ago, a very long time. Much before the hummingbirds were recognized as the jewels of the bird family. Much before the hummingbird was known as the *colibri* in both the French and Spanish languages. It comes actually from the Caribbean language. Furthermore, the hummingbird has another term in French besides *colibri* . It's *oiseau-mouche*, bird-insect, an appropriate term for this tiny creature. Aztecs wore hummingbird talismans emblematic of vigor and energy. Even before the Aztecs, there was a small group of people living in the Caribbean waters, on a tiny island called Violetear where the living was easy and filled with happiness. No one knew violence. There was no war, no struggle of power and no harsh words between neighbors and friends. There was peace, a soft and tonal peace that vibrated throughout the land as small as it was. People were always ready to accommodate others and willing to share whatever they had or owned. There was perfect harmony between man and beast, between woman and man, between human nature and environmental nature. Just harmony of voices in unison, so-to-speak. Singing was heard throughout the day and at night there was the low humming sound of birds which the natives called hummingbirds. When these birds slept in perfect tranquility, there were a few who stayed awake just to hum their song in the moonlit air. You see, this continual humming gave rise to the harmony among people who slept to the harmony of the humming. Nothing could derange or dispel this gentle and soft sound. It generated sleep among the humans and without sleep humans could not work properly, could not be energized and could not work to their full capacity of human endeavors. Nothing can be done harmoniously without gentle sleep, is what they believed. Sleep is the required aspect of staying alive and well, they said. Sleep deprivation was an evil that counteracted with their nature as human beings, they thought. So the hummingbirds and their gentle sounds or singing was a gift from the gods, it was said.

The hummingbird, although much beloved by the people, were practically colorless. They did not have the jewel quality that they have today. They were plain, dull in coloring and nothing to speak of except for their hovering breathless noise. They did not catch anyone's eye. They were simply ordinary and dull. The hummingbirds themselves had no pride in their look and their appearance for they thought themselves to be plainer than plain. Just a very plain species of dull-colored birds. They looked to the heavens to claim some sort of grace to be granted them in order to gain some coloration that they might enjoy displaying their diversity as miniature birds. They had nothing to lose, they said, only their dullness. Days and months went by, even years and nothing happened. They began to despair. The heavens seemed closed to them and their request for color dismissed.

One day, a small wren-like bird flew into their midst and introduced himself to the hummingbird flock. Some hummingbirds wanted to shoo him away since they thought he was an intruder. They did not want an intruder in their midst. The little bird had dull plumage and sang an ugly song for a bird. He lost all confidence from the hummingbirds that looked to him for some kind of uplifting. Is that all the heavens could afford to send them, they said with mistrust. The poor dull creature tried in vain to insert himself in the company of hummingbirds, but to no avail. Try as he may, he could not win a single hummingbird to his point of view. He felt distraught and wanted to fly over the mountain ridge, but he knew he could not do it. It would have been a most difficult attempt on his part. He thought of flying into the big cat's mouth and be swallowed or eaten by him. He couldn't do that. He wanted to stay alive and well. He only had one life to live, he told himself. Until one day, one of the hummingbirds came to him and offered him some consolation.

The name of this hummingbird was Veru, and he was a descendant of one of the hummingbird line of eye-catchers. The eye-catchers were the oldest of the line of hummingbirds that had crossed over the borders of distant shores where they had been in search of new blossoms that would give them pure nectar. They were called the explorers and discoverers. They had the guts to fly in the face of danger in order to find the sustenance they needed. Not just for themselves but for all hummingbirds to come. The had finally found the new and rich blossoms that offered them the rich and much sought after nectar they needed to survive. They called it the divine nectar because they considered it to be sent to them by the gods. Veru told the young wren-like bird not to hold on to his worries and that he would help him negotiate a deal with the other hummingbirds. The deal being that the so-called intruder would no longer be an intruder but a member of the family. The family of the hummingbirds. And so, Veru accomplished his task and his promise by allowing the intruder to talk and discuss at length his reason for being alone and practically an outcast. He was so eloquent in his discussion with the hummingbirds that he convinced many to subscribe to a new policy of understanding and compassion. Some older ones complained that they were opposed to this new policy because it allowed outsiders to intrude into their lives and harm their traditions of being ever conservative and head-strong about intimacy. "What intimacy"? asked the others. "The intimacy of staying firm and unwavering in our identity as a species, never faltering and never wavering." "But, we must be supple and understanding in moments of change. We must not be intransigent." "Then don't bend, don't be supple to the demands of time and newcomers. Remain stuck in the past and do not believe that things won't change, because things do change. Birds change. All birds will someday be allowed to change and flourish. It's a matter of destiny." And so, the discussion went on for days if not months. The headstrong ones would not change their attitude and their mind about the situation. They were stuck in the mud of their unwillingness to bend and be supple in their thinking.

Finally, the wren-like bird left the hummingbirds to their endless discussions. He could not tolerate their stubborn attitude and their pride. The hummingbirds remained dull and plain in their plumage. Nothing was ever going to change. Not until the hardness of heart changed. Some of the younger hummingbirds began to think about the situation and they thought of a way to turn things around. But how? They turned to Veru. He had been cast off like an unwanted stranger and he waited for things to change. He didn't want to influence the others with his plans and he waited until someone would inspire the others with enough confidence in themselves to make matters better than they were. That would take courage and deliberate action. He waited for a savior, one who would save the species from itself. Then came a young hummingbird called Joviah who came into the lives of the hummingbirds one day in late May. He was born of a humble and very modest female. Her name was Mayatia. She had laid two eggs, as tiny as they come for hummingbirds. She had taken good care of her two eggs until they finally hatched one bright morning. The two tiny hummingbirds grew and became adult hummingbirds. One flew off to somewhere never to be seen again. Some said he was too adventurous, and that he had been eaten up by a predator. The other, Joviah, grew to be a fine bird with a delightful personality and a heart of gold. He was a generous soul and supple in his mind and heart.

One day, Joviah was found on the ground helpless and wounded. He had suffered the ruthless attacks of some so-called friends, and they had left him dazed and stupefied. "Why would they do such a thing to me?" he asked himself. He knew the answer, but refused to accept it because it touched upon the seriousness of his affair with others who knew him and wanted him dead. He would suffer for his mistakes, they said, suffer because he made people suffer by his insistence on keeping harmony within the ranks. They did not believe in social justice and harmony. The only justice they believed in was that of tit for tat, or an eye for an eye and a kick for a swift kick in the face. In other words, revenge. It was all due to the fact that Joviah wanted harmony among each one of his kind. He wanted to live in peace and resolve differences by soft and tender words of mercy, not hard and difficult slam dunk retorts that hurt everyone. Joviah was of the peaceful kind, not one to offend anyone or put their sense of dignity at risk. He was indeed a peacemaker. He was willing to sacrifice everything and anything for justice and peace. But justice and peace come at a very high price sometimes. The price of one's self-sacrifice. Joviah was willing and ready to do that That is why he lay on the ground suffering the insults and injury of those who could not stand what they called his platitudes and purposeless taunts. He just wasn't like them and they could not stand for that. He told them that the reason for their dullness and plainness of plumage was that they were too dull themselves and hardly knew how to behave with others who did not agree with them on any account. How can harmony reign if there is no sensibility to mutual understanding. How can one exist in total disharmony, he asked himself, fearing that harmony would never come to such a gang of thugs and feeble-minded beings. They had to accept the foibles of others and their differences if they wanted others to accept them unreservedly. They too had foibles and various different tendencies. Joviah asked them, one day, what was it that they wanted. They did not know. Did not know! "What a predicament," Joviah said. He could not get them to understand that their real problems came from themselves, not others. The struggle or the battle was not lost because heaven saw it fit to send down the wren-like bird to the hummingbirds, specifically to Joviah.

You see the wren-like bird, the plain and humble one, was part of a level of little angels right after the Cherubims, far below the archangels in dignity and might, but considered little messengers of good omen. They're the ones who chased after the manna-eaters who were disgusted to eat what the Yahweh had sent them in the desert. These little ones convinced the disgruntled ones to eat what was given to them or else. They also rewarded the obedient children who followed the dictates of their mothers and fathers who wished to follow the Lord's commandments. These little ones had a great influence in the lives of all human and beastly creatures.

This little bird of angelic quality flew down from the heavens and contacted Joviah and told him he could save the entire species of hummingbirds by taking on the charge of enlightening them with kind and mystical words, words of clarity and guidance. Joviah asked him what were these special words. The little bird told him that they were engraved on every hummingbird's heart, but that too many had erased them by not listening to their hearts. The words became effaced never to return again. It was only by enlightened instruction that the words would reclaim the hearts of so many. But, these hummingbirds must have a clean heart and a clean spirit, the bird said. They must wipe away all prejudices and all ill-intents. It must become a clean slate. "But what are the words?" asked Joviah. Here are the three words the little birds told him: **love**, **purity of heart**, and **forbearance**. "What does that mean?" asked Joviah. "It means the following: love is a virtue of the heart as well as the soul. You see, even birds like you have souls, a very special soul. Love is always aimed at others and not the self, but you must love the self that you are before you can love others. Where does it come from? Well, it comes from the Creator who is, love itself. Pure love. *Agapè*, as the ancient Greeks called it. **Purity of heart** means that the heart is not duplicitous and not against itself. It must not work counter-productive. A pure heart is one that has no uncleanliness of intolerance, strife, hatred, and the mischief of envy. Purity of heart means straight as an arrow that goes directly to the truth of things. No deviousness. No bending from the truth to falsehood. As for **forbearance** it means self-control and patient restraint. One must not lose sight of the fact that creatures are prone to be out of control sometimes and they are not able to restrain themselves from bursts of willful anger or outbursts of meanness. They must learn to persevere in their energetic flight throughout life. They have to appreciate the everyday things that come along on their path to perfection. Its a long and sometimes dreary path must it must be faced with candor, deliberate and honest assessment of one's strengths and weaknesses. Not everyone is perfect. Actually no one is. The road to perfection is strewn with imperfections that fall beneath the the pathfinder on his way to seeking perfection. Perfection comes from practice and long endurance. It cannot be gained with outbursts, bad intentions, cowardice, and hatred of self and others. Hatred is a beaten path to imperfection. Only love can smooth it. Love comes from a pure heart, a heart that is simple in its intent, warm in its practices, and full of energy that stirs up the belonging in every society. Either one belongs or one not. One cannot not belong. It's only the thing to do as a creature of the one who created everyone of us. The bond of belonging is love, sharing and restraint from abuses and self-deprecation. You must learn to love self, truly love, and then it will flow to others. You hummingbirds must learn to love differences. I don't mean necessarily to like them, but to love them when they appear in others. Everyone cannot be the same nor can they prevent from being different. Differences make the variety in us creatures. See how I am different from all of you hummingbirds. I am small, plain, dull in plumage and not very exciting as a creature of God." "But you are an angel, you cannot deny that." "Yes, one of the lowest order of angels. The most humble of the humblest." "But, you are indeed different from all of us." "Of course, that's what makes me who I am."

The wren-like bird then explained to Joviah how to convert hearts so that all of the hummingbirds can have the malleability and flexibility to change for the good of all. Its took time and much effort but Joviah, through his own efforts, sacrifices and ardor managed to change the hearts and minds of his fellow hummingbirds. Those who rebelled all the time and those who reneged from their sense of belonging as well as those who just did not appreciate differences, all were confronted by their own weakness and the power of change and they grew more tolerant and malleable and less dull in their mindset. It is then that the much appreciated extravaganza occurred. Rather than all being dull, plain and muted in heir plumage everyone was transformed into jewels of the species, the hummingbird. Some were transformed into small birds of bright and colorful plumage while others really shone and glittered in the brilliant light of the sun. There were those whose plumage reverberated with color and the magic of brilliance. There were more and more species of hummingbirds that were formed, the Anna's, the Black Wizard, the Blue-throated, the Broad-tail, the Calliope, the Ruby-throated, the Violet-crowned, and many more. And then, the hummingbirds started to migrate to many parts of the world so that many many more people could enjoy their luster and delight. So many of them and so many differences. *Vive la différence*! Was shouted from every rooftop and from every tree and branches if not from every nest. That was the extravaganza of the hummingbirds. That was the great manifestation of the love of the great creator for his hummingbirds. Love can even make hummingbirds shine and sparkle like jewels in the rays of the sun. For love can be an extravaganza of differences at work. Throw caution to the wind and LOVE became the motto of the hummingbirds. Is this trite, plain romanticism and cautionary-less like the plain and simple tales? Where does he get all this stuff might ask the reader who seeks rational and entertaining stories. Well, I get it from the hummingbirds themselves. Trust me.

14.

The Tale Of The Magic Of Stirring A Pot

Once upon a time in a far land and a far country of beings, there lived an old woman who loved to cook, bake and collect all kinds of recipes. Her name was Dora the stirrer-upper. She just loved to stir things up, rumors, disagreements, pitiful little stories of people scrambling to earn a living and so on. But, she was a good cook, an enormously talented person with mounds and mounds of recipes in her head. She had accumulated them over the years. She had gathered recipes out of the minds of so many people who shared her life simply by being friends and exchanging the brightest of brightest of words in lengthy conversations and, of course, recipes. She had culled many of her best recipes from an old friend, Charles Elliott Carmody, whom she met through her friend Fanny-the-recipe-maker. He had died several years ago and left her his most cherished recipes. Dora did not have children nor did she have many relatives since most of them had died young. She had never gotten married. Some people called her a spinster, an unwed chump, a single person, *une vieille fille* as it was said in French. She did not mind the taunts of people who called her anything but her name. She loved her name. It had been given to her by her great aunt, Isabelle-la-fleurie, the flowered one. My, my, my, how she loved flowers, that one. Her entire life was spent cultivating, pruning, admiring, and collecting blossoms for her garden. Her house was always full of fresh-cut flowers. She loved their exquisite perfume.

Moreover, the magnificent and wonderful colors of each blossom sent her reeling with awe and inspiration. Blossoms inspired her to think of her childhood days when she lived out in the countryside and enjoyed strolling in the wide-open fields where there was always a bounty of wild flowers.

Aunt Isabelle had given her the name of Dora simply because she liked it very much. It reminded her of *dorure,* in French, the gold jewels of her young life like the beautiful locket that her father had given her when she turned sixteen. *Les dorures* of her tender years and of her later years when her husband showered her with gold and silver jewelry were reminders of the love that some people had for her, Isabelle. So, she gave the name Dora to her little niece, the daughter of her grand-niece, Flora.

Dora was a lovely child, a soft-spoken, obedient and mindful child until she grew up to be a willful, loud-mouth, and wicked old witch of a grown-up. However, Dora was a good cook and baker. That was one good quality she had. How she loved putting things in a pot and just let them simmer for a while until the blend smelled good and appetizing. She had all kinds of recipes in her ever-grasping mind, never had written them down for she did not know how to write. She could read, but she could not write. She wasn't dumb, as some people called her. She simply had had no chance to learn the art of writing words down on paper. Besides, no one had taught her how. Growing up for Dora meant helping her mother who was a widow and struggling to put food on the table. There was the washing, the ironing, the folding of clothes, and the dusting and polishing of furniture. Dora and her mother lived in a tiny and very plain dwelling place on the outskirts of town. They had very few neighbors and they hardly ever went anywhere. Dora led a very sheltered life.

One day Dora met a woman whose name was Fanny-the-recipe-maker-and-scribe. She made up her own recipes and people enjoyed her cooking. That's what Fanny did for a living, cook for others. She had no one else in her family except her father who was growing blind and could hardly move his body. Fanny was lonely and felt abandoned until one day a hunchbacked old woman came to her and instructed her how to bake and cook. Fanny believed in fairy princesses and fairy godmothers, but not in fairy dashing princes who come to gather princesses to go away on horseback somewhere in a distant kingdom. Surely, the old hunchback was not a fairy princess, not even a queen in disguise sent from some wonderland somewhere. Fanny only believed in what was true to her and what her heart told her. She admired stories of wonders and delight like the tales of knights and ladies in distress. She enjoyed hearing about them as told to her by her neighbor, Dora, who knew by heart so may medieval stories and legends. Dora was a charmed person who devoured the fabulous tales of the Middle Ages. Her favorite was that of Lancelot and Queen Guinevere. She had played the role of the Queen in a school play and she had memorized all of the dialogues of the long play. Her teacher had commended her for her skill at learning by heart pages and pages of the script. The role of Lancelot had been played by Kurt Longhorn, a cute blond kid from across the way who was the idol of so many young school girls. They had envied her for her role as Lancelot's lover. She had gotten the role not because she was pretty and had a good figure, but because she was the only one who could read well and learn the text by heart in a matter of weeks. Her friends envied her capacity to learn and to memorize so quickly. They called her the intellectual sponge.

Dora reminded Fanny of the time both of them had sneaked in the local theater to watch an old film about kings, queens, knights and ladies They had both enjoyed the film. They had sneaked in because they did not have the money to pay for the tickets to get in. They knew that it wasn't right, but they just had to see this film. It was a spectacular film with horses, meadows filled with blossoms, knights in armor, and ladies playing songs of love on the lute. The oh's and ah's came out of their mouths until someone sitting in front of them told them to shut up. They kept quiet for the rest of the film.

Fanny loved all stories dealing with ladies and young men courting them. However, she would never accept any plea from a courtier to enter into her service. She was a determined young girl who did not want to be bothered with boys. She did not resent boys, but she just did not like them. That's all. She liked lollipops, ice cream cups with movie stars inside the lids, penny candy, colored popcorn in a brick-like shape, black licorice, and sour pickles that her mother bought at Zanzinia's store on Waterfall Street. But, she did not like boys. They were a mean sort, she said and they made little girls cry. Not her, because she was not a cry-baby. Most of all she delighted in stories and legends that offered her a way out of the ordinary into the magic of wonderland.

Fanny began to tell Dora her life story simply because she felt she had to tell someone about it. Besides, few people like Dora and her mean spirited way of looking at things and people.. Fanny could easily tolerate her since Dora listened to her story quite attentively. Fanny told Dora that as she grew up, she became more and more desperate to have a chance to spread her wings for she wanted to explore all of the avenues that were being offered to her like a chance to get into the Ladies Society of Benevolence and the Sports Club of her town as well as the Tolerance Society of Good Faith run by the ladies of her parish, but none would have her. They all thought that she had no credentials to her name and that she was not educated enough to belong. Fanny began to feel excluded from the network of *bonne entente* (good friendship). She grew more and more impatient and even worse exacerbated over the refusals of all those who wanted her excluded from their tight-fitted groups She saw in that intolerance, injustice, and bullying. Bullying because these people were bullying her and not at all compassionate. They taunted her, called her names under their breath, and made fun of her while being hypocritical in public by smiling indulgently and pretending to accept her in their circles without ever offering her the slightest invitation to join them in their endeavors. So Fanny went her separate way and decided to make her own way, her very own little world of baking and cooking. However, she grew more and more intolerant herself and crusty, vain, bitchy, and disdainful of almost every gesture of decency. From a humble, benevolent, kind, and sweet person, she evolved into some kind of a witch. She concocted schemes, took delight in offending people, argued with almost everybody about minor things, used profanities to get her way, and started to get hot under the collar every time she did not agree with someone or something. She turned out to be exactly the opposite of what she had been before. People thought that something or someone had bewitched her. What made her turn into something she would never have thought of becoming? How can a fine and talented individual change over the span of a few years, they asked. Certainly there was something behind all of Fanny's negative propensities. But what was it, they said despairingly.

Fanny was told repeatedly by some of her close friends, and there were few of them, that unless she changed and became less hateful and more likable, she would lose all of her friends even those who had remained close for years. She asked herself how she could possibly change given the endless struggle within her and the many hurdles she would have to face. She could not and would not change. How could she? She was determined to try and remain the way she was . After all it had taken years to mold herself into the strong woman she had become. Let the others change, she told herself. Not me. I am who I am, she muttered.

Dora tried repeatedly to convince Fanny to change her attitude towards life and especially others. What attitude? asked Fanny. Your unpleasant attitude that you have towards everything and everyone, Dora told her. "Am I unpleasant?" asked Fanny "You certainly are," added Dora, "the most unpleasant creature on earth. I cannot even stand you anymore." So, Fanny risked losing everybody that mattered in her life and she now realized it. First, she decided to change even though she was convinced that she did not need change. She tried and she tried but nothing worked. What was she going to do?

Well, she was going to see someone, who was going to help her change and become less unpleasant, less brutal in her attitude in life. That someone was an old wizard of a man that she had gotten to know and his name was, Charles Elliott Carmody, a poet and a gardener. He was also a lover of good food. "Food, my dear Fanny, is not only the way to a man's stomach but the way to his soul," he once told her. "But it has to be good food, not only good but excellent. You see excellence is the key to everything that touches the soul and keeps it in harmony with the vibrations of human endeavors. All that is worthwhile on earth must at all costs rely on the measure of excellence." "But exactly what is excellence?" asked Fanny. "Oh, it must be learned and I will teach you the best I know how."

Charles Elliott Carmody was born in a small village near London and his parents respected royalty and the high expectations they had of their own. After all, they said, expectations breed excellence. The harder one tries to excel the harder it is to miss out on coming to the point of excellence. Excellence requires hard work and tough discipline, they said. So, they made it a point of submitting their son to the trials and tribulations of achieving excellence in work, play, intellectual pursuits, and artistic endeavors. They were going to mold their son into the clay of supple and easily swayed desires that comply well with exhortations from the soul, a disciplined soul. Charles Elliott grew up as a well-disciplined, obedient and learned child. He read every book his mother laid before his eyes from Rousseau's *The Social Contract* and *Reveries of a Solitary Walker*, Voltaire's *Candide*, Zenon of Elea's Paradoxes, Marguerite Yourcenar's *Memoirs of Hadrian,* William Golding's "*Lord of the Flies,*" to Flaubert's *Madame Bovary.* At a certain moment in his life he fell in love with the intriguing and luscious foreign film, *Babette's Feast,* and never waivered in his desire to imitate the woman who prepared the mouth-watering and soul-fulfilling meal for her ultra-conservative guests whose abstemious nature of the congregation led them to abstain from the luxury of food until Babette enters their lives. It is then, they all manage to devour every portion of it up to the fine wines and the final enjoyment of coffee with vieux marc Grande Champagne cognac. The entire meal is well sequenced: *Potage à la Tortue,* turtle soup; *Cailles en Sarcophage,* quail in puff pastry; *Savarin au rhum avec des Figues et Fruit Glacé,* rum sponge cake with figs and candied cherries. What a delightful meal and a sumptuous one at that. Babette spends her entire winnings on this exquisite meal in order to please and mollify her guests. It's a meal of an extravagant gesture on the part of the kindly Babette. It's the tale of an sumptuous feast and can be interpreted as a parable of grace. Charles Elliott not only admired the film but he had to view it every day for two months until he got fed up with it and discovered yet another charming film, a film about what could be called, food porn, *Chocolat.* He so enjoyed this film that he never stopped eating chocolate for almost a year. Then came *Like Water for Chocolate,* a film about two lovers, Tita and Pedro, and forbidden love. Charles Elliott learned about Mexican cooking and the way to cook with one's moods and emotions as Tita does in this film. Finally, he fell upon the story of two cooks, French gastronomy and the iconic cookbook of Julia Child. He always thought that Julia Child was a bit loony at times, but he enjoyed her recipes although he laughed at her mumbled jargon as if she was sloshing around hot food in her mouth.

Charles Elliott had become an artist as a cook and chef. He had refined his skills and was well prepared to teach them others. That was the heaven-sent moment for Fanny when she found herself in desperate need of a refinement of soul and personality. That's when Charles Elliott stepped into her life. She was in much need of this transformation. She could not continue in her much frustrated lifestyle of abrasiveness and self-deprecation. Things had to change, but how? Through the grace of food and food preparation, as Charles Elliott put it to her one day.

She learned not only how to cook but how to prepare food, how to mix and blend. How to serve delicacies such as roasted oysters with calamari on a bed of warm brown rice. She also learned how to concoction *amuse-gueule*, make *hors-d'oeuvre* delectable, serve delicious and mouth-watering *entrées*. In other words, she learned to turn her life around by the cuisine she had never known. Charles Elliott even showed her how the *table d'hôte* worked: a set menu and set way of eating with usually a set price in a given restaurant. He also told her about *le service à la russe*, meals served in sequence from a variety of platters from which guests serve themselves with as much as they want. There were many a lesson to be learned and digested and Fanny did them all. She came out of her learning experiences with her head held high and her soul purged of any misguided tendencies. She had become a likable and friendly as well as thoughtful human being....through the *rapprochement et le salut de la cuisine bien cuisinée*. Through the closeness and salvation of well-made cuisine. Charles Elliott had warned her about the misshapen and spoiled fruit falling off the tree in the orchard when the tree lacks good soil and good sap. The fruit falls to the ground early and rots there without being ever useful or tastefully appetizing. If the soul does not flourish then it rots, Charles Elliott told Fanny. And so, Fanny was saved from the many scars of a misshapen life ...through food and *la cuisine*. The tale of Fanny, the pot-stirrer, has spread throughout the land and many mothers tell it reverently to their daughters as part of their growing-up education. It's a magical tale because it creates magic and stirs creative moments in the lives of those whose moments of magic and warmth have eluded them or simply have not been accepted early in life. Magic, after all, is a way of seeing things through a colorful looking-glass and discovering either *la magie des mots, la magie de la cuisine ou la magie de vivre sa vocation,* the magic of words, the magic of good cooking or the magic of one's vocation. Fanny needed no more lessons after her encounter with Charles Elliott; she had become a teacher...*une maîtresse de l'art de la cuisine,* a teacher of the art of cooking good food...with the most pleasant and warmest disposition that a saved-by-grace person can have. After all, Charles Elliott had told her before he passed away, an artist is never poor. "Look at Babette," he told her, "she's a model of artistry and beneficence." Dora too had changed. She was much more malleable, less contentious, less abrasive and more like a genuine human being. She had learned her lessons from Fanny who had learned from Charles Elliott. Dora never forgot the words spoken by Charles Elliott; that an artist is never poor and never lacks the warmth of real friends. She never forgot *Babette's Feast* either. Dora keeps this tale in her heart and in her never-failing memory. It's her iconic cookbook, Culinary Friendship, was to be her cautionary emphasis from then on. After all, good and compassionate deeds go very well with good cooking. It's a marvelous combination for those who have evolved from being old nags and witches to good cooks that delight palates with splendid recipes. Dora and Fanny live on in the memory of those who knew them and stirred the pot like both of them. *La bonne cuisine n'a aucune faille*(good cuisine never fails), remember that my children.

15.

The Delight and Despair of Armand, the Flower Maker

Armand Desrosiers was a born artist. He loved to make flowers in every single way that a flower looked to him. Of course, he preferred natural flowers, but when he could not get them because he did not have the money to spend or he could not grow them on account of the soil or the bad weather, he fabricated them. He made them with whatever material was available to him, paper, silk, cardboard, metal, cotton, or even unknown sorts of material such as wired trays that come from shipping boxes. Nothing was a challenge for him; nothing mattered if others refused to accept his ideas. Nothing... except the environment in which he found himself sometimes. He hated an environment negatively challenged by soot, dirty air, smog, filthy particles or worse, ugly smells from paper-making plants or coal industries. He once complained about the terrible smell of garbage along the side of the roads where he took his morning walks. He championed those who took it upon themselves to fight for clean air and clean environment. His heart was not in politics nor social media because he could not stand infighting or hypocrisy. He could definitely not stand greed, those whose life control was amassing money and things that they called treasures..He read about the big pharmaceuticals that robbed poor people blind by their high prices blamed on the cost of research, so they said. Armand could not stand for all of these things that bothered him beyond hope, and exasperated him to no end. He thought of "Flowers for Algernon" where research takes a vicious turn for the worse just because the researchers thought of their own pride and climbing up the ladder of successful and rewarding scientific research. They did not take into account the psychological and spiritual, even the ethical ramifications of their dealing with a reluctant and intellectually challenged human being. "The problem, dear professor, is that you wanted someone who could be made intelligent but still be kept in a cage and displayed when necessary to reap the honors you seek. The hitch is that I'm a person," Charlie tells Professor Nemur. Nemur in turn tells him, "You know we've always treated you well." "Everything but treat me as a human being," answers poor Charlie Gordon who felt abused and neglected by the savoir-faire and the savoir-cacher(hide) of his research team. That is why Armand retreated to his small cabin in the woods just so he could meditate and reflect on the things that bothered him endlessly. Someone once asked him why he did not join those who struggled outwardly and openly to combat the evils of the abused environment. He told him that there was nothing to gain by it since most politicians had us by the throat and ended up stashing away so much cash from partisan contributions that they ended always as being incumbents and winning the race. Some called the game fake news, but it wasn't fake most of the time, it was merely doctored to fit the constituents into the sleeves of the politicians. Armand said that there was nothing to be gained by playing politics, and that politicians always won on and over the heads of the poor people who would have liked to really get together a real democracy. Armand said that true democracy doesn't exist and that Plato was right in his judgment about such a type of government. Sure, the people turn over their voting privileges as a people to those who would take over the reins of a democratic government. That, they said, was true democracy at work. Not everyone can become mixed in with the running of government, so that's why they hand the reins over to those who are supposed to make the right decisions for them. But, that does not always work, and that is simply "fake news." "Why?" asked Armand. He answered his own question by saying, "It's because there are crooks and will always be crooks, wolves in our midst, who find a way to deceive others by their sly tactics and the mass media goes along with it. It's called deviousness through sensationalism." That's what Armand said alone in his quiet cabin in the woods far away from politics and politicians as well as the media. No news is good news, he would say. Right! But, why remain so impassive and ignorant of things, some people asked. Because, things will never change and things change only for the worse, replied Armand. Just take a look at "Animal Farm" and its devious switch of so-called democratic rule that degenerates into what one could call devious "animalocracy." The animals themselves become arrogant politicians and claimants if not beggars of so-called rights to power, and we all know that power corrupts. Basically, corruption leads to the abuse of power which is abuse in itself and of others. So, Armand took things into his own hands and started to make flowers instead of fighting wars and struggling with the politicians. Making flowers made more sense to him.

One day, Armand began to realize that making flowers could not end the prejudices, intolerance, bullying, and other conspiracies that were fabricated by men and women of little sense of ethics and spirituality. You see, Armand thought that spirituality was the very foundation of the soul and that a dead spirituality was the death or stagnation of the soul. Armand was convinced that the soul was the link to eternal awareness and strength of life. That human life was but a passageway to eternity. He could not see how politicians and other devious creatures could miss the point about being truly human, and live in total harmony with the eternal link. He also thought that ethics and aesthetics lived together in perfect harmony if allowed to flourish. *La beauté côtoie l' éthique*, beauty rubs shoulders with ethics, according to Armand. A flower is as ethical as human thought and action because it follows without faltering the aim of the Creator who does not want disparity in his creation. The disparity of what the created one is and what it must be. So, Armand conceived of a plan. He was going to teach a lesson to the devious ones with flowers, but fabricated flowers. Flowers that try to imitate nature, although they fail to be true to their essence. Real flowers follow the path of responding to truth and majestic beauty. They do not deviate from this path in order to proclaim their power over other flowers. At least, he was going to try and mitigate the awful truth of destructive callousness on the part of politicians by means of ethical truth and beauty.

Armand set himself to work by first selecting the materials he needed to make the flowers he was going to design and eventually make. But, why was he making fabricated artificial flowers when there were millions and millions of real flowers in the world. To teach the devious ones a lesson: learn not to deviate from the truth and the ethical standards of humanity. It was that simple. However, the deviates were not accustomed to not deviate from these simple but worthy rules of conduct and behavior. First came the adherence to truth. Never ever deviate from truth no matter what the situation or the person or persons involved. Then came the ethical standards. Never compromise with ethical behavior and situations no matter what and no matter how. Moral dictates are not to be compromised and never cast aside. Humanity deserves these standards and merits the worth of being addressed in all situations with dignity and straightforward awareness of the importance of not being devious in whatever means or ways. Armand firmly believed in that. He so hated deviousness and hypocrisy that he was ready to sacrifice everything for the integrity of truth and straightforwardness. As straight as an arrow was he, but not so straight so as to comply with and even become the slave of the unwavering tendencies of ultra-conservatism. Yes, he was upright, but also resilient, accepting, and understanding. Much like Pascal's *roseau pensant,* the thinking reed, Armand was the thinking arrow. He knew how to get to the point.

Armand started to fabricate with all the chosen materials at his disposition, the many flowers he thought of. Tulips made out of tiny colored teacups; gladioli made of metal shafts enameled and bright with color; tiny violets made of the strips of purple streamers; large ornate women's powder puffs to resemble the big blossoms of the peonies; small jeweled pink hearts made of some jewelry items to resemble the lovely string of bleeding hearts; multi-colored pansies with flat faces that were made from the paper faces of children peering in a store window; red spears of dried red peppers for those flaming red salvias; multi-colored paper posies made to resemble carnations; bright red eye-catching fabric, plastic or crepe paper poppies made to resemble the variety of poppies that veterans wear on their lapels at fund-raising time; pieces of wire all meshed with tinfoil made to resemble cacti; pots and pots of multi-colored and multi-shaped discarded buttons to be like posies with pipe cleaners as stems; popular marigolds of yellows and oranges with tints of brown, all made with paper mâché. Of course, there were the roses sometimes made of a variety of fabrics and even plastic, all made grossly or not too delicately by someone wishing to duplicate roses and fail most of the time. Roses are unmistakably non-duplicable, as Armand said. Armand did not attempt to duplicate roses. He did not dare mar the beauty of a rose by fabricating it and mistakenly trying to render a true rose in any shape, form or made-made-material. "A rose, is a rose is a rose is a rose," said Shakespeare. And, that's that, said Armand to himself.

Armand would then take his collection of fabricated flowers and distribute them surreptitiously wherever he would judge fair to all who were voracious for flowers. He dropped some off at certain desks in several offices, on work benches in the surrounding industrial park, on church pews, on park benches, in local banks, in schools where both students and teachers were most joyful in accepting them, and in many places that were open to receiving the fabricated flowers . Of course, he did not drop them off at local florists or even supermarkets that sold fresh flowers for they would have not been receptive of artificial flowers. Everyone who got such flowers seemed pleased with them except for those who wondered what was going on. There were some who were suspicious of Armand's moves and motives. Was he doing this to gain popularity or gain something in return, they asked themselves. When someone gives us something with no strings attached, then we begin to ask questions. What is the motive behind such a gesture, for instance. We all know that nothing is truly gratuitous. You have to pay the piper or the price, don't you. Well, Armand left them in a quandary. What were these flowers all about or what did the flower-giver have in mind. Most people thought that the fabricated flowers were nice and colorful and especially well-made. They admired the skill of the craftsman.

Armand let the flower-receivers stewing in their thoughts. He knew what he was doing. He wasn't devious nor was he hypocritical about his moves as a flower-maker. He just wanted to teach people a lesson about flowers: fresh and natural or artificial. What was it going to be and why. First of all he was proud that most politicians accepted his offerings with what he considered pride and gratefulness. At least, it seemed that way until he discovered that most of the politicians threw the flowers in the rubbish cans. He knew because he inspected the receptacles where the politicians got rid of unwanted items. He found many of his flowers crushed or torn apart. Armand then realized that politicians did not respect gifts of flowers artificial or natural. Of course, there were a few who did keep them and respected flowers as a gift. But, they were few. What was going to be his next move, he asked himself.

His next move was to get rid of all flowers in the politicians' gardens by spraying them with contaminants. He did not like doing this, but he figured that the politicians did the same thing with the air, the soil, worse with the environment. It was a big job but he succeed by hiring young people to help him in his efforts especially those who were fed up with governmental policies and laws that contradicted the will of the people. What was democracy all about they had asked repeatedly. *Demos*, the people not the individual politicians, that's what democracy was all about, they claimed. The young people were delighted to help Armand out in his lesson to politicians. Would they learn though or just wonder what all of this was about. Armand told them that when the gardens are gone, when all the natural flowers are wiped out, then perhaps the politicians will realize that something strange was happening and that it was time to wake up. Would it be the environment or the politicians, and would they be ever at odds. Of course, some politicians swore they were deliberately and unequivocally for fresh air, clean water, good soil and a sound environment. Were there enough of them enough to be truthfully, sincerely, ethically, and unambiguously affirmative in their support .Well, Armand discovered that money and profits, especially money gotten by the awfully convincing bias of hidden litigation and persuasive lobbying were the motor behind what propelled the actions of the so-called engaged politicians. *Engagement* sounded very political

Sartrian existentialism to Armand. He had studied Jean-Paul Sartre and his cohorts in philosophical literature and had found them unconvincing in their theories and philosophy. Why Sartre had even refused the Nobel prize in literature and said that he much preferred to get a sack of potatoes instead. That's how true to his sense of existentialism he was. Sure, a big show, a big deliberate show of unconvincing political absurdity on his part, thought Armand.

When the flowers started disappearing in the gardens, private, governmental, civic, and so many others, the politicians put together a committee to investigate the cause of such a catastrophe. It took weeks, months and even years to deliberate, seek recommendations from the committee, and finally enact a law regarding such deterioration of natural resources: the flowers of our gardens. The formula that Armand and his young friends used to wipe out the flowers was such that the agricultural and conservation agencies, both federal and state, could not discover and unfold the reasons behind the disappearance of the garden flowers. Armand had concocted a special formula that could not be deciphered nor decoded under microscopes, and that left the so-called experts totally unable to counter Armand's formula for getting rid of the flowers. The public started complaining and many constituents went to their elected officials to get an answer to this bewildering situation. Most of them were afraid that such a catastrophe would endanger all fresh and natural flowers everywhere. It would mean that this land of theirs would become a land of desperation and environmental disaster, they said. Some politicians told them that flowers were not that important to the vital economy nor were they a necessary item for national security. So, they ignored the complaints of their constituents.

Later on after all the flowers were gone and replaced by the artificial ones, there was no need for bees those pollinators who thrived on flowers for the making of their nectar. Without the bees there was no propagation of growing things such as fruits, vegetables and even trees who required the energy and stamina of bees. There was an overall standstill of growth and flourishing in nature. Armand was troubled by this and worried that things would worsen if there were no natural flowers at all. No soft and silken petals, no fresh scent of various genuses of flowers. But worse of all, no beauty in nature in a vast panorama of prairies, garden scenes and all over the land. Why didn't the lawmakers care about that, Armand asked himself. All they had to do was to step outside and view the disaster of a flowerless land. But no, they were too preoccupied with bickering and bolstering their egos with worthless bills and inappropriate laws that they enacted for the sake of keeping their jobs and their emoluments. "As long as we get the vote, who cares about silly flowers anyways," they asked themselves. The constituents did and they were about to revolt when someone thought of the idea of throwing all of them out of office by the power of the democratic vote. Flower power, they called it. They urged Armand to stop killing off the real and natural flowers and give them back to natural scenery so that they would be able to enjoy them again. "On one condition," Armand told them, " that you never allow again the politicians that do not give a hoot about ethics and aesthetics, about beauty and morality." They all agreed that they had been too careless and non-committal with their votes. Votes mattered and votes got the right people in power. "But, make sure that power is not allowed to corrupt the very people you elect. Power without greed and ego-stressing systems are a must," said Armand. "Let's get the flower power going," urged Armand. And so the people got their choice of politicians who now did the will of the people and were committed to what was called from then on, flower power, the power of natural beauty and the ethics of truth in all and everything. "What is truth," some one shouted. "It's the way of the will of the Maker who provides and nourishes all, humans, animals and plants...and even the politicians who need constant nourishment," cautioned Armand delighted at the result of his small but very important revolution. The revolution of flower people like himself. Armand told his followers that the word revolution meant just that, to revolve, but to revolve around the core of human life and dignity. However, the core or wholeness also meant the environment. Flowers are an integral part of the environment, and he cautioned them never to give up in protecting them from silly if not greedy-for -power politicians, the kind that lord it over all especially the good will of people and their democratic choices, not of hypocrites like the lobbyists and other dyed-in-the-wool hunger-grabbers who tear away the fabric of true democracy. From that moment on, Armand wore a bright red artificial poppy on his right lapel and a fresh rose on his left one. It made people smile.

16.

Henry's Dilemma

What's a dilemma? someone asked the school teacher. Her name was Miss Sachebien, a French name that meant knows it all. Her answer was, "A dilemma is a quandary of sorts or a *tourne-en-rond* situation that has no meaningful end to it. It just turns in circles." Well, people were not satisfied with her answer because they could not make any sense out of it. So, they turned to Henry, Henry with the owl-shaped face who had the peculiar gift of turning things around and making sense of almost everything that was presented to him. You see, he was endowed with the knowledge and perspicacity of a wise one. It was said that wisdom flowed from the mind of the one who best imitated Solomon, the wise biblical king. Henry told the one who was asking him to define "quandary" that he had the right definition for it. However, Henry told the one who was posing the question that definitions were always vague and not to the point, and that the best way to define things was to give concrete examples. Examples are like definitions, but clearer and more concrete and less indefinite when done with words only. "You see," said Henry, "when I define things, a problem, or whatever, then I go right to the point and tell the enquirer that he has to use his imagination and render concrete what I am manifesting in the example given. For example, and here is the nice ingenious part of the example, if I use words that convey real, concrete and senses-based things, then it becomes easier for the interlocutor to imagine what I am proposing to him. You see, we humans are not only imaginative, intellectual and prone to ideas, and quite often to ideals, but fundamentally we rely very much on our senses."

----Yes, I see, says the interlocutor, but how can we find sensible, concrete ideas that can define what is wanted?

----First of all, you must not rely simply on words that are associated with ideas. You must clearly see with your mind's eye, the concreteness of the idea proposed. You must see, feel, touch, and even smell what you are to define. That is, if you really want to define what you truly want. Definitions are not simply words, and words are not simply ideas, they are what can be perceived through the looking glass of human perception. Things are transparent inasmuch they are seen clearly and introspectively. There are so many ways of perceiving things, really perceiving them as they are meant to be. But, what can I tell you that you may grasp as your own? Nothing. I can only suggest things, ideas and even words. YOU are the one who controls the perception of things you want to see and define. But, you will tell me that one sees what one sees. Yes, but how do YOU see? That's the question here. I realize that the eyes convey what you are apt to see and that images can be distorted or dimmed by light and darkness. Sometimes our eyes deceive us. They're only sensitive to what the true image is in our looking at things. You must admit that we do not always see straight. I'm not talking about being inebriated, under the influence of drugs, or even sleepy or groggy, and whatever causes our not seeing straight. I mean, seeing things as they truly are out there in the light of day. As the saying goes, what you see is what you get What you get may be disconnected to your seeing eye depending on how you feel or how you are able to receive the full picture clearly and perfectly attuned to your way of perceiving things. Does one always see things concretely and factually? It depends doesn't it. Depends on what? On many situations or probabilities. You see things can be perceived and then dismissed by the mind as trivial or unimportant. They become, at times, mirages in the desert of arid perceptions. You see, I truly believe in human creativity. I believe that without some influence of one's creativity, there can be very little clarity of perceptions that reveal one's sight or even insight into things. Am

I dreaming or am I hallucinating? I sometimes think that I am . You see, there is a very fine line between reality and illusion. However, creativity is not illusion. It's the gift of imagining things and casting our imaginings or the full power of our imagination into the light of wonderment. What I call the power of amazement and awe. When we perceive things, events or happenings or whatever you may call it, we cast the spell of perceived reality on it. I mean we see reality within the perspective of what is in front of our eyes and we run it through the mind's eye processing it through the brain power of developing what we see. But, there is also the power of the imagination that comes into the process. Some think that the imagination is seldom frank with us, and that it's only way of casting doubt on the fact of seeing what we truly see. That we imagine things or imagine that we see something when in actuality we haven't really seen it. We imagined it, but I say, imagining is a way of seeing in depth what we truly see. It's just another dimension to our way of seeing. Must everything be factual all of the time? Men and women of science say, yes . It's either black or white, they say, not colored by the imagination. I may add, that certain scientists do rely on the power of the imagination and creativity. I bless them and more power to them for they see with the full range of the ability of not only seeing things but the power of seeing, and I mean grasping fully the power that the Great Creator himself has and has imparted to us human beings in certain measures depending on our God-given talents and how we have nurtured them and proceeded in our attempt to flourish and grow. I perceive the art of "seeing" in the measure that Oedipus "sees" when he gouges out his eyes and becomes blind. Then he "sees." What a marvelous way that Sophocles is making us see the power of true perception even when we have lost the ability of sight. We see through the intellect and the power of the imagination. We have reached the power or the ability to "understand." "I see, I see," says the blind man. Yes, he sees clearly and faithfully according to his faithful power of reason and intellect as well as the power of the imagination. You see, I do not think of the imagination as a trickster or a deceiving agent of the mind, but as a true creative agent of the power of the soul. Ah, here's a new concept that I have not yet introduced.

What does all of this that I have been talking about and what significance has it to do with this particular cautionary tale. The tale of Henry and his dilemma or quandary. Well, it has a lot to do with what I have been telling you about specifically, the power of the creative imagination.

What does create and creative actually mean, you might ask. I often ask myself this very question. It's an idea, a thought that we get through our intellectual powers. It's also an idea conceived by other powers such as the senses, intuition, and other abilities that we have as human beings. Cogito *ergo sum, je pense donc je suis* says Descartes. Thus, if I am able to use the power of the intellect and conceive ideas, I am also able to conceive colorful and imaginary ideas that I am able to bring out of my conception such as images, ideas that elicit other ideas, and thoughts that stimulate words in order to express these images and ideas. The mind works in so many ways and facets of creativity. So, for me, creativity is the power to conceive an idea or an image totally from scratch or maybe not totally from scratch since everything is based or linked to something else already conceived. There is nothing new under the sun, says the proverbial saying, and it's so true. We all stand on the shoulders of the giants, is a remark colorfully depicted in one of the stained glass windows of Chartres. So true. However, as you may already know, we can create from what has already been created before but in a different light or a different mode of expression. Artists do that, poets do that also and so many talented people given the fact that they have the power of expressive creativity. *Cogito ergo creo*, you might say. I think therefore I create. All in all, I state that the creative imagination is founded on the human power of using our imagination for purposes of creating and embellishing what has already been said and done. *Tu m'as donné de la boue et j'en ai fait de l'or*, to paraphrase Baudelaire. (You gave me mud and I made gold out of it). What a mighty power the creative imagination is if one can change mud to gold, from base and commonplace mud to the glittering gold of the artistry of poetry and the chemistry of fabricating new stimuli for the brain at work. Our brain needs stimuli in order to remain alive, truly alive. Yes, *homo faber* is indeed man/woman at work making things and not only making them but CREATING them. The power of gods, if you believe in them and of God the Creator as so many people believe . We create, we fabricate, we work with our hands, our minds and, I want to add, our souls. The spiritual dimension of the human being is also very important to our existence. Since the soul is the stimulating factor of life, I may add. This I strongly believe. Without the soul, a human being is a robot, a computer computing things and formulas, a machine of sorts or simply put, somewhat an artificial thinking organ. Some will not accept what I'm saying about the composition of the human being and probably leave out the soul factor thinking that the mind or intellect is proof enough of human existence. But then, I say to them you have no real life, just a shell of existence that thinks, yes, but does not spiritualize[I'm fabricating here] its existence. The power of the spirit is that of transcendence and thinking above and beyond the clouds of material existence. Ideas may be of the mind and intellect, but creative endeavors and accomplishments are of the soul. The imagination is for me the handmaid of the soul. This may sound "whacky" or stupid for some, but I maintain that the imagination is a prime factor in determining what shape or form our creative endeavors will take. From the spark of the creative soul comes the imaging strength that makes everything come to light. Without light there is no painting, no colors, said Monet, everything is black, and the same thing is true for imaging and creativity. The natural and manufactured light is necessary for painting as the spiritual light of the soul is not only necessary for the imagination but it nurtures it and fosters images that far surpass anything that can be created by human intelligence. Even in the brightest light of day. Some people accused Henry of being too much the Platonist. Yes, Plato and his "cave." The cave of bewilderment, they said. Why? Because not everyone can see things the way Plato conceived. Plato the idealist, they said. Plato who saw things other people don't. That he saw with his mind and not with his eyes. What's wrong with that, asked Henry. "Never mind," they answered back.

Now, what does all of this has to do with the cautionary tale at hand, «Henry's Dilemma »? Well, it has much to do with the tale. First of all, it cautions us to be wary of definitions not well defined or not well worded by anyone who wants clear and understandable definitions. Definitions that can be and should be grasped clearly by the mind without any misconceptions. Henry's dilemma is one that defies all preceptions of words and definitions since it's a quandary that cannot be fully assessed and resolved. If we take the word dilemma and study it from an intellectual observation, then we have another word or words that try to define the given word. These other words try to resolve the issue at hand, a definition, but it cannot clearly and definitely address the issue, that of a cogent and reliable definition. You see, definitions are meant to be understood by all who seek them. Quite often, dictionaries do not resolve the issue, they only supply words that may or may not satisfy the situation. Am I being too picky here? If so, then I withdraw my contentious words and cede to those found in dictionaries. After all, dictionaries are made to clarify and define aren't they? And so, I end by saying that this particular tale called « Henry's Dilemma » finds its very meaning in the word dilemma or quandary, if we choose to add another word to it. It's a puzzlement, as the King of Siam, says to himself and to Anna who tries to instruct him about geography and the mythical science of the King's concept of the univertse. Here's another word that could be added to the definition of dilemma, puzzlement. Now Henry has yet another word to deal with. Poor Henry, he's in a dilemma now isn't he? I'm sorry if this tale appears to be an essay rather than a tale but it serves as a reinforcement of a cautionary tale, this particular one about quandary. Tales need a backbone of reasoning and imagining. There you have it, dear readers...in a quandary.

17.

The Tale of Jude the Misgiven

I know that the word misgiven does not exist in any dictionary, but as a writer, I give myself the privilege of making up words that I feel need to be devised or created for writing purposes. You see, words not only come out of dictionaries, but from the heads and mouths of people. That is why so many new words are added to dictionaries year after year. Misgiven, a word to mean one who conveys fear, doubt or suspicion. The past participle of "to misgive," I suppose. Whatever its grammatical implications, the word misgiven, as applied to Jude, means that the fellow named Jude is a person around whom hovers implications of doubt and concern, quite mysterious in their continual expectations of probability or improbability. You see Jude was a loner and a man of tales who loved to fabricate stories about anyone or anything. It didn't matter if there was truth in them as long as they entertained the people who listened to them. After all, they were meant to entertain not discourse on certain truths or dogmas. Jude fundamentally was an entertainer. He loved to have fun and make people laugh. He always had a wide smile on his pudgy but friendly face. People called him Jude the podge-pudge. He didn't mind being called podge-pudge because it made him feel good inside. People loved him and they even made good fun of him. He didn't care, he simply loved people and he entertained them with his stories. Quite often made-up stories. Some people thought that Jude's stories did not make sense, but they listened and did not dare to pass judgment. They felt sorry for him. He had very few friends and no one to guide him along the way of his growing-up, it seems. His parents and his sister, they said, were continually not there to accompany him in his struggle with his identity. They said nothing and remained silent about the real Jude. He was Jude the obscure just like Thomas Hardy's hero. But, Jude was no hero. Not even the protagonist of a famous novel. He was considered a nonentity by many.

The reason he was known as Jude the Misgiven was the fact that nobody seemed to know why. This epithet started to surface when someone said that Jude was a queer type, an odd-ball. Instead of using the terms queer or odd-ball, people preferred to use the epithet of misgiven. It sounded so much better, so decent and so academic of sorts for a being that people loved and even respected, even if Jude was deemed somewhat of a dunce at times. Misgiven was a term made just for Jude, they said. It suggested an aura of mysteriousness and redemption. Yes, redemption from all of the strange behavior patterns that were exhibited by Jude. Misgiven could cover the faults of misbehavior caused by not knowing how to behave in front of people. It was all a crazy game. The game of learning how to deal with someone who showed potential, but lacked the spirit or, should we say, the intelligence of developing that potential. What potential, you might ask. Well, the potential of becoming a thoughtful and creative person. What did they expect from Jude anyhow? Some said that they expected more from him than just tomfoolery and queerness. Others said that queerness and queer had disappeared from the scene years ago when the term applied to homos. So Jude was odd not queer. But misgiven, that was another term with several layers of meanings. The answer to all of this was to define misgiven accurately and without confusion. So, this is how the term misgiven was defined for us as applied to Jude: filled with certain doubts, cannot come up with the right answers or pertinent questions, misunderstood, and hard to fathom since there was an element of mysteriousness in his character. Some people thought that the definition was much too complicated and obtuse for the average person. Give us some concrete words with concrete examples, they said. How can we understand the meaning of misgiven if all we have to deal with is a bunch of crap? But filled with doubts, no right answers, no pertinent questions, misunderstanding and difficulty of fathoming things are concrete words and easy to grasp for anyone with an average intelligence, they said. All in all, the answer was to let Jude speak for himself, define his being misgiven by his own words, actions and deeds. So Jude was given the task of defining himself as a misgiven person.

----I'm misgiven because I don't know how to express myself in some given situations. It' s hard for me to explain my feelings and thoughts when I 'm confused about what I'm expected to say.

----Just say what you feel and what you think. It's as simple as that.

----Simple for you, but not so simple for me.

----Can't you just put into simple words what you feel and think at any given moment?

----No.

----Why not?

----Because my mind doesn't work that way.

----What do you mean by that?

----Well it doesn't. It's simple for you, but not at all simple for me.

----Why not?

----Why not? Why not? It's because it's not the way I feel and think.

----What is the way you feel and think then?

----I don't know if I can explain it.

----Well, try.

----It's like this. When I try to define myself, all I come up with is a blank answer or worse, a babbling refrain of stupid mumbles. I cannot come up with well-defined explanations. I cannot think straight. I falter in my choice of words and my train of thoughts.

----But you see, you can talk rationally.

----But, I cannot explain why words do not translate my being nor my brain in motion. I simply cannot put into words, clear, precise and meaningful words together in order to explain my being a misgiven.

----So why are you a misgiven?

----I do not know why except that people started calling me that years ago.

----Why?

----Why? I do not know why.

----You must have some inkling of the reason why.

----Inkling?

----Yes, inkling. A suspicion, a small idea of sorts.

----I don't suspect anything.

----Surely, you must have an idea why you are called misgiven.

----Well, it's because I'm afraid all the time, afraid to come out of my shell and afraid of what people will think if I open my mouth.

----You're not afraid now, are you?

----No....and yes.

----That's not an answer.

----I do not know. I do not know anything. There.

----Yes, you know something, but you're afraid to let it come out.

----That's it. It won't come out of my mouth because my brain will not let it. I'm not being stupid, but I hesitate and falter. That's all.

----You mean you're perhaps retarded and not quite like the others?

----I am not retarded and I am not stupid.

----Then, who are you and what are you?

----I am Jude and I am a misgiven.

-----Don't give us that. We already know that about you.

And so, conversations like this one went on and on. For days. For weeks. No one could extract from Jude the reason why he was called the misgiven. Except for his sister who was reluctant to explain why her brother was called the misgiven. Until, one day, she was forced to explain what she did not want to explain about her brother, Jude.

Jude's sister's name was, Henrietta. The sister did not like her name, but she had to live with it. It had been given to her by her father who wanted his daughter to be called Henrietta after his great aunt, Henriette de Valois, an offshoot of regal thinking and desires by a mother who had dreamed of being a princess or a duchess. Since the family resided in an anglophone milieu it was decided that the daughter's name would be Henrietta.

Henrietta was a talented child, a child of beauty, charm and wit. Unlike her brother, Jude, she was outspoken and frank in both her words and demeanor. Everyone loved her. Everyone thought that someday she would marry a high-class young man of power, fame and money. Eventually, she would have children and live happily ever after. Just like a fairy tale ending. However, it was not meant to be. When her parents died, she was left with the constant care of her little brother, Jude. So people said at the time. She had a hard time adjusting to a servant's life, as she called it. She couldn't go out much and she certainly could not bring suitors home. Besides, she did not have suitors. All of the boys she met did not want to go inside the house and deal with her brother who was like a log or a boulder, stiff in behavior, rigid in manners, and cold in thought and words. That's how they described him. Their thoughts and words about her brother hurt her deeply. So, she decided that marriage was not for her. She would stay with her brother and take care of him the best she knew how, for the rest of her life. She had no other choices, she told her friends, the few she had and could keep.

One day, Henrietta met this handsome prince of a man who was called, William Henry. Masterson the Third. He was a gem of a guy and a talented person who loved traveling and the study of ornithology. He simply loved birds. He especially loved the blue jay and the robin. Nothing exotic, nothing flashy and unexpected as far as birds are in their domains. He didn't have to travel far from home so see these birds. He could watch them in his backyard. He often invited Henrietta to watch with him, for hours. She grew tired of watching birds, especially the blue jay whose cry was like a piercing and wailing sound in the echo of the air. It affected her nerves, she said. She could not stand it. As for the robin, she liked the springtime harbinger who liked to pluck worms from the green sod. He was a proud bird with his orange-colored breast and dark beady piercing eyes. Henrietta stopped watching birds after her brother told her that he didn't like her leaving him alone. She tried to please him in every which way she could. So, she stayed home most of the time knitting, playing word games or doing the house chores even though she had done them repeatedly during the same day. It simply a means of whiling away the time. The drab, listless, and somber time, as she called it. Time went terribly slow for the young woman, especially since she had practically nothing to do that interested her. Oftentimes, she would sit on the edge of the large window sill and stare outside to see if there was something that would catch her eye. She would see the neighbors go by and the newspaper boy as well as the mailman do their rounds. It was always the same routine. She did not enjoy any of it. It just whiled away time and monotony. She did take care of her brother's needs, but they were becoming less and less demanding of her. Jude could take care of most of them and he did without murmuring or being sad about it. He was a resourceful young man. Relentless in his pursuit of tending to his immediate needs and careful not to bother his sister too much. Why did his sister insisted in taking care of him all the time, he wondered. He could easily take care of himself now that he had reached adulthood. However, Henrietta thought it to be her duty and her pride in the service of her brother. She really had no life of her own.

Henrietta started to be more and more a daydreamer. She often sat down and began to show her sense of listlessness and deprivation of interest in anything worthwhile. She had nothing to live for, she told herself. Except to take care of her brother. But that had become a duty that had faded away with time and the growing-up of her brother. And furthermore, even if the epithet of misgiven still applied to Jude, no one, but no one, could define what the term meant as it applied to Jude. Not even himself. So things went on as they always did until one day Henrietta decided to open up and spill the beans, as they say. What beans?

Well, it was a matter of telling all and everything about her dear brother, Jude. He wasn't her brother after all. He was her son. She had gotten him out of marriage at sixteen, and the biological father had dismissed her and taken off to some faraway place without providing for both the mother and the child. Henrietta's parents had taken her in after the boyfriend had gone. She had no place else to go. People did not know that she had a child out of wedlock, and they certainly didn't realize that she had been pregnant. Her tummy bump had never shown. They didn't even know that she had lived with her boyfriend in some dumpy place, a tenement house off the beaten path, it was said. Her parents made sure that no one knew about the birth of a child who was baptized Jude at the insistence of her parents. A baptism of un-choice on the part of Henrietta. Jude the patron saint of the misgivens and the disparate individuals, she thought. People got to know him as Henrietta's brother and the parents' child, a latecomer no less. No one dared to question it since women of Henrietta's mother's age, mid-fifties, had given birth to children late in their years. It was just a given fact that mothers of advanced age did very well as mothers, especially if they had support from other children like Henrietta.

So, Jude grew up as Henrietta's brother and everything went fine until the mother died of cancer, and two years later the father passed away of sheer loneliness and grief, people said. Then it was disaster. Disaster because Jude would not accept the fact that Henrietta was his birth mother, and that she had not acknowledged him as her child. Disaster because Henrietta refused to remain by Jude's side until he would reach the age of full maturity. Jude was fast approaching maturity, and he wanted Henrietta to be with him a while longer until he could fend for himself. He had never done it by himself and for himself. Both Henrietta's parents and herself had never dared to offer poor Jude the opportunity to become independent and proud to be so. They had never supported him in his attempt to live his own life. They never wanted him to get a job as menial as it may seem, such as newspaper boy or grocery boy. They did not even trust him with money. Sure they gave him a dollar a week as an allowance, but even then he wasn't allowed to spend it all by himself. There was always someone there to tell him what to do. He hated that. Jude grew more and more afraid of others and of himself, afraid of doing something wrong, although he didn't even know the difference between right and wrong. He was that naive and uneducated about things. They did not even allow him to go to school for fear that people would question his real identity. They home-schooled him. Mother, daughter and even the father took control of Jude's life and learning. They did not teach him any sense of ethics, no religious values, no cultural ideas or knowledge of western nor eastern civilizations. No art theory and no artistic works were discussed with him. Jude knew no art, no culture, no history, no real sense of real life and living. He grew up an anomaly of learning, an empty vessel of discipline and reasonable adherence to the intellect. Everything seemed to hang on his reaction to feelings and one such feeling was fear. Added to that were the feelings of mistrust, suspicion and a begrudging sense of being cast aside. He felt like an outsider, especially when people called him the misgiven..

The reason why Jude could not define himself as misgiven was that he knew just enough to begin to define himself and his own feelings, but he could not convey it to others. There was no conduit to sharing what he felt and what he knew about himself. The message was blank and the messenger missing. So how was he to survive such a standstill, a meaningless existence so-to-speak. Jude was completely lost and entirely unfit to live an existence of meaningful actions and fulfilling adventures in life. He was simply devoid of creativity and imaginative thoughts that might lead him to some healthy means of being who he was really meant to be. He didn't know anything about being creative enough to fulfill a sense of ardent and dignified living. He told himself that he wasn't human; he was simply a biological being given life by a mother who denied him his own identity and by a biological father who had planted his seed and then abandoned him as a throw-away creature. He felt like all of the human fetuses that are aborted and left to die unknown and unwanted. At he very least, he considered that life is life no matter in what condition or form. Human life is fragile from conception and it cannot tolerate un-love. Not wanted is not being human at all, Jude thought to himself. Being wanted, being cared for as humanly as possible, being loved is being truly human, he thought. Jude the Misgiven was true to his name. He was truly misgiven for his heart was filled with fear, his mind full of illusions about belonging, and his soul taken up with a great lack of spiritual direction. He was a young man without a spiritual compass and he wandered in the vast domain of lost souls.

Henrietta felt relieved from the burden of having to hold in secret the true identity of her son/brother, Jude the Misgiven. Everyone knew about her situation and her plight as as a mother abandoned by the man who had fathered her son. She had hidden her secret from everyone and it had festered in the deepest crevices of her heart and mind for years until it had reached a breaking point. Everything, every forcibly hidden thing, every ugly lie that's lived day after day reaches its breaking point at one time or another, or else it kills the person who is stigmatized by it. The ugly head of the serpent spits blood and devours the one whose fate it is to live with the beast.

As relieved as Henrietta was after her revelation, she felt traumatized by it. She felt the coldness of emptiness and being unloved by the one to whom she had given birth. Although she had tolerated her being a sister to Jude, she never experienced the joy nor the love of being a mother to him. Jude had experienced that lack of motherly love even though he thought that he had gained it with Henrietta's mother. However, it was a trumped up love, a false love that does not reveal sincerity and trust. He had felt it all these years, and now he realized that the love he had longed for was indeed an un-love, a made-up love created to hide what was considered either a scandal or a bad affair. After all, society would not ever tolerate such an affair, an affair of the heart gone wrong. Masking it, hiding it and even whitewashing it did not make it any better. Jude knew that and he simply could not swallow the truth. He could not digest the venom of lies and hypocrisy.

Jude appreciated the care that his true biological mother who had become his false sister had given him, but nevertheless, as much as he tried to stomach it, it always turned out to be sour. Now that he knew the full reality of his birth and the attempts of trying to shove everything under the rug in a manner of speaking, he realized that he had to do something about it. Something that would wipe out the anger within him, alleviate the pain and redeem him from all the perversity of the deed committed against him. In his mind, it was perverse and ugly. A deed to be avenged by the vengeful acts of the despaired. The rage inside Jude reached such a high pitch that he could no longer sleep. He was afraid that it would devour his mind, heart and soul before he could do anything about it. He had to do something, not just something slight or inconsequential, but really serious and even hard to reason. It had to be real and it had to hurt both the doer and the victim. He had been the victim long enough, he told himself. He didn't mind being hurt because he had felt the sting of hurting deep inside himself for a very long time without knowing what to do about it So, Jude started plotting day and night. How would he resolve the rage within him and be at peace with himself afterwards, he asked himself. There were no measures of mercy and compassion in him. Nothing was out of bounds for him. Everything was permissible in a world of lies and deceit, he told himself, and he believed it. He did not need permission from anyone to rectify the situation. He had to come up with something deliberately ugly and hard to atone for the hurt he had suffered for years. Nothing, no nothing would be too ugly nor impossibly horrendous to satisfy the ugly worm that gnawed at his brain and his heart. Anything, anything would be better than nothing, he thought. Was he getting immeasurably too deceptive with himself by letting thoughts and desires control his doing something concrete and real? Was it all a dream, a nightmare where reality is turned upside down. No, he mustn't let himself be torn by ideas and thoughts about doing something, but actually do it. Right then and there, he knew what he was going to do. Enough worrying, enough plotting, enough of foolish strategies. Enough. When you are full of everything either through obsession, inner gnawing, or worries you to death, well, it's time to get a hold of yourself and declare not amnesty but war. You have to fight and fight it was for Jude the Misgiven. He declared himself no longer a prisoner but a conqueror. Rather than give in and cease to be active in his pursuits of retributions, he became a conqueror of windmills, the windmills of his imagination and fabrication of a mind seeking remission from ugly plots and vile daydreaming. Enough! But was he only daydreaming like the Man from La Mancha. Nothing but a dreamer that one, he said under his breath. Dreamers are such bores. They only dream and do nothing, he continued talking to himself.

Jude was was trying to find cutting shears in the shed when his sister came up to him and asked him what he was doing.

----I'm looking for a pair of cutting shears.

----Why?

----Because.

----Because what?

----Do you always have to question my thinking and my actions? You always pry into my doings and pry into my reasons for my behavior. Enough!

----- O.K, O.K. You don't have to snap at me. I'm just trying to see if I can be of help.

----I don't need your help.

----Fine, and she walked out

Jude was looking for a cutting tool so that he could cut piano wires. Piano wires were strong, durable and at hand when one had a piano. His sister played the piano occasionally and sometime he liked to listen to her playing a favorite song, a patriotic one and especially a Mozart composition that enraptured him. She didn't play that often, so he missed hearing the music that she provided on the old piano in the living room. Jude only wished that he could play, but he did not have the talent nor the encouragement to play. He stopped wishing and even stopped thinking about it.

Jude found a pair of shears, strong and with a good grip. He had seen Henrietta's father cut thick wire with them, and he knew that those shears would do the work that he wanted. Cut a long piece of piano wire. He told no one about it and his plans for using the wire once detached from the piano. But, he had a plan. It was a morbid one, but he didn't care; he didn't wallow in self-pity or a troubled conscience. He was going to wrap it around somebody's neck and strangle his victim. He had seen it done in an old black-and-white movie. Not that he wanted to kill somebody, but he wanted to experience the delightful thought of doing it and getting away with it without too much fuss. It was all a exercise plan, not a real plan of action. He wanted to see how things like that worked. He wasn't scared and he wasn't intimidated by and act of violence. To him, it was not a violent act but an act of sacrifice and mercy. Perhaps it would be the man next door who was always getting on Jude's nerves. Perhaps, it would be the grocery man who used to put his thumb on the scale and cheat customers of a few ounces of meat. He had seen him do it without remorse or concern for the customer. That was cheating, Jude told himself. Perhaps it would be Madame Theriault from Oakland Street who made fudge and never gave him a piece even though he craved for it and told her about it. Why, she would bite into a large piece of fudge right in front of him, rolling her eyes at him. He hated her for that, the old bitch! Maybe it would be Henrietta's close friend, Norma, who would not allow Jude to even come close to the two young women while they played cards on the dining table. Jude liked cards and wanted so very much to join in the fun. Norma insisted that if Jude joined them she would leave. As hard as Henrietta tried to persuade her friend to make allowances for her brother as she called him, Norma never relented. The two women played alone with poor Jude watching them from the corner of his eye simmering in his thoughts and wrestling with his motives for disliking the two of them. Whoever it would be, the whole thing would amount to an act of tasteful revenge. Jude the Misgiven did not have a disposition for revenge but he did have a propensity for getting even. Tit for tat. Unjust deed for an unjust deed. Unfair calculation for an unfair attempt at not playing fair. That's how Jude saw things and he abided by this philosophy of fairness. He did not tolerate people and things that were out of the circle of justice and fairness. At least, that's how he saw things. Justice and fairness meant that both sides dealt the same blows and both sides rendered the same deed. Jude could not tolerate unbalanced accounts. All had to be either rectified or balanced in the right way. That was his way. For him, unbalanced or crooked deeds were not right. Even the lack of righteous deeds or the acknowledgment of not having played a fair game was outlandish from his viewpoint. Jude was very demanding when it came to measure people and deeds. He liked the statue of justice that he had seen, the one holding a balance while blindfolded. She is measuring well and doing justice a great service. Jude liked that as an ideal. But people did not always abide by her standards. Some tilted the balance or used crooked ways to measure actions and deeds. Jude was going to measure things correctly and fairly by abiding by the rules of the game, that of being alive and filled with a sense of justice and righteousness. He didn't exactly know how to express this in particular and meaningful words, but he knew the formula for exacting justice. I'll see to it, he told himself, that things will be squared off the way they should be. He knew what to do and how to do it. He had to choose the right time.

The right time came when Henrietta was about to go to bed one evening in early March when the wind was blowing swift and loud outside., She was tired and had spent much time reading some book that she had gotten from the local library, It was a book about elephants and whales. She loved animals and had a fondness for large animals. She had not spoken to Jude for days leaving him to his own senses and his own plight as a hermit without a sense of belonging. She even fought with him about the question of where was he going to stay once she left the home where they stayed. She was tired of supporting him and taking care of him, she told him. She wanted to be free of any responsibilities inflicted by her fate as an unwed mother, she said. She had had enough of being the mother/sister of a misgiven creature like Jude. Yes, to her he was a creature and not a person. She thought of him as a created being sent to harass her and to make her miserable. Her entire life had been wasted on him, she had told him in no uncertain terms one day when she was fed up with her situation in life. Jude had felt the tension in her voice and the terrible hurt of a mother/sister telling her child/sibling that she had never loved him. It was like a slap in the face for Jude, a cold and vicious blow to his ego as a person misgiven and misallied. A misalliance that had grown out of fateful circumstances. Enough of this he told himself. I've got to do something. Something to rid myself of this terrible lack of love and alliance as a person seeking the strong bonds of friendship and love. He didn't even love himself, he said. What was the use going in circles all the time? Why tolerate life and and not savor it? What is my true destiny in life? Why was I born? All these questions and more swam in his distraught mind. At one time, he thought he had strange cobwebs in his brain. Cobwebs that prevented him from thinking straight. Was he going mad, he asked himself. Being a misgiven meant to him being close to insanity. Things kept spinning and spinning in his mind so that he felt nauseous and unsteady. Was it vertigo? What was it that made him feel that way, he wondered. He had to do something about it. What?

Henrietta had put down her book, shut off the light and immediately fell asleep. The bedroom was dark except for the glow of the outside street light that filtered through the curtains of her bedroom. Everything was quiet, the quietness of a room empty of any sound except the muffled sound of the open mouth of someone sleeping. An hour or so later, Jude stepped into the bedroom and checked if Henrietta was truly fast asleep. She was. He had in his hands a piece of piano wire that he carried with diligence and care. He did not know what he was going to do at that point, when he realized that what he was contemplating was not quite what he wanted to do. He backtracked and went out of the bedroom only to return some moments later. He knew now what he was going to do. He hesitated at first, but he decided that he had to do what he had to do, slip that wire around Henrietta's neck and hold on very tight while twisting it until no sound came out of her throat. Could he really do that, he wondered at first. Snuffing out a life was not of his choosing, he calmly thought. But, he had to do what he had planned to do over the space and time of several days if not months. He feared not doing it for he did not want to be a misgiven even at a time when he could prove himself to himself. He wasn't a coward. Besides, he had to eradicate the ugliness of being a misgiven. He was sick and tired of being someone destined to remain off the track, he told himself.

Jude approached the bed, took the piano wire, slipped it very carefully around Henrietta's neck and throat until she started moving her head. She woke up, opened her eyes and saw what was happening. Her eyes bulged with horror. She tried to scream but could not move or utter a single sound. Jude could feel the delight of strangling a person who had cast him aside for years and had never, not once, shown any love for him. Without remorse and without any sense of compassion, he twisted the piano wire so that it felt tight and secure around her neck. Her legs and her feet started to shake in convulsion and her head went from side to side. Her entire body shook like leaf. Then the shaking stopped. Everything was still and very quiet. Henrietta's bulging eyes were still open and looked like two huge eggs in the faint glow of the light streaming through the curtains. A chill went up Jude's spine. His deed was done and over with. He could not think of anything else. He slipped quietly out of the bedroom and went to bed in his own bedroom across the way. He felt drained and somewhat listless. He lay there on his bed his eyes wide open. Then his eyes closed and he slowly fell asleep. No remorse, no feelings of pang and anguish. His entire body felt like it had gone through a wringer so drained and limp was it. Deep sleep came to him without any interruption until he heard a knock at his bedroom door. He woke up suddenly, somewhat dazed.

----Who is it?

----It's me, Henrietta. Breakfast time has long gone. Get up you lazy bones.

Jude trembled at the voice. "It couldn't be. It just could not be," he whispered to himself.

----Get up and come downstairs. I have something to tell you.

He started to talk to himself, "It couldn't be. It must be a dream. No, a nightmare. Oh, God, I botched the whole thing. Now I know that I'm a misgiven creature. A creature who went awry and died. Am I dead? No, I'm fully conscious. Now, I know I'll never get to where I want to be. In the land of the living where dreams of being loved and wanted are but a step away. Now, I've done it. I botched it for good." He fell back asleep. Reality for the misgiven Jude had played an ugly trick on him.. Always be careful of what you think you might have done and not truly done because it can cause not only anxiety but real discomfort..

18.

The Elephant and the Whale Go For a Stroll

Once upon a time, long before fairy tales were known, there was a storyteller who loved to tell the story of the elephant and the whale who liked to take a stroll at daybreak. Of course, one had legs while the other one had fins and could not walk. However, the whale could accompany the elephant by swimming along the coastline while the elephant trampled the sod at a given pace right alongside his strolling companion. The water's edge was deep enough for the whale to swim while the elephant walked near the edge of the sea trampling along in the cool waters. They were not too far apart so that they could see one another and, at times, even speak a few words in their own language. It was a language of harmony and subtle communication. It was indeed an odd couple, the other animals said. A large pachyderm with a very large creature of the sea. Who would have thought these two creatures would share the love of a morning stroll since one was a creature of the vast overland while the other a large fish that lived in the waters of the sea. As odd a relationship that was theirs, it was a relationship of mutual admiration and trust. The elephant admired the whale for its prowess in the waters and trusted him as a friend. The whale only had high praise for the elephant and was very confident in his friend, the huge elephant with a trunk that could lift up any heavy burden for a being in need.

One of the earliest names for the elephant was Waterspout since he did have a large trunk with which he could spray himself, especially when it was hot outdoors. He drank water with it and he managed to help others out when they needed an elephant trunk to carry a load. Waterspout turned to roll-around-carrier, then to high-in-sky-finger although the elephant had no fingers. When he lifted up his trunk straight and stood on his two back feet, he looked like a huge triumphant creature that could shoot water in the air and take on the appearance of a sprouting fountain for all to see and enjoy. The elephant was proud of his trunk turned fountain in the sky. Everyone said that the elephant was a mighty rough-skin boulder of an animal with an elegance unmatched by other creatures on earth. The whale agreed with the compliment and added to it by saying that the elephant was indeed a giant of an animal that made everyone proud and merry. Merry because the elephant was always joyful and full of trumpet blasts that awed the entire jungle and wooded plains.

As for the whale, he was considered to be a giant himself capable of swimming thousand of leagues and crossing distances never before known to the other creatures. It was said that the whale ranked uppermost in the realm of the giants of the earth, sky and water. He was way up there with the soaring eagles, the lofty volcanoes, the tallest mountains, and all the created beings that reached for the stars. The whale was indeed a mighty and respected creature by all. His friend, the elephant, could not express his deep sentiments for such a friend for fear of not being good enough or able enough to meet the high standards of laudatory expression. He had never learned how. Neither his mother nor his father had taught him the rules of singing the praises of others. Elephants were like that, proud animals filled with self-reliance who had high and mighty ways of celebrating themselves in all the glory that a huge animal like the elephant presumed he had, and that no other animal enjoyed. The elephant was not the vain and haughty one like the male lion who proclaimed himself king of the wild, master of his pride. No, but the elephant was nevertheless an animal of superior strength and a mighty believer in his own capacities. No one would have dared deprive him of the honor of superior strength in mind, heart and abilities to rule over the entire planet on which he was put. As for the whale, it was considered a genuine task to try and invent compliments worthy enough for such a beast, a worthy and sublime creature, they said of him.

The elephant and the whale were what constituted part of the harmony in God's created nature. The realm of nature was indeed a king's domain ruled by justice, peace, and understanding. Some said that was the way the Great Creator had meant it to be. The friendly elephant and the benevolent whale were the symbols of nature's harmony in action. However, things changed over the years. They changed on account of a colossal misunderstanding. A misunderstanding over the rights of some creatures like the ape, the crocodile, the giraffe, and especially man. The worse was on the part of man. Man had read somewhere that he was given dominion over all even the domain of animals. He had given a name to each one and had subdued, if not enslaved, some of them. Man managed to tame the horse, the cow, the falcon and even the eagle, and with time, even the elephant. Whatever he put his hand to, man controlled. With time some animals, like the elephant, were locked up with chains, and were forced to entertain entire families just to make them smile and laugh in a circus tent. Even the lions and the tigers were tamed forcefully with whips so that they would obey their masters. Force, brute strength and especially willpower ruled. Some animals like the horses and the cows did not mind the taming since they felt useful to man who took good care of them in general. But, along the way some animals were terribly surprised to find out that they had become the prey of man. Like the "game" plan. Yes, animals became game for humans. It was distraction at its best. Going out in the forest, the savannas, the African wilderness on a safari or anywhere else where so-called fun is attainable and hunt your prey of choice. There is a lot of money involved and much energy spent on getting trophies to append to a wall somewhere. Why? To show one's personal grandeur or exploitation of nature and its animals called "game." One woman recently killed a lovely and graceful giraffe for whatever reason. Why? Aren't giraffes noble and wonderful creatures out in the wild? So why kill them? Why put them in a zoo where they do not seem to fit at all? Pleasure of taking animals from the wild to place them in a cage or an enclosure for the pleasure of kids and gawking individuals? How would you like to be kept in a cage or a stifling enclosure and have people look at you and try to give you bits of their food just to make the situation palpable? Zoos are incredible spaces where man has placed animals in order to get the pleasure of having a city menagerie at hand. If you cannot travel to go and see these animals in their own environment, then borrow a book, go see a movie, watch a television documentary or whatever venue available, and enjoy the visual and audio experience. There are ways of enjoying nature that do not disrupt the everyday life of creatures meant to live elsewhere than a zoo. Use your imagination and thrive, used to say my uncle Joshua.

Then there's the slaughter of certain wild animals for the money that can be had in selling their rare and expensive attractions such as elephant tusks for ivory, crocodile skin for purses and luggage, cobra, boa, or any kind of serpent skin for the pleasure of having expensive attaché cases, a rare piece of luggage, or shoes made out of these skins which makes them fashionable.

Then there's the slaughter houses where thousands if not millions of animals such as cattle from the vast farmlands, are slaughtered each day for meat. Meat sells well. A lot of protein in red meat. [How many hamburgers can America eat each day, I wonder]. We all need to eat but do we need to eat that much? Of course, when we go to a restaurant and order a steak or any meat dishes, do we envision the animal that that cut of meat comes from. Of course not. We see the nice juicy steak, filet mignon, the best and the most expensive, and we delight in having an expensive and outrageously sublime meal. You will say that everyone needs to eat and why not eat what we like. Sure, as long as it does not take away the food from mouths of children, and hide their eating habits of junk food and junkyard leftovers. Why are so many starving, you may ask, when there is enough food for everyone on the planet. Is that part of the poverty cycle? It is a cycle for it keeps coming and going, coming and going and never seems to end. The poor you will always have with you, you might add. Yes! But do we need to keep increasing the numbers? We usually do not like to reveal those statistics because they inflame the politicians who are ensconced in their comfortable lifestyle in plush offices and fat salaries with benefits that belie their political assurances that they are indeed preoccupied with the welfare of all constituents. Well, we are getting away from the main ideas of this tale aren't we. Let's get back to our *moutons,* our sheep, as Pantagruel the Rablaisian monster says. Not the sheep but the elephants and the whales. We have heard much about elephants and why don't we concentrate on the whales for now.

Of course, we all know that the whaling ships of yesteryear were specialized ships. They usually had two or more whaleboats or open rowing boats used to capture the whale and brought the captured whale to the master ship to be flensed or cut up. Blubber was extracted and rendered into oil. Oil for lamps prior to fossil fuels were used. It was a very profitable industry. In olden days before the modern equipment, the whale was harpooned and led the sailors on a very long adventure since it took a very long time for the whale to die since it bled to death. A very inhumane way of capturing the prey. It was a chase much like the chase of any prey, an adventure of men out at sea for months and even years. The chase, the adventure, the monster of the deep and the tales of whales and their capture by men who lived lives of sea-worthy often mythical adventures are all part of the myth of the whale and its capture out at sea. The chase was part and parcel of the very core of whaling. Sailors of the vast seas were enthralled by the chase. Without the chase there was no adventure. Men are adventurous creatures from way back. Take, for instance, Odysseus and his ten-year adventure. That's an adventure to capture the imagination of men seeking the glory of the chase and the ultimate adventure of seafaring experiences. There is nothing as fascinating as the myth for it deals with human emotions, the human seeking of grand illusions of sorts, and a determination to charter one's identity in the world. The quest for ideals and ideas is the greatest adventure of all. Thus, whales exemplify this quest by giving us the leviathan of all sea creatures being sought in a magnificent hunt until the end either of beast or man. Nowhere is to be found such excitement and adventure as in the chase and capture of the great monster of the deep, the whale.

Furthermore, there was the concrete gain in exploiting the whale such as the bones for purposes of fuel, baleen for women's corsets, men's collar strips, buggy whips as well as dice and dominoes made out of whale bones. Not to forget the killing of elephants for their tusks for the ivory industry. The slaying of elephants simply to obtain their tusks because it pays a modest sum of money for the poor African native who needs to survive the inadequacies of poverty and want is a definite crime against nature.

I read somewhere recently that there was a slaughter of a protected blue whale in Hvalfjordur Iceland. It came as an article in the world news. The largest animals in existence, blue whales are a protected species and have not been deliberately captured since 1978, said the article. There was a debate over the killing of this blue whale whether it was indeed a blue whale or a fin whale. Conservationists argue that it was a blue whale by its lack of a white lip that characterizes fin whales. Moreover, the mottling on the whale's flank was an identifier that acts like fingerprints that the animal in question was likely a blue whale.

According to statistics presented by the World Wildlife Fund, blue whales were nearly wiped out by whaling fleets before regulations were created. A staggering 360,000 blue whales were killed in the 20th century in Antarctic waters alone. The rogue whaler argued that Iceland is a big fishing nation of the ocean and that the U.S. has deer hunting so Iceland has whale hunting for its game chase and capture. It's all a matter of political and financial excuses to capture what has been protected for a long time. Greed and the bypassing of regulations as set up by conservationists are the reason behind the killing of such a beloved and protected animal. The possible extinction of the blue whale is yet another cog in the wheel of destruction of the Creator's plan. He did not create to put enmity among creatures, but harmony and peace. Not destruction but construction. Human beings need to construct rather than destroy and divide. They need to let the elephant and the whale stroll side by side. It would be a disaster if all animals of land and sea were to be set on a collision course by dint of human interference and especially unharnessed greed and uncontrolled pride. The elephant tusk and the whale bones are just as important to the survival of the harmony of species on this earth. Not one part of either elephant or whale must be sacrificed for the industry of bargaining or selling for profit. Furthermore, yet another game for profit is the poaching of rhinos for their distinctive horns. We are told that these horns are worth more than gold in certain cultures. And so, the African native is once more used by big money to slaughter an animal for its tusk, its horn, its hide, or any of its distinctive feature just so that profit can be had. Poverty, starvation, fear of losing your hut or your shack, as well as many other reasons impel the natives to slaughter any animal that's on the trade list, just so that he can earn a pittance. Moreover, the cycle never seems to end in spite of the energy and devices of the conservationists.

It also has been reported that humanity has wiped out 60% of global wildlife in the past 45 years. That's incredible! This is indeed a threat to humanity and the planet, as scientists say. We are on the brink of disaster, aren't we. This added to climate change is a warning that we have to stop spoiling the planet, its wildlife, and it's human endeavors as far as being creative in our efforts to manage and preserve what has been given to us by the Creator. Some may not believe in the Creator but there is a creative beginning to all, it's not just a BIG BANG as some people put it. Just happenstance? Think the way you want, to but I do not think so. There is a beginning, a design and a purpose to all. Philosophers from way back to the Greeks and most probably further back than that have cautioned us to be truly rational in our rationality and use our strength of inductive as well as deductive reasoning to fathom this universe that has withstood the irrational doings of some who proclaim that all is in the hands of we the people and not of God, and we can solve all mysteries and harm. But can we? Do we have the capacity to wipe out and even eradicate all cautions since we have the power to do so? Do we? Cautions are simply warnings or flags being raised to prevent human irrationalities. *Cogito ergo sum*, yes, but once aware of our existence as human beings do we act like one or do we plunge into our irrational selves and profess by our words and deeds our lame presumption of being almighty and all powerful. Like gods gone haywire. I know, some of you may think that I am now in the essay mode, but there are things that need to be said even if they're said in the context of a tale.

The elephant in the boa's big belly as well as the whale that swallowed Jonah must remain as the symbolic reminder of the plausible strength that all humans have in order to find some equilibrium in the powers of controlled rationality and the productive imagination. Boa constrictors, elephants and imaginary whales help to fulfill the need to keep intact the world of creativity. Do we need a cautionary tale for that, you might ask. Well, reader, what do you think?

19.

Why Does the Peacock Have a Fan

I have often wondered why the lordly peacock has what we could call a fan. Yes, a fan of rainbow-colored feathers with large spots that look like eyes when he struts around. I am told that only the male has such features; the female is more modest and more simply attired. The peacock is the male while the female is called peahen. It makes sense. But why does the peacock have such an extraordinary plumage, is my question. I am told it's for mating ritual purposes. The female is attracted to this display of the brightly fanned plumage. The peacock goes around hauling this long and must be heavy train behind him until he chooses to fan it. I am told it's not for vanity, but for natural purposes, the purpose of mating. Although we associate the peacock with its train and fan of extraordinarily attractive feathers with vanity and pride, the peacock is not a vain creature. People can be vain, and so people are the ones who associate the so-called proud peacock with the vain and proud human being. Pride is a natural quality, vanity is not. I mean natural pride and not over-done pride. I would rather associate this kind of pride with the French word, *fierté* and not *orgueil*. Be it as it may, the peacock exhibits the beautiful qualities of a rare bird with the blend of the most satisfying of colors and the most enviable dress-plumage. Only the Creator could have conceived of this. The Creator has the most vivid and colorful of all imaginations far surpassing that of the human being. All you have to do is look around you in all of nature. We no longer take the time to really look, I mean truly look carefully at the miracles in nature, miracles of outstanding shapes, sizes, colors, etc. We have become passive and carelessly mindless in our observation of natural phenomena. We seem to take everything for granted, for we think that we have the power to substitute, copy or create what the Creator has already done or even worse, we tempt the forces of nature by eliminating what is good and plentiful, and by assuming that we can easily replace it with artificial and not absolutely necessary properties or modes of existence. Our development of science has emboldened us to think we can overstep our human capacities and create what has not been created before like the atom bomb. Atomic science and atomic energy is fine as long as they aren't used to destroy humanity. But that's another story. I want to tell you a tale of immense value and interest for those of you who enjoy tales and stories wrought by the creative imagination. It's the tale of the peacock and it's fan of brightly-colored feathers. It's a cautionary tale, so do not think that I'm telling it to you for moral purposes only. That's only part of the tale. The other part deals with the genuine purpose of telling tales.

Once upon a time, no that's too old-fashioned and absolutely cliché. That was used too many times and it smells of the long-ago past when children were induced into the wonderland of dreams and tales. Let's say, once a long time ago when the peacocks and the other birds were placed on this earth, there was a confusion about the plumage of all birds, since the Creator did not fully realize that some birds belonged here and other birds belonged there. It became a geographical nightmare of sorts. Although the Creator claimed perfection, there was something to question about his talents and properties as a creator. He himself realized that. Not all creators are deemed perfect. That's an ideal that prevails all over creation. So why do we think that the Creator was so perfect that he insisted on being the supreme being who manifests wisdom and unalterable rights to perfection. I do not know enough about perfection to render any judgment, but I do know that perfection exists, and involves the knowledge of imperfection. How does one acknowledge the very fine line between them. No one knows. But, the Creator has to be perfect since like Aristotle's definition of creator almighty, perfection calls for the unmoved mover. There has to be a first cause, he said. Alright, we may attribute perfection to God, but perfection does not exist on this earth. Not for animals, not for things and certainly not for human beings. Let's get away from philosophical discussions shall we not? They can be boring, if not maliciously intrusive to our telling of tales.

One big question in all of this is why did Lord Krishna choose a peacock feather specifically, and not another bird's feather. One of the reason is the peacock is the only creature in nature that observes complete chastity in life. It is told that when the peacock is happy, he dances with his wings and his eyes are filled with tears. Peahen drinks these tears and conceives. Peacock does not have even a tinge of lust in his heart. So much for mythical chastity. Lord Krishna identifies with the bright colors of the peacock, and he wears a peacock feather on his head signifying that the entire range of colors are in him . In the Indian calendar, the days that follow the Full Moon day until the New Moon day are considered sacred since they represent the Blue of daylight hours and the Black of nighttime symbolic of the peacock and his array of colors.

Now, how did the peacock get to have a huge train or fan of such colorful feathers? That is the question or the issue at hand. Well, I will tell you a tale of how the peacock got to have the peacock fan. It started with a terrible rumor that all cocks and hens were to be exterminated by one fell swoop. Why? Because the Creator had made a mistake. But, creators are not supposed to make mistakes it was said in whispers, and all over the newly created world. The Creator, a mistake! Really! Creators are not supposed to make mistakes, or else everything created becomes suspect and can be interpreted as lies. Nothing, absolutely nothing must stem either from an error or a mistake. Absolutely not! Then, how did it happen, the newly created people said. Its was a mistake, that's all. But there should not be any mistakes because the Great Creator, the Infinite One, the Most Holy One of all nations and ethnic groups wherever they may be planted to serve the Creator, they rely on his most reliable strength of character and unmistakable properties of creativity. He is the One and Only Lord of all creation, it was said. Nobody else is supreme in the entire universe celestial and earthly, as well as transcendental. The universe to the Creator consists of absolutely everything under the sun, under the stars, even under the watchful eye of the Great and Almighty One. Everything! Absolutely everything! So how did a mistake of colossal dimension and importance happened, people asked. Was there an answer to this problem? Who would and could discern this problem of the fallibility of creation and its ramifications? Who? If God makes a mistake, then he's not God, is he? Whatever the matter or the question, there was an error made at creation and that error caused great concern among the created ones, human and fowl. I said fowl because the other animals, except the fowls such as the peacocks and the peahens, were not affected by it or did not show much concern. Only the peacocks and the peahens seemed to be touched by the great mistake and that error was: one could not tell between the male and the female of this species. There were no means of gender identification. So with time and patience, the mistake was rectified and the cock got his tail while the hen laid eggs as appropriate for the female. The female, the peahen, was attracted to the peacock, not because he was vain or haughty in his manners, but she was attracted to his highly colorful and marvelously designed fantail that seemed to explode as a fan when the peacock decided it was time to mate. What an erection! So, people asked, what is the caution in all of this. What is the moral of the tale or is there one? You, my readers if you cannot interpret this tale and find a caution or a moral, I cannot give it to you. I ran out of advice and cautionary examples when I ran out of ideas. You see, ideas do not always come to a writer freely and simultaneously. I mean when he is writing, sometimes ideas run out. They just fade away. I suppose they'll come back. They usually do. Right now, they're gone, and I am left deliriously and magically without words. Words without ideas are nothing but tools without a master plan. They just sit there, waiting. For what? For ideas and that takes creativity and imagination at work. Not idle or wasting time for the writer. That's a cautionary tale in itself. Do not wait for ideas to come, create them. But how? If you wait for ideas to come, you will wait a long time. Draw them from experience, and do not wait for something new. There is nothing new under the sun, as they say. Neither under the moon(I made that up). We artists, if I call myself an artist-writer, we all stand on the shoulders of the giants. We cannot plagiarize, steal ideas, wring out all the juice from a story, or even make up a story as if it was inspired by another writer. We must be original...can we?...must we be? I leave that up to people whose task is like the critic who assesses the merit of writing. Sometimes, even they make mistakes and call a piece of writing "purple prose." What color is good writing, I ask myself This writer is very much like the peacock,. I like to strut myself and show my fan of colors, eye designs and mythical feathers that prompt me to illustrate the art of good writing. Now that's a cautionary tale if there is one. The myth of writing is the truth of the creative imagination at work...if one is writing tales or even a novel. I caution all of you though, be cautious about the art of writing for writing is an art and a skill that will not be compromised by bad faith and tomfoolery. It must be strait and not narrow, but open to a vast array of plenteous peacock feathers. Let us suppose that is why the peacock got his huge colorful fantail...to inspire writers like me.

20.

Pas de deux, Pas de gars

There are some who will tell you, and they insist, that ballet is not for boys. *Pas pour les gars* (not for boys). Why?, you ask them and they reply, "Because it's not for boys. Boys will be men and men don't do ballet. It's a girl's thing." That's their answer. They've never seen ballet, nor did they ever think that some day one of their sons would announce that he wanted to become a ballet dancer. Ballet is for girls and that's all. These people did not consider that some great music was composed for ballet by renowned composers, and that traditionally every French opera had a ballet sequence in it, for it was the rule. Furthermore, there were men's roles in almost every single ballet. Great opera houses like *l'Opéra de Paris,* Covent Gardens and La Scala were built for operas and ballet. There were concert halls too. People were interested in music, ballet and operas. There were even ballet schools established in order to give young people the opportunity to learn and practice the art of ballet, an art form that is highly technical as a dance with its own vocabulary based on French terminology such as, *pas de deux, jeté, battu, piqué,* and many more, all terms specifically wrought for ballet. Unfortunately, stereotypes were formed for male ballet dancers such as, wimp, snob, neurotic, vain, creature of the night, and artsy. Even so, some people did not like ballet and they thought that ballet was for sissies, not for real boys. "What's a sissy, or who is a sissy?" "Well, a sissy is a boy who acts like a girl or a man who does women's things like…" "Like what?" "Like, I don't know." "Like cooking and baking?" "No, I don't mean that." "Well, like what?" "I don't know," et cetera, et cetera, et cetera. The term sissy is never well defined, nor is it a name that means anything of consequence, except that it could very well be classified as bullying at times. Anyway, bullying is always stupid and a thoughtless thing. That's what some people say. Not those who do not like operas and ballet for boys. They're in a class by themselves. They could be classified as malcontents. Oops, that's not the right word, I suppose. I would like to inject a small reminder of some very good films about ballet and dancing. "Billy Elliot" for instance. Not to forget "Shall We Dance" about hiding learning how to dance as if it was meant to be hidden. Anyways, the writer now proposes a tale about ballet for boys. *Pas de deux, pas de gars.*

His mother had him baptized William after his uncle, her youngest brother, who was nicknamed Bill. The boy grew up as Billy-Joe. Billy-Joe had no siblings, and his father had died in an industrial accident years ago. The widow worked in the mills for years until she could not do it any more. Mill work was debilitating and strenuous work for a frail woman like Molly. That was her name, Molly Madore. She had married a Frenchman from up north in the Saint-John river valley of upper Maine. Molly loved her husband, Sammy, and they had moved to the southern area of Maine where Sammy Madore had found work in the mills. His wife, Molly, also found work there for she had insisted that a wife had to help support the family. The wages were small and they could not survive on only one paycheck what with the rent, groceries, the purchase of gas for the 1940's Ford Sedan with the wide white walls(they were both excited about this car), and the doctor's bill that came up once in a while. Molly had a bad back and a weak stomach that acted up now and then. However, she had still insisted in doing her own housework as well as making all of the meals without exhausting the weekly income. She had even managed to put some money aside, "For rainy days," she had said. When the first baby came along, it was a girl, the couple had to spend money on hospital bills that kept piling up. But the baby girl died anyway, and the couple, Sammy and Molly, were terribly afraid to have another baby because the doctor had told Molly that it would be best not to have another child, due to her frailty.

But Molly had insisted on trying for another child anyways even if her husband did not want to put his wife in danger. She did conceive of another child and this one was healthy and strong, and the mother had recovered very well in spite of her frailty. Molly was ever so happy. Happy to have a beautiful boy with golden hair. Just like her own hair, golden like the morning sun and curly like a little lamb, she had said. Molly had beautiful hair growing up and everyone said so. All she had to do was wash them with soft soap and the curls would come up as she was drying her hair with towel She would then brush them and then she could look at herself in the mirror and be joyous that her hair usually turned out to be so golden and manageable. Molly hoped that her son's hair would be the same. Billy-Joe had beautiful hair. Just like his mother, people said. When Sammy died, Molly was devastated. Billy-Joe was still so very young. He could not understand why his mother cried all the time.

Billy-Joe grew up tall, lean, muscular and lithe for a young man. He loved music, took a liking for the arts and dance, especially ballet. Molly did not know why ballet, but she encouraged Billy-Joe in his every choice of activity. She specifically tried the best she could to encourage his deep sense of creativity and his capacities to imagine things such as dragons, pirates out at sea, dwarfs and magic creatures of the woods. Billy-Joe had a vivid imagination and a rare capacity to express himself in art and music. His teacher, Miss Blandon, had told him how she was impressed by his talents, and she tried to encourage him to explore music and dance. She suggested ballet for she was a big devotee of ballet. She first introduced him to Tchaikovsky's **The Nutcracker.** At first Billy-Joe was hesitant when he learned that tickets for the performance were very expensive. He could not afford to buy one, but the teacher had already purchased a ticket for him and for herself. Billy-Joe loved "The Nutcracker." Afterwards he tried to imitate some of the ballet steps, even a pirouette artfully accomplished to his delight. When Billy-Joe attempted to show his ballet steps to some of his elementary school friends at recess time, they all laughed at him. They could not see how a boy would do such a thing and take delight in it. That was a girl's thing, they told him. Billy-Joe insisted on keeping his ballet exercises every day all by himself. His mother was the only one privy to his private performances. She always told him that he was becoming a good dancer, and that she would give him all the help needed to learn from a professional by taking lessons. She thought that her son was a talented child out to make a success of himself in the world. So, she went to Billy-Joe's school to consult with Miss Blandon.

Miss Blandon reassured Billy-Joe's mother that her son had indeed talent for the performing arts and that she would do everything in her power to assist him in getting to a good school where ballet was being taught by professional people. She had contacts, she told the mother. The mother was happy about this result and she hurried back home to tell her son about the good news. Billy-Joe wasn't home. The mother was worried since she had expected her son to be there waiting for her. She was concerned because Billy-Joe was supposed to run an errand for her. The mother started calling some of his friends and some of hers. No one knew of his whereabouts. No one realized he had left the house without telling anyone about it. Now, the mother was really worried. Late that afternoon, the mother received word from a neighbor that she had heard that Billy-Joe had been hurt in an accident. Her husband was a policeman and he was a witness to the accident. She told Billy-Joe's mother that her son was in the local hospital and that the hospital was having a hard time identifying the patient since he did not want to respond to their questions. Billy-Joe's mother rushed to the hospital and ran to the desk to ask where was her son. They told her that he was still in the emergency room. She started crying for fear of a terrible thing happening to her son. A nurse came to talk to her and told her that her son had suffered a broken leg. Someone had hit him in the back while driving. He was alright but his right leg had been severely broken if not shattered. The doctors were not quite sure if they would be able to save the leg. Now, the mother was frightened and she begged the nurse to be able to see her son. The nurse told her that it would be a while before she could be admitted to her son's bedside. When time came, after a two-hour wait, Billy-Joe's mother stepped timidly into the room where Billy-Joe was and started asking her son why he had not told the hospital staff about his identity and why he had not told them about her being contacted. He told her that he was sorry about the accident and he did not want to frighten her. Billy-Joe was writhing in pain, she could see it. Besides, he was terribly worried about his leg even though the doctors had been able to save it. That night, the mother stayed at her son's bedside and prayed that her son's leg would improve so that he would be able to go back to school and attend the ballet school also. That was his dream. The mother honestly supported her son in becoming a ballet dancer but had always cautioned him not to wish for the impossible.

After months of therapy and determination on Billy-Joe's part to get well, and especially make his leg function again as it should, the therapists, as well as the doctor, told Billy-Joe and his mother that the leg would not get to be limber and functional as in the past. That Billy-Joe would have a limp in the right leg for the rest of his life. Billy-Joe was devastated. His mother was now in despair that her son would be a cripple all his life and that his dream would vanish into thin air, just like that on account of a dirty, crazy accident, she said. What would happen now?

Billy-Joe did not want to give up his dream and he fought tooth and nail, as they say, to find someone who would set his leg straight so that he would be able to walk straight. Doctors and therapists all told him that it was impossible since the break had been bad and all they could do for him was to make him walk Nothing more. No dancing and especially no ballet. Why would a boy like him want to dance ballet, they asked him. Billy-Joe made no reply to this question for he knew that they had a strong bias against boys and ballet. Ballet wasn't macho enough for boys. He had heard that over and over again. Billy-Joe told his mother that he was going to show them, all these cowardly people, that ballet was not just for girls but for boys also.

As Billy-Joe grew older and stronger, he realized that his leg had changed and had grown straighter, especially his foot. He started exercising both leg and foot rigorously and found that all of his work and determination were paying off. He tried a few ballet movements and they worked, not ideally but modestly artistic, as he told himself. Months went by and even a few years and Billy-Joe was no longer a cripple, as people said. He walked straight and could even dance well.

However, both school and ballet companies dared not take him in for fear that his leg had not sufficiently healed. They did not want to risk the professionalism of their programs and dancers, they told him. Billy-Joe told himself that he was going to show them that he could become a professional dancer in his own way.

A few years went by and Billy-Joe had greatly improved both in his walk and his dance, enough to form his own ballet school of dance, and try to go for an audition somewhere, not just a mediocre school but a really good school of ballet. He attended every possible ballet performances that he could go to and learned the techniques of professional ballet. He started attracting some students that proved to be great students. His school began to attract attention not only to himself but to most students he taught He was proud of his endeavors and happier than had ever been. He did not mind the bullying anymore, the bullying of those who ridiculed male ballet dancers like him. His efforts were rewarded by the attendance of familiar faces in the ballet world. Even the Arts section of the New York Times mentioned the virtues of his talents and absolutely professional performances by his students. People started comparing his school to the famous ones like the Balanchine company of ballet, the Joffrey Academy of Dance, the Julliard School, and the American Ballet. Of course Billy-Joe's school was certainly not in the league of the Paris Opéra, or the Royal Ballet. Surely not the Bolshoi Ballet Academy. But, his school was growing in reputation. It was proof that his students were getting admirable and professional teaching and competence in ballet dancing Of course, Billy-Joe was not alone in the teaching and the mastering of ballet dance. He had hired some truly professional people who were very competent and demonstrated exquisite talent for the performing arts. Billy-Joe knew what he was doing.

One night as Billy-Joe was preparing to open the latest ballet performance of his now well-known ballet school, he sat there in the audience wondering how his mother would have loved his success as a dancer and as a ballet teacher. He was waiting for the curtain to rise when, all of a sudden, a hand touched his right shoulder. He turned around and saw standing there his hero, BALANCHINE. His dream had indeed been realized, just as his mother had repeatedly told him. "Be careful of what you wish for, it may come true," she had told him. She had not told him that in a cautionary manner, but in a jubilant way of encouraging Billy-Joe to never give up. Giving up was the sissy way, Billy-Joe had told himself in defiance of adversities and misconceptions... *pas de gars* became a cry of daring and insistence for male artists in bloom. Billy-Joe had showed them the way. *Pas de gars... il n'y aurait pas de ballet*...no guys, no ballet.

21.

The Blue Popsicle

Were you crazy about Popsicles when you were young? I was. I especially loved the orange one, and I still do. There were also the red ones, the cherry flavored, the purple ones, the grape flavored and then came the blue ones, and I do not recall their specific flavor. I have a close friend name Louise, who recently divulged to me that her very favorite Popsicle when she was young, was the blue one. She and her friends loved the blue Popsicle. Why? I asked her. She didn't remember. All I know about the blue Popsicle is that it left its color blue on your tongue and on your lips.

I remember, as a small child, one little boy named Ronnie who liked Popsicles so much that he begged his mother, his grandmother and even his aunts and uncles for a nickle in order to buy a Popsicle. Popsicles then came in twos, just like conjoined twins. You had to separate them in order to eat one at a time. Some just took the two of them into their mouths and chewed on each one as they went on chewing and slurping the Popsicles. I could not afford to buy Popsicles because I had no allowance, and my mother did not have the money to buy Popsicles all the time. So we made our own in the freezer tray that made ice cubes. We used to pour Koolaid in the tray compartments and let them freeze overnight. However, they were definitely not like Popsicles. Each little frozen squares was rock hard like ice and they were not soft enough to sink your teeth into them. You had to let them melt in your mouth. They did not taste like a good Popsicle bought at the corner grocery store. One day, little Jonah, that's how I will call him, bought six blue Popsicle twosomes and sat down to eat all of them all in one sitting. His mother had told him to save some in the freezer for another day, but he had insisted on eating them all. She had left him to his own demise for it was indeed a demise for poor little Jonah. First of all, he had a belly-ache. His tongue and his kips were frozen cold all day long. Worst of all he had a blue tongue and blue lips that would not go away. Kids laughed at him; older people smiled when they saw him in his blue state. His grandmother vowed that she would no longer give him a nickel to buy a Popsicle. His mother tried to console the poor little boy, but he was disconsolate. As much as he tried, he could not get rid of the blue coloring. His mother tried to wash his tongue and his lips. She even rubbed the washcloth hard but nothing doing. She then scrubbed and scrubbed, and it hurt the little boy who cried and hollered out loud, but the blue coloring stayed. The mother was as much discouraged as Jonah was disconsolate. He promised her that he would never again eat blue Popsicles. As fate would have it, the company discontinued the blue Popsicle perhaps because kids no longer wanted them. Little Jonah never forgot the blue Popsicle and, to this day, there are remnants of the blue coloring on his lips. Kids started calling him "Blue Lips, the dying kid." Jonah didn't like that. He still doesn't like it. CAUTION: Do not eat blue Popsicles. They may leave a remnant of blue that just will not go away. The mark of "Blue Lips, the dying kid." Jonah was not actually dying, but he had the mark of a frozen-blue-lips boy. Nobody likes that, not even Jonah. Especially Jonah who at one time loved blue Popsicles. Have you ever wondered why they don't make them anymore? I'm sure some people like my friend Louise still remember them and perhaps would like to get some even though they leave a blue remnant . But Louise is a grown-up today and only loves the memory that blue Popsicles of her younger days when blue Popsicles were somewhat of a craze. Popsicle memories fade away or rather melt away easily like the frozen delight they represent. Trust me.

22.

The Days of Cheap Wine and Wild Roses

Lest we forget the days of wine and roses, let us remember that the wine was not always good and the roses, gloriously red and imbued with a fragrance that only roses have, do wither and die. They were not always fresh and delightful. Roses, roses, the most desired of all flowers, it seems. Their silken petals, their fragrant aroma, their delightful colors, and their symbolic worth of love, caring and admiration are ever on the mind of those who give them and receive them. A rose, is a rose, is a rose says the poet. What more can you say? As for the wine, a good bottle of wine is priceless and it inspires the *bon-vivant* to sip it carefully and not gulp it down like a madman. A good wine is meant to be savored, through slow, cautious and deliberate sips. It has to profoundly affect the taste buds before it can be or should be swallowed. A bad wine can taste like vinegar or sour grapes, and it should not even be offered to anyone, especially to those who are *bon-vivants.*

Christ recognized good wine at Cana when he turned water into wine. He wasn't going to have the host serve inferior wine at a wedding feast, was he. A good wine can soothe the pangs of woe and the pains of love when things go wrong in a relationship. The French and the Italians have known that for centuries. Nowadays, everyone knows it. Of course, except the so-called winos. We celebrate with wine, we give accolades with wine, we baptize ships with wine, we teach students how to uncork and decant a good wine. A good wine must age and gather in very slowly its taste and aroma. It must lie dormant in an oaken barrel or keg for a very long time until it reaches the ultimate extent of its maturity as a true and tasteful wine. After all, a good wine must be tasted with the taste buds that demand and crave authenticity in a wine. The good servant or waiter knows how to serve it with gentle and adroit handling, perfect uncorking, decanting so that the dregs are not allowed to rise to the top, and finally the gentle pouring of the first to the taste host, so that the second pouring will not have tiny pieces of cork in it. It's all a marvelous ceremony of good taste for a good wine. Wine is an absolute necessity for those who relish fine wines on a daily basis. There is a French saying that captures the essence of fine wine: *"Une journée sans vin est une journée sans soleil."* So utterly true in my estimation as a connoisseur of good wines. I love wine and I go for the good and exquisite ones that refresh the soul and give of its full body to it. I'm not the only one, I'm sure. You can call me *un bon-vivant.* My name is Alfred, an ordinary name, but a man of exquisite taste buds.

As for the roses, one has only to look at a rose and detect its beauty and charm. Garden roses, hedge roses, wild roses and all roses that grow in a good soil. One can buy roses, grow roses and sell roses. Growing roses is not an easy thing to do. There are famous roses with famous names, and then there's the Little Prince's rose on another planet, he tells us. He took very good care of her, watering it and putting it under glass for cold and frosty nights. Once he was away, far away, we all wonder what happened to his rose. Eventually, he does return to his asteroid, at least, we deduct this fact from the ending. He returns to his planet with some good learning and teaching from the fox. Friendship, that's the main word and central theme. Loneliness is yet another theme. When one is lonely, one cannot exist whole. I mean entirely humanly whole. There's something missing. A friend can help to solidify one's existence. Oftentimes, a real friend helps to bolster the meaning of one's existence. Without true friendship there is no bonding in life. Just acquaintances.

Here's a tale of true and genuine friendship that parallels that of the Little Prince. It is true because it happened some time ago in a small village in France, northern France in upper Normandy near the *falaises,* those remarkable cliffs This village attracted artists and creative poets and writers of all cultures and geographic distances. The village did not advertise itself as an artist's delight, as a spot to paint or draw or whatever the artists wanted to create, but it did welcome those who having discovered the village, its beauty and seclusion from all unwanted distractions decided to live there. There was a woman whose name was simply Mariolle, La Belle-au-visage-de-laine-blanche, she was called by many. Her complexion was soft and white like virgin wool. Her place of origin was unknown to all except herself. She wanted to keep it that way. She led a very private life hidden away in some small cottage, a former bakery that she had converted into a dwelling place. She had no sleeping quarters except for some kind of a loft without stairs. She used a ladder to go up there. She slept on a pile of thick blankets and quilts when she found them. She lived by the skin of her teeth, so-to-speak. All of her time was spent creating and painting.

Mariolle spoke French but the local natives thought she was from Québec due to her accent. She did not mind being called "*la Canadienne*" as long as they accepted her and her art. She was indeed an artist who excelled in watercolors. She said that she loved watercolors because when she posited the colors, any color on her specially treated paper, the colors bled and showed her the direction she was to take as a creative artist. She did not like drawn forms and shapes and especially the so-called art of drawing. "It's like painting inside the lines and shapes," she used to say. "My paintings are the consequence of a structured composition and spontaneous effects...a blend of intellect and instinct. I use color, gesture and form to express an observation, a sensation, a state of mind, a strong emotion. I love experimentation . I let myself be guided by the unexpected with an attitude of confidence. I work with oils, aquarelles, and with mixed media in a style that is of lyrical abstraction, influenced by Kandinsky and a need for personal expression." Those are her words on personal creativity with colors. She also claimed that art is not unlike nature; it is not simply a decor of our existence. She also used to repeat every time she was invited to a show or a workshop, that art, as far as she was concerned, calls one to the freedom of being and nature is the breath that allows this freedom. This, she said almost vehemently, this is the reason I live to paint in Varengeville-sur-mer. She goes on to say that when she uses watercolors, she lets the colors guide her hand and her creative imagination. Watercolors are made for that, she insisted. They flow and spread themselves on paper. She was convinced of that. Of course, she has the guiding eye to help the work of art establish itself as a work of true art.

Mariolle lived to paint. It was not a job, but a calling from the spheres. People who knew her claimed that she was a poor woman who often went without bread on the table. It was said that she often went to bed hungry. Some people told her to get a job, a real paying job, but she told them that she had a job, that of creating works of art. She preferred to go without food than spending time earning a wage. Time was precious for her. She did not want to waste it on spurious jobs. Sure, she wasn't too practical nor was she mindful of all the things people said about her. She did not care. She did not sell too many of her works, but she continued painting. When things did not seem to be too rosy, she turned to workshops, sometimes traveling hundreds of kilometers to reach her destination. She was thus able to not only earn much needed money but gain friendships for which she craved. She loved teaching not only her artistic skills but her ideas about painting and her commitment to creative arts. She was so deeply engaged with her art that she spent many hours explaining to students the reasons for her artistic accomplishments. COLOR that was her central idea and emphasis. Color was everything to her as an artist

When she stopped doing watercolors, she devoted herself to a larger canvas and oils. This was a new adventure for her. She produced painting after painting until it was time for her to explore personal artistic shows hoping to entice art lovers to admire her art and at the same time sell some of them. She needed the money, but not at the expense of rushing through her paintings. As she conceived, she selected from her mind and from deep within, then she applied when she found the time had come to execute a painting. "A work of art is not a commodity, it's an expression of the creative soul at work," she once said.

She and I once conceived an opportunity of working together, I as a writer and she as a painter: Mariolle and Alfred, the creative artists in full bloom. We were to offer workshops of the creative imagination and measures of art with oil and canvas and words on a given page that expressed both artists' sensitivity to and application of creativity as a means of expression. We each had our own thoughts on art and had worked for years trying to express ourselves in the manner best perceived as an artist in flux. We were both excited about this project; it never materialized. I used to tell Mariolle, *"L'homme propose et Dieu dispose."* She replied in turn, *"Non, la femme dispose et Dieu propose...s'il le peut"* [Man proposes and God disposes...No the woman disposes and God proposes, if he can]. She was a true feminist at heart.

As to the cheap wine and the wild roses, both applied to her and her determination to do everything methodically ideal. She used to say that she had a method to her madness. Nothing worthwhile was left unattended by her vivid and gutsy determination to create not from the brain but from her guts. She was convinced that art, her view of art stemmed from her guts deep inside, ran up to her brain and flowed through her fingers. That is how she viewed the expression and talent of her art as an artist Mariolle lived for her art and with her fiery eyes, she proposed near lyrical expressions from her melodic mouth. That was her endearment to others who listened to her every word, Mariolle was indeed a self-made artist of consequence. At least she tried to convince herself of that. But she did not sell. She only had a few possibilities of sales on a market that was not seriously open to her. She did not seek money as such. She needed it to survive and pay for her art needs. She sought recognition as an artist of worth. She rarely got it, but she kept on working very hard at generating the work of art that would bring her this recognition. She needed a market, longed for an agent who could sell her work, desperately sought contacts but there were none out here. It was indeed a cruel market that did not recognize true talent She never got discouraged, and she never despaired. She relied entirely on her artistic projects that she conceived. Quite possibly there would be one show, one exposition of a new series of paintings that would stir up the art lovers enough to gain recognition and, of course, some worthwhile sales. Mariolle spent hours and even weeks setting up her exhibit in a small Paris salon. She was not satisfied until every frame, every corner, every inch of every painting was to her liking. She had trained her eye to observe the dictates of her brain and her guts in a disciplined and committed way. No one else could see or understand her hard work for an exhibit that would last but a few weeks. But she cared, and she would not compromise her artistic ideals and determination to succeed in her pursuit of identity and trust in her art. To her, her art was like good wine, for the taste of wine had to be perfect or else it would have been vinegar and sour grapes. Matched to this were the roses. She cultivated them and loved them. She even liked the wild roses on the hedges next to her cottage, but the roses she grew took precedence and she admired those precious moments she spent cultivating them. She loved going to *Le Bois des Moutiers*. Lovely gardens in a large park overlooking the sea surrounding a manor house. The gardens are well known for their blossoms: rhododendrons, azaleas and magnolias. She did not find roses there but she marveled at the cultivation and ardent care that was worthwhile to produce such lovely flowers, she said to one of her neighbors. It was indeed a place, a heavenly place unique in France, she once told me.

After the exhibit she was so exhausted that she lay in bed for an entire week so bad was her back. Her energy was entirely spent. She was a slave to her art and to any exhibit that would display it with aplomb and style, the style of a genuine artist in search of the ideal measure of excellence and creative expression. Her drive and her ambition to excel in her work was what kept her going,

Eleven years ago, she was confronted with major surgery when the doctors discovered cancer in her abdominal cavity. It was more than serious; it was life threatening. The operation lasted thirteen hours. She lost her rectum and her vagina. She felt she had lost her womanhood, but she reconciled herself to her bodily condition feeling that her true womanhood resided not in her body, but in her gut feelings and in her receptive mind. Her guts were where the very source of inspiration could be found, as she said. It took her a very long time to recover from her surgery, but her art and her determination to survive in spite of it all was what made her cling to life. She said that she had discovered in her critical moments of her operation and her therapy that she knew that all that mattered was that she was of this earth, bodily and physically. As to one's spirit and transcendental allegiances, she thought nothing of it, for it no longer mattered. Life was for the here and now, and not for some hereafter. That's how she saw things. Very concretely, not spiritually. If she was to remain sane and lucid, she had to be practical and live in the present. Hope was for the uninitiated to proven reality and the cloud-lovers who hovered like meaningless balloons in some wilderness. She cautioned people about living in a conjured reality of dreams and artless endeavors since they were the ones who pandered to others with their irrationality of dreamed up realities. Religion had become part of those ill-conceived realities, and she wanted no part of it, although she had been raised a devout Christian. Art was her religion and her constant companion in life. Art brought her sanity and worth. Her sense of creativity made her resolute in her pursuit of what is beauty and the delight of being able to capture it through her art, *"L'art c'est la résonance de tout ce qui est pur et beau, simple et intimement franc, et la nature nous les donne libéralement."*[Art is the resonance of all that is pure and beautiful, simple and intimately frank, and nature gives them to us liberally]. In certain moments of clearsightedness, she would expound on her philosophy of art. However, she never thought that art was a philosophy in itself. The mind and its thought provoking qualities and processes could never be fully associated with the culture of art, she maintained. Art was much more than the brain. It was infinitely couched in the realm of the gut-feeling crevices of one's own body and strength of feeling rather than simple thinking.

Little did Mariolle realize that all of her experiences in life, all of her deep and luxuriating feelings and all of her creative efforts over the years would come to a single and powerfully charged moment when despair would set in. Despair that her creative works did not matter anymore and that her taste for painting, rather her drive for painting were not there. It was as if there was nothing there. Nothing. Nothing mattered anymore. Gone was the necessity to find enough funds for her art work, gone the need for specially treated paper, canvases, watercolors, oils and brushes, and even the easels and frames that were once a fundamental necessity for her as an artist. It was all a bunch of meaningless tools.

Despair had turned into a devastating sweeper of all to an artist like her. She had so wanted to perform her role as a creative spirit filled with vigor and determination to show the world how good she was in art. When one is devoid of hope, determination, the vigor of creating and imagining, and especially the will to live, then there is nothing left but to die. So Mariolle went back to some darker moments in her life when she had contemplated suicide. Not by her own hand, but assisted suicide. She knew this lady who could help her. She once had overcome the deep and dark shadows of living and creating, and her art had given her the will to live. But now, there was nothing left except the will to die. Why would an artist like Mariolle want to end life and the art of creativity? Her mother and her sister Eileen had cautioned her about losing all spiritual values that make one climb the stairway to transcendence and eternal truth much like the *Tao*. She had flatly refused to indulge in such hocus pocus, she had said. Now she stood on the brink of life, and not really knowing what to do. No amount of cautioning would make her change her mind. There was only one way...DEATH. The finality of it all. Would she or wouldn't she? An artist is already dead once she abandons her art. Despair creates nothingness. Nothingness begets nothingness. We now have a blank canvas. No colors, no brush strokes, no movement from guts to brain to hands. The fingers have become numb due to idleness. The need to create must never be allowed to stagnate and die. *La vie et l'art forment une alliance dominatrice qui engage l'être humain à satisfaire le besoin de créer, et ce besoin est viscéral.* [Life and art form a dominating alliance that engages the human being in satisfying the need to create, and that need is visceral].

Mariolle died on a Monday around three in the afternoon, a summer day when the sun warms the earth with its rays of bright light having discarded the shadows of uncertainty and doubt in a being once given to expressing herself in the mystery of art. Mariolle, you see, was never a real person . Oh, sure she did exist in a reality that was more real than real. Reality can be multi-layered and multidimensional. Layers upon layers and dimensions so vast and so challenging to the mind that it can blow your mind thinking about it. Truly, she was the figment of my imagination, me Alfred, the dreamer. *Une imagination cotoyant la réalité,* an imagination bordering reality. It can and it does happen, you know. However, an imagination gone wild like the wild roses that grow by happenstance. If Mariolle did not truly exist, then what happens to this tale, you might ask. Well, Mariolle did exist as an exemplar, an artist living out her art body and soul. *L'art peut par lui-même séduire le roseau pensant et lui accorder une réalité hors de l'ordinaire.* [Art can by itself seduce the thinking reed and grant it a reality outside the ordinary]. CAUTION : Never imagine what you seem to imagine as real. The imagination can play tricks on you, dear reader. Then all that is left is cheap wine and wild roses. I know, for I, Alfred, is the product of this writer's imagination...but he lives...like the aroma of a fantastically rich and tasteful red wine that lingers and lingers and lingers. Can you smell the roses too? Forget the cheap wine and the fading roses. They only belie the true essence of things. The caution lies in the fact that wine needs to mature to gain its full body and taste while roses need to be ever fresh. I know. I make the rules of the game and I dare say that it's the rule maker who wins over those who do not even follow the rules. They crash. That's all. They simply fall into the cheapest of the cheap. Like cheap wines and faded roses, they are soon forgotten. However, the rich and fragrant wines as well as the sumptuous roses live on. They're part of our collective memory for they shine like the starry night of creative wonder and luxury. The luxury of splendor and being able to capture wonderment. Wonderment, you see, cannot be captured so easily. It's only caught by those who dream dreams of marvelous delight and in union with the heavenly spheres that mitigate the cheapness in our lives. That's all.

23.

Chagrin

The word "chagrin" can be employed either in French or in English. In English, it's a borrowed word from the French and it comes from the Old French *chagreiner,* to become gloomy, said of the weather. Also from the term *graignier,* to mean sorrow, trouble or a feeling of disappointment, humiliation, embarrassment caused by failure or discomfiture of some kind, mortification. So much for the dictionary's explanation and definition of the word "chagrin". My name is Ethelbert and I want to look at this word from the perspective of the French definition of suffering and pain, and especially what is meant in French by *chagrin* as *un état moralement douloureux,* state of moral or ethical sorrow. *Douleur* in French has the connotation of deep pain and profound dolor, and that is what I want to direct my cautionary tale towards. I have experienced chagrin once in my life and it was truly painful in my heart, in my very guts and in my soul. It has lasted to this day. But, I do not want to relate my own chagrin experience. I want to tell you about the chagrin of a young boy who became the very essence of a human being deeply hurt by certain events in his life. The hurt was so bad that the pain lasted until his death. Chagrin lasts and lasts because of the never-ending memory of it deeply embedded in the minds and hearts of those who live the pain. How can such a painful experience last so long, you might ask. Well, I will tell you all about it in this cautionary tale.

His name was Michou short or rather turned into an endearment term for Mishael, the name he was given at birth. His parents loved the name taken from the Old Testament, and they were enthralled by this name, the name of one of the three young men in the fiery furnace condemned by the king of Babylon. The parents preferred this name to that of his Chaldean name of Meshach. The parents understood that the story was part of the folklore of the Hebrew people at that time, but they took it as the creative efforts of Yahweh's people following the Lord's commandments as given to Moses. The story of Mishael and his two young friends were part of the myth of God's covenant with his chosen people, a myth as daring and truthful as the nose on your face, affirmed the parents. That is why they gave the name of Mishael to their son. They wanted their son to be bold, daring and wise in his commitment to his faith in the Creator, and to his loyalty to whomever would lead the young man in his pursuit of his calling in life. That someone was Mirwana, a native-American artist who lived at the end of the 20th Century in a small village called Maupiwistan. It was an Algonquin village inhabited by some two hundred people of that tribe. Mirwana was a very talented and wise person who had lost her husband during the Second World War somewhere in France. She had never taken another man in her mature life. She had raised two daughters and they had moved away from the village, and had been assimilated into the world of the white culture never again to return to their native village and tribe. The tribal customs as well as the fidelity to family ties were gone as far as they were concerned. That had hurt the mother deeply as she continued her way of life modestly with a perseverance that never faulted. Mirwana had taken to painting small scenes from nature on canvas, and then had tried her hand at painting larger canvases that produced an enormous following of hers and her art. She did not paint to gain financial profit but to gain solace of her loss of family. That is why she cherished the friendship that she had developed over the few years she had gotten to know a young man by the name of Mishael.

Mishael had encountered Mirwana at a country fair just outside of her own village where she exhibited her well-known canvases that portrayed animals in the wild, running streams or even blades of tall grasses that had caught the bright light of day on an early autumn morning.

Mishael had stopped at the stand where stood Mirwana and admired the painting with the tall grasses. He had asked his mother to give him money so that he could purchase the painting, but his mother told him that she was not going to waste money on a painting like that, a canvas showing nothing but grass. He told her that he loved the painting and that he truly wanted it Mirwana looked on as the two argued over her painting. She felt sorry for the boy who truly loved what she had captured in the scene she had painted. According to her, the boy saw the real magic of art in splendor and light with his inner creative eye that the mother had not seen. Mirwana offered to give the painting to the boy but the mother refused. She thought that the painting had no real value at all, financial and artistic. The boy left disappointed and confused for he did not understand his mother's refusal. It was free, the painting was being offered free and yet the mother refused. One could see the sadness on his young face. Mirwana saw it. She returned to the village a bit saddened that her painting had delighted one and tormented the other. Mirwana put the painting aside thinking that one day she would find the boy and she could give it to him in a gesture of warmth and friendly persuasion.

The days, the months and the years went by until one day in the spring Mirwana met the young man that had grown up to be a child of nature and who wandered from place to place, village to village living in pursuit of a woman he had once met at a country fair, and who had enthralled him with her painting of tall grasses in the sunlight She had moved away and he could not find her and her painting.

Mishael had long blond hair now, a bit shaggy with a mustache and a beard with clothes that were baggy, worn and frayed. Some people called him a hippy, not that he minded being called one of those who lived life as they saw fit for free spirits. All he cared for was the splendor of tall grasses in the wide and open fields. He loved living free and not shackled to everyday commitments even though his mother had somewhat disinherited him and had left him by himself and to himself eking out an existence that was deplorable to the mother. Mishael just had to learn the hard lessons of life, she told herself. No sentiments of compassion and love were ever expressed by her. She had never learned to do so.

Mirwana had offered her painting of the wild grasses to Mishael but he refused saying that he did not want to take it away from her. What would he do with it, he asked himself. Besides, he had the painting engraved in his soul, and that was a cherished memory that would never fade. He would carry that painting inside him until the day he died. He left Mirwana smiling at him and telling him to live with peace in his heart the way nature and the Great Manitou had fashioned it. He went away feeling blessed by the artist who painted tall grasses. He set out to explore the wild country and to find what his heart told him to do, inner peace and tranquility.

Michou the boy, now called Mishael by those who know him and respect him, survived both the difficulties of living from day to day without too much to live on. He did chores and mended fences as well as chopping wood for whomever paid him a few dollars. He never anticipated that one day he would be rich and famous. That was for those who had dreams of climbing high in society and being rich with loads of material things. Mishael did not care to wallow like a swine in the deep mud of greed and the entrenchment of misguiding forces. He much preferred the soft and quiet air of far distances and the green grasses of hills and meadows where the wildflowers grew and the grasses got taller and taller until they magically blended in with the shimmering sunlight of earthy days.

Mishael still continued thinking about the much desired painting of the tall grasses by the artist Mirwana and he often contemplated searching for her somewhere somehow but unfortunately he could not attain his goal of finding her. It had been years since he had last seen her. Was she still alive? Was she defunct? Was she hidden somewhere by her own tribe, alone and suffering the pangs of loneliness? These and other questions were constantly on his mind. Until one day he met a stray Algonquin friend of his who happened to be in the vicinity of the yearly fair that exhibited paintings of artists of all talents and all creativity. The young man's name was Chibouyawi and he had some information about Mirwana since his grandmother was a distant relative of the artist. Chibouyawi informed Mishael that he knew for sure that Mirwana had died some years past and that her body had been burned in a tall pyre for the wind to scatter her ashes. He also told Mishael that the poor lady artist had to give up her painting sprees on account of poverty and a lack of strength on her part. That's all he knew about her.

Mishael asked his friend if he could see the grandmother and talk to her about Mirwana. Chibouyawi, although he did not encourage Mishael to do so, he nevertheless gave him the place where he could find her. It was a village far away in the mountains. He himself had not been there for years. Mishael was determined to find the old grandmother and have a conversation with her about his artist friend. He undertook the journey to find her. It took him 345 days to finally reach her, almost a full year. Once he found her, she was sitting in her tent by herself. He introduced himself and told her that he was her grandson's friend. She was pleased to hear about him, pleased like a mother who recovers her long lost son. Chibouyawi's mother had died a long time ago. The father had fled the village leaving his wife to her own struggles and fears of dying. It was the grandmother who had taken in the boy and fed him, washed his clothes and reminded him of the fidelity to tribal traditions and customs. The boy Chibouyawi had left the tribe and his grandmother as soon as he could leaving his grandmother painfully to her own devises.

The grandmother told Mishael that as far as Mirwana was concerned, she had died after a terrible struggle with the local tribesmen who did not pity her nor did they take care of her and her immediate needs. Rather they resorted to the old way of handling an old, childless, widow who had no male support to take care of her. They abandoned her and threw her out of her tent without blankets, without any clothes and without any food. It was total and cruel abandonment, she told him. During the winter months she had to go begging for shelter and food, and only received bits and scraps now and then. She froze to death since her frail body could not take it anymore. As for her paintings including the one of the tall sunlit grasses which was destined for Mishael, they were all burned by the shaman of the tribe who thought of them as fodder for witches and besotted old women. The grandmother told Mishael that Mirwana often spoke his name calling him to her and her plight as an an abandoned woman. Of course, the grandmother had never heard of the name Mishael and did not know him in the slightest. So Mirwana died alone, forgotten and filled with chagrin, said the grandmother. The tribe did not burn her on the pyre as decreed by Indian custom. Rather, they threw her body to the wolves who ate her limb by limb leaving only some scattered bones here and there. Terrible thing said the grandmother holding back her tears.

Mishael was dumbfounded by the news of his dear friend the artist of tall sunlit grasses. He did not know what to say nor how to feel at that precise moment of chagrin. Yes, it was chagrin, that terrible feeling of hurt, pain, and soul-drenching sorrow of abandonment. He truly felt abandoned by all he could think of, relatives, friends, tribal people, even nature herself. Why had he not tried to find Mirwana before she fell into the pit of her own chagrin, he asked himself. He blamed himself for everything. He left the grandmother with a huge hurt in his heart and a terrible sore on his conscience. But the worst sore and pain was in his soul, for he could not absolve himself of the terrible sin of abandonment. Yes, he considered abandonment a sin. The worst kind. Worse than torturing others and worse than greed. Abandoning a woman like Mirwana, an artist and a marvelous creation of the Great Manitou, the Creator, was indeed a defiant stroke of a lack of love and charity, he told himself. He did not know too much about charity, a word the Christians used, but he knew a great deal about love.

You see dear readers, Mishael had once been in love, deeply in love with a beautiful child of nature, as she was called by the followers of free love and free wanderings out in nature. She might have been called a hippy like Mishael but she lived the life of a pure and unblemished woman of her time. She did not fall into the trap of indecency nor the awful net of deceit and collusion. She lived her own life and did not and could not find a way to limit her capabilities of being true to herself and to others. She was transparent in her motives and sincere in her effort to make friends who could appreciate her tenderness of heart and soul. Mishael; discovered in her a soul like his, one that could not hide from the truth nor run away from it. People loved her for that particular reason as well as for others too. Mishael fell in love with this beautiful young woman the moment he lay eyes on her and especially when she spoke of her commitment to living in nature and with nature in a subtle and absolutely remarkable way. Mishael saw it in her deep blue eyes and detected it in her soft siren-like mystifying voice.

Mishael and the beautiful Miranda, that was her name, moved in together and made love a constant gesture of their affiliation. Within the next six months, Miranda discovered that she was pregnant. She did not want the child but Mishael convinced her told keep it. It was also his child, he told her. It was a girl and both of them relished the fact that they were parents.

With time Miranda grew more and more restless and she wanted to get away from it all. "What about the child?" asked Mishael. "What about her? retorted the mother.

And so. Miranda went away one early Sunday morning never to be seen again. The ugly worm of chagrin made its way back into Mishael's heart. This time, it was as if the intensity matched that of the time he had experienced the feeling of abandonment due to the loss of Mirwana. The chagrin of loneliness coupled with a discomfiture of the soul. It would not go away as much as he fought it. And so Mishael placed the child in an orphanage thinking that it would be best for her and for him. The mother was nowhere to be found. The child's name was Mirwana after the old Algonquin artist much revered by Mishael. It hurt Mishael to lose Mirwana a second time but there was nothing he could do about it. It was Manitou's decree that fate had imposed it upon the the one who was destined to suffer deep chagrin. It got to be so bad that Mishael thought of making short of his life by taking enough drugs to drown his chagrin and put an end to his life. However, he could not bring himself to do it.

Mishael's chagrin intensified when he fully realized that he had lost his child for good. The child, he was told, was adopted by a couple that moved away to Newfoundland. The authorities at that orphanage were not allowed to give him the information he asked for. It was a case of privacy, security and privileged information, they told him. Mishael told himself that it was a bunch of words spoken by educated people in order to mollify the situation. He wondered why such people could not follow the rules of the heart rather than the dictates of legalistic regulations.

The years went by and Mishael wandered from location to location never finding a place that felt like home to him. Chagrin, deep emotional and moral chagrin had invaded his soul and he never recovered from it. He started drinking heavily and soon realized that he was a sot, a drunk without any ethical bearings. His spirit was completely demoralized and he began to think of suicide. His only hope was in the AA movement that someone suggested to him. At first, he did not want to hear of it, but what other options did he have. With the healing of time and perseverance on his part and on the part of his sponsor, Mishael was able to reclaim his sense of spirituality and find love and compassionate mercy of the Christ he had never really known but got to know through AA.

One day, as Mishael was glancing at the artwork on one of the walls of the AA meeting place and he recognized a painting that had been once familiar to him. It was a painting of tall grasses in the bright sunlight. It wasn't Mirwana's but someone else's creative work: Toni Anderson, a reborn Christian he found out later. As he was catching his breath, he looked at the bottom of the art work and read the following "Unless a grain of wheat falls to the ground and dies it remains by itself." It was taken from the parable of the Grain of Wheat from the Gospel of John and he realized right there and then that his soul-life as well as his chagrin had to die so that his growth as a man and a creative person be allowed to flourish a hundredfold. That was precisely Mirwana's symbolic message ever present there on her original painting but ignored by so many who lacked a sense of creativity and spiritual discernment. Mishael told himself that he had found the key to the healing of his chagrin and that was rejuvenation through creativity and a love of the fine arts. Love heals, the discovery of self heals and the giving of oneself heals, but so does the expression and creativity of the fine arts. That's why the tall grasses in the bright sunlight continue to stimulate the creative juices of one's ability to imagine and to create. Mishael discovered that chagrin can be overcome and its pain and discomfort blown away by the mere touch of a spike of the tall grasses in the sunlight. Mirwanda, the artist, had shown him the way but it took time and effort to discover the path to healing since chagrin is a vicious and downright terrible sore that can only be healed very slowly and deliberately if one chooses to make an effort in the healing process. Eventually, Mishael passed away in an unknown territory known only by a few friends of his. Mishael's ashes were buried on a hill where the tall grasses of autumn swayed to and fro in the gentle breezes of daylight and even nighttime. The Great Manitou had ordered his child back home to rest in the peaceful quietude of creative tenderness and peace. All chagrin had been wiped away from the heart and soul of the one called Michou, the Mishael of later years. The one with the sun-filled soul. The lover of tall grasses and tall wonders of nature. The path of chagrined hearts filled with pain and discomfort has been leveled and smoothed. Mishael has accomplished his task on earth. Mirwana the Indian artist has shown the way. Art and its influence on human souls has finally convinced people that there is a way to smooth and benign approaches to life in all its complexities and winding roads. Which way?----no, not that way----this way. *L'art est la voie de l'exigence de vivre et de créer*...art is the way of the necessity to live and create, were the last words of Mishael. He had written it down on a piece of paper that had stayed in his shirt pocket He had found this quotation in a book of poetry and had written it down word for word. Unfortunately, the piece of paper in his shirt pocket was burned in the cremation process and so it was never read by anyone. However, it remained in the ashes of a once chagrined man who loved tall grasses in the sunlit meadows. His daughter who somehow had discovered her father through many searches had taken the ashes and buried them with deep sorrow and love even though she had never gotten to meet her father and talk about a love relationship that Mishael had so wanted all of his life but had never developed in full bloom. Mirwana the younger became a poet artist of considerable fame and she never forgot the man who was once afflicted by chagrin and loved the tall grasses. She wrote a poem about her father entitled, "The Chagrin of the Man With the Heart of Sunlight and Tall Grasses." The poem became a favorite of not only the white people but especially the Indian tribes of the descendants of the Cherokee family and particularly the Ho-Chunk Nation/Winnebago who were forced into exile against their will with canons and rifles at their backs. You see, they knew what chagrin was since their tribes had not only known about it but had deeply experienced it in their Trail of Tears. That, my friends, was true CHAGRIN.

24.

Out of the Soul of Africa

Africa is a continent where dark-skin people live and thrive in their own way. They do not all live in luxury and wealth since many of them are poor and at times suffering the anxiety of abandonment and being left behind in the upward climb of society. One could say that most of them lead a dignified life filled with the cultural values that have been preserved for them by their ancestors. Many have suffered the thrust of greed and corruption by white colonists who sought to line their pockets with gold, diamonds, and whatever they could get out of a land rich enough to make anyone wealthy at the mere touch of a grabbing hand while the poor and destitute natives suffered the trials and tribulations of being taken over and enslaved by men with guns, power and might. Corruption seeped in very easily like a giant boa slithering into their lives, swallowing them whole and digesting them for the benefit of white supremacy. We all know about the sad history of the blacks being swallowed by the whites, but do we know the history of blacks swallowing up other blacks. That history is hidden somewhere under the bushel baskets of denial and shame. No one wants to talk about it. No one can talk about it since it's a history not meant to survive the chaotic tremors of conscientious beliefs that black African history is worth preserving no matter the time and place. Once it is hidden, it remains hidden because some people want it so. Those people are the dead consciences of the those who learned to be white. The skin may be black but the soul has turned white. What, you might ask, is this all about. Well, it's about the phenomenon of turnaround and it can be best exemplified by the following cautionary tale.

One day, the devil in hot pursuit of a kingdom where he could dwell in comfort and serenity, a place outside of his own domain which is hell or some call it Hades. That was right after Satan had offered Christ in the desert after his lengthy fast: one, hedonism, hunger and satisfaction; two, egoism, might and power to exist; three, materialism, kingdoms and wealth. He is tempted to change stones into bread to end the fast and satisfy his hunger. He is told that if he throws himself off the pinnacle, the angels will catch his fall and not hurt himself. Then, he is told that if he worships Satan he will obtain all the kingdoms of the world. He is tempted because of his humanity. Satan could not tempt his divinity. God cannot be tempted by Satan. Humans can and easily so. Temptation in itself is not evil; it's the succumbing to temptation that's is wayward and against what is right and true. The temptation to eat a candy bar is not wrong. It all depends on the situation and its mode of operation. There are much more evil to an act of unkindness and even a willingness to avenge oneself mercilessly than biting into a Milkyway

Depending if one believes in God, his Commandments, his alliance with the human race or any other link to ethical behavior, evildoing is by itself wrong. However, we have to define what is evil, don't we. I do not want to get into all of the moral precepts and all its countermeasures, I only want to tell a cautionary tale about the soul of Africa. That's a tall order, you might say. Well, it is, but I want to hone it down to some very specific and concrete examples in order to make things more relevant and more to the point.

I know that you will caution me about insisting on only one faith, that of the Judaeo-Christian faith. I am not leaving out other faiths such as Islam because I want to cast them aside for lack of better understanding and even worse for some kind of religious prejudice. No! I will let the Prophet Mohamed and his followers tell their own stories. They have a very rich story to tell.

First of all, the soul of Africa is not evil nor is it irrelevant. People and their culture are never irrelevant. Everyone belongs to the human race in general, be they white, black, red, yellow or whatever the color of skin being referred to. Skin color is not that important when it comes to the quality of the human person. We are born with it and cannot do too much about it. We accept it and that's all. However, some people believe that the color of one's skin matters when it comes to human relations and business ventures. Some even think that justice is not always served when it's a matter of race and color. When prejudices become part of judging people, then justice is not well served. So, how does one handle prejudices. EDUCATION through. SENSITIVITY to human feelings and creative endeavors, and that covers both heart and soul. If a person is not given freely the freedom to exercise his/her own human rights and if she/he is not allowed to be creative in a milieu that encourages human creativity, then freedom is jeopardized. Colonizers keep their slaves and the rest of the population uneducated so that they can better control their destinies as slaves and what they called low-life. These colonists had only one thing in mind, make money and claim power over people and the environment. If you keep people poor, uneducated, and without hope, then anything is possible in line with lording it over hundreds if not thousands of helpless human beings. They are helpless because they're ignorant of the fact that they are being treated as slaves and cannot make a move since they do not know how. They have no idea of claiming their rights as human beings. They are plain uneducated. Not dumb as some people put it, but they lack the means of bettering themselves. There are no opportunities to fly over the nets of derision, fear, hopelessness, and, above all, a great lack of self- reliance.

Here is a tale that exemplifies what I have been speaking about. Tales and or stories are so much better when it comes to putting in evidence the crux of the matter. After all, as I have said so many times before, human beings are story-tellers by birth and culture. We invent stories, we tell stories to our children, we energize others by telling them about their own stories, we proclaim historical facts and their importance in life by telling stories that are based on the essence of history. Stories matter. Well let's return to our initial intent, a cautionary tale about the soul of Africa.

There was a man who professed to be a Christian and was admired for his diligence, charm and sense of duty by all of his neighbors in the small village in southern Africa. They said that he was a model of probity and diligence and that he was kind to everyone, kin and strangers alike. No one could find fault in him. Except, that he was one who could find fault in others; he would not mince words. Although kind in gestures of friendship and helpful in actions of generosity, he oftentimes showed his weaker side by his insistence on making remarks on people's human frailties be they small and hardly noticeable by others. He was a man of discipline and stalwart sincerity when it came to human behavior. He expected everyone to behave without a hitch on what he called good behavior. No one seemed to be free of his remarks sometimes pungent sometimes mellow, but he could not help himself from making them. It was his duty to do so, he used to tell people. He insisted that his sense of duty warranted it and he wasn't going to flinch one bit when it came to duty and self-pride.

His name was Futurou-Luke, named after the great evangelist that his parents admired and cherished as evangelical Christians. They so trusted the word of the Gospels that they would not have understood why some people did not affiliate themselves to Christian teachings. They proclaimed that they were die-hard Christians, and they would not aspire to do otherwise so strong and unbending was their faith. The parents as well as the son were so rooted in their faith that it would have been treason for them to even consider other beliefs especially Islam. They considered Islam evil and destructive of any revealed doctrine that was part of the true faith. True faith for them was Christianity based on the Gospel truth. They accused the followers of Mohamed of being superstitious with their five pillars and their prayer rugs. They thought that going to Mecca was a frivolous journey for thousands of pilgrims going to venerate a huge rock. Christians went on pilgrimages but they were holy places with venerable heritages such as Santiago de Compostella, Lourdes, and Rome. Why would anyone throw themselves into a riotous situation where mobs ran around a rock with so many getting killed and mauled by frenzied people. Christians did not do that, they claimed. They did not remember the killing of many so-called non-believers in various parts of the world by so-called good Christians. They did not recollect the history of the slaughter of the Huguenots in

France, of the killing of the Jews in those well-known concentration camps by Nazis who claimed to be Christians.

Futurou-Luke could not stand Islam as a faith and especially its followers, the Muslims. He claimed that he was surrounded by them in most neighborhood that he knew. Although they behaved with the best behavior and were ever so kind to all, and gave to beggars and homeless people as well as providing means of literacy to those who were too poor to go to school and learn, Futurou-Luke could not bring himself to acknowledge their charity and compassion towards others. He thought that they were doing such deeds to gain political strength and be recognized by those that were in power. He liked to judge people by his own standards that he had concocted years before he got to know what ethics were in general, and by strict rules that he called Christian commandments. He had cast aside the traditional Judaeo-Christian commandments and had substituted them with what he considered more up-dated with Christian beliefs and ways of doing things. He eliminated the commandment of loving neighbor since he claimed that he could not trust everyone. He got rid of total commitment to father and mother since not all of them were worthy of love, he said. Then he claimed that killing another man was at times commendable since some men were dangerous and killed others themselves. He also eliminated the one against fornication and the taking of someone else's wife because he said that was up to individuals and their thoughts about having sex since sex was a natural instinct. As to taking someone else's belongings, well some called it robbery and some appropriation of necessary property for well intentioned purposes. Perjury was alright as long as you did not get caught doing it. You see, Futurou-Luke played by his own rules and liberal standards, although he claimed that he was a conservative person with traditional beliefs. He thought himself to be god-like and altogether a law-abiding Christian, so he claimed. His parents commended him for his sense of propriety and God-loving measures of good thinking and good deeds.

Futurou-Luke had a friend who was called Mohamed-Gabriel. He was Muslim. Although both men were black, Futurou-Luke thought that Mohamed-Gabriel was blacker than he on account of his faith,

Islam. Muslims were darker and blacker than Christians, Futurou-Luke said. Their souls were blacker than Africa itself and black was black when it came not only to the color of the skin but especially to the color of the soul, according to him.

----You're so damn black, Mohamed-Gabriel, that your soul is transparently black. I can see it through your garments.

----You must be kidding, my friend. No one sees through layers of garments.

----I tell you that I can see that you are inner black with my inner eye.

----What inner eye?

----The one given to me by God.

----God gave you an inner eye?

----Yes. Not everyone has one, you know.

----I should say so. Are you sure you have an inner eye?

----I can see the within of things and especially people's inner selves.

----What do you see?

----I see people's sins and blackness.

----What do you mean by blackness?

----Black, black, don't you understand?

----No, I do not understand your seeing blackness.

----Then, you're stupid if you don't see what I see.

----But you said that the inner eye was given to you by God, or was it Allah.

----Not your god, gawd, no.

----There is only one god and that is Allah.

----The true god is God himself. The Christian God.

----That's what you believe, but I believe otherwise.

----Then you're wrong.

----Why? Why can't I be right?

----Because you're wrong. That's all.

----That's what you think. Who made you god?

----I'm not God but I'm pretty close to Him.

----How is that?

----Because I'm right and God tells me what is right and wrong.

----How?

----By by being close to him and seeing with my inner eye what is black. Black is sin. Black is whatever is black as a reflection of sin.

----Then we are black-skin. Does that make us black as sin?

----Yes.

----Are all black people sinful?

----It may well be.

----You cannot say that and think you are right. People are people and black-skin people are just like other people inside. If sin exists then it has to be inside the human existence.

----But it shows on the outside.

----Do you see that with your outer eye or your inner eye?

----Both.

----How come? I cannot see that.

----Because you're a follower of Mohamed.

----What?

----Yes, you people do not have the truth.

----How do you know that.

----By my faith and mine alone, not yours.

----You're an ignorant and prejudicial fanatic if you think like that.

----I am endowed with special gifts and I believe that I will be saved.

----Then only the ones with special gifts will be saved?

----I suppose so.

----You suppose so?

----I know so.

----You are mistaken if you think that way.

----My faith is rock-bound and heavenward.

----What do you mean by that?

----It's just that I know and I know it's hard and unbreakable like a rock and destined to leap into heaven with the angels.

----You're a damn fool, you know that?

-----You're the fool, Mohamed-Gabriel.

-----Go ahead, call me names. I don't care. You can throw stones at me, you can shout names at me, and you can think whatever you may think about my being black but I am just like you, I am a fool because I tend to believe in you and your so-called educated ways. You think that I am dumb and stupid perhaps because I do not have a formal education, but I'll have you know that I am educated in so many ways.

----Like what?

----Through my own heritage that is African and through my values and Allah-given rights as a firm believer. I can read and I do read voraciously. You hardly read at all.

----I read magazines and financial news.

----That's not reading. That's entertainment for pseudo progress.

----Progress is progress.

----True progress is human progress, intellectual, spiritual and emotional, and of course, cultural progress.

-----What exactly is cultural progress?

----Cultural progress is the benefits our whole human existence has by regenerating itself in the cultural elements that have been given to us by our ancestors.

----That's all passé. Useless for us the younger generation.

----No! If you give up on your past you fall into the pit of forgetfulness and ignorance. Then you are truly black . You have a blackened soul, not a true African soul.

----Words, just meaningless words.

----No, Futurou-Luke, words full of meaning, but you do not get it.

----I'll stick to what I know and what I know is right. Evangelical Christians are always right. You people are wrong to think that we are off the track. We're on the right track.

----The Christian Gospels may be right, but people like you who claim all kinds of manufactured beliefs based on the gospels are mistakenly wrong. You're not followers of Christ, but followers of the sly devil gone awry. Christ was Christian in his teachings as far as I know. He wasn't so fanatic about his teachings and beliefs that he condemned rather than accept good faith and good will.

----Don't you go blaspheming us. We are the true believers and that's all.

----Return to your African roots and find your true soul before you start calling others black as sin and not faithful to the Creator. There is only one Great Creator and He is the one true God and we call him

Allah. You can call him whatever you want. Is God black? I do not know. Does He have an inner eye? I do not know. He may be full of eyes and he may have the all-seeing eye ever watchful on his creation, black, white, yellow, red or whatever color skin. All I know is that I am black African with an African soul. White colonists may have influenced our way of life and beliefs, but we are deep down African no matter what the color of our skin is.

----I'm African too but I do not think like you do.

----Of course not. You are different than me. We're all different in whatever way, but deep down we as Africans are alike in our deep down soulful culture.

----I don't get you with that word culture.

----Well probably someday you will. I do sincerely hope so. Do you know what *négritude* is and means?

----What?

----*Négritude*, a French word to mean a literary and philosophical ideology.

---- Who came up with that?

----Francophone poets, Aimé Césaire and Léopold Sédar Senghor. They were both Africans and both are from the northwestern part of Africa. Senghor became president of his country, le Sénégal. Later on, he was elected to the *Académie Française*. That's how learned he was and culturally sensitive to the African soul.

----I never heard of them.

----Of course not. You don't read poetry and you don't read French.

----Why should I?

----To be better educated, that's why.

----I'm educated enough as I am.

----Trained but not educated.

----What do you mean by that?

----Someday I'll explain it to you.

----I still don't know what negrotude means.

----Not negrotude. *Négritude.* It's defined as a consciousness and pride in the cultural and physical aspects of the African heritage.

----What does that have to do with us?

-----Everything, *mon ami*, everything. It touches directly on the African soul. But you don't know that yet. Maybe someday you will when you get out of your conservative and ignorant shell of a human being not yet a man.

----Are you downgrading me as an African. Is that an insult?

----I'm not insulting you, I'm trying to educate you.

----I'm not stupid and I don't need you to tell me that I don't know enough about our culture. Culture to me means high standards and high living.

----Here you go again, off the track.

----Let's get off the train and the tracks. I'm getting tired of it.

----Allah be praised.

The two men went away each to his own neighborhood. Before leaving each other, Mohamed-Gabriel said to Futurou-Luke,

----Be cautious, *mon ami,* too much of a good thing can lead to indigestion.

----What do you mean by that?

----If you don't get it, I can't give it to you. It has to do with the soul.

Futurou-Luke went home bewildered. Scratching his head he hollered, "That guy is crazy. He doesn't know what he's talking about. He's completely insane when it comes to explaining things. Besides, what does he mean by 'be cautious'? I'm always cautious about things and about people. What's to be cautious about anyway? I don't get it. I just don't get it."

When Futurou-Luke got home he rushed to get a comic book that his cousin from the States had sent him. He opened the cover and there in big bold letters were the words, SOUL FOOD.

25.

you know...you know

It has become a way of speaking or the continual odd oral expression of some speakers to interject here and there to the great consternation of some of us, if not annoyance, the two words "you know." "You know," "you know" twists my brain and lowers my resistance to quirky annoyances that affect my sense of good and clear speech. "You know", yes, I know, what is it that you want me to know, I usually answer not always audibly, but in my silent thoughts. I hate it when I keep hearing these two words punctuating and slicing up someone's speech patterns when they speak. Can't they simply talk without interrupting their train of thought and speech, I ask myself. It just becomes a mode of imitating others who have the same habit. It's simply annoying, I think. "You know," yes, I know, now stop saying that over and over again at every fourth or fifth word. It becomes a frightful habit, I think. It frightens my sensibilities for good speech and listening. It rubs me the wrong way. I may be over-sensitive, I don't know.

Then, there's the other annoying pattern of speech when someone keeps injecting "euh", he or she doesn't seem to know what to say next. To me, it means that they do not have a clear train of thought to back up their talking fluently. It is truly annoying to the listener. Isn't it? Then there's the unmistakable pattern of speech deficiency that I call audible lack of cohesiveness, that of jumping from one topic to another without finishing what has already been said. It's like a hare hopping and hopping without any sense of direction or clear-mindedness. My thoughts are usually well organized and if not so, then I try my best to stop and organize them so that I can speak rationally and with a sense of cohesiveness. I do not jump here and there like a lame-brain hare. And forget that my interlocutor has to be able to stitch things or patterns together in order to better understand what I am saying. Cohesiveness in speech means being able to connect things together and make sense out of whatever is said. Don't expect the listener or interlocutor to be able to make plausible connections to something that is being said without rhyme or reason. Out brain is not made up of out-of-control wiring. Speech, listening and being attentive to what is being said is what makes a good listener, but what is being said must cohesively rendered. If one keeps interrupting the flow of what is being said with "you know", or hesitant "euhs," then the listener keeps being put on guard for the next hesitant moment without being able to keep his "cool", as some say. What if I caution you about such difficulties of speech and bad habits of delivering any form of speech be it an oration, a small talk in front of an audience, or even a face-to-face encounter where words are used without being concrete and direct about it. Then I lose the true meaning of what I am trying to tell you readers. Well, the best way to to this is to use examples and provide the necessary patterns of interrupted speech. Here is an example that I will use and I will attempt to punctuate Abraham Lincoln's Gettysburg Address and see how you respond to the irritating habit of using "you knows" here and there. This is not necessarily a cautionary tale but an example of how to use caution when delivering words that affect one's listening and paying attention to what is being said. See if you can stand it for a short while without being somewhat irritated or even mildly perturbed.

Read it out loud to get the full impact. Here goes:

Four score and seven years ago, **euh**, our fathers, brought forth on this continent, **you know**, a new nation, **euh**, conceived in Liberty, **euh**, and dedicated to the proposition, **euh, you know**, that all men, **euh**, are created equal.

Now we are engaged, **you know, euh,** in a great civil **euh** war, testing whether that nation, **you know**, or any nation so conceived,**euh**, and so dedicated can long endure, **you know** . We are met on a great battle-field, **you know, euh,** of that war, **you know.** We, **hmm,** we have come to dedicate, **you know**, a portion of that field, **you know**, as a final resting place, **euh,** for those who here gave their lives, **you know,** that that nation might, **euh,** live. It is altogether fitting and proper, **you know,** that we should do this.

But, in a larger sense, **you know**, we can not dedicate---**euh**, we can not consecrate, **you know**, we can not hallow this ground, **you know**. The brave men, living and dead, who struggled, **you know**, here, have consecrated it, far above our power to add and detract **you know** . The world will little note, **hmm**, nor long remember, **you know**, what we say here, but it can never, **euh**, forget what they did here. It is for us the living, **euh,** rather, to be dedicated here, **you know**, to the unfinished work which they who fought here, **you know**, have thus far so nobly advanced, **euh.** It is rather for us to be here dedicated to the great task remaining before us—**euh**, that from these honored dead we take increased devotion, **euh**, to that cause for which they gave the last full measure of of devotion, **you know** ---that we, **euh,** that we here highly resolve that these dead, **euh,** shall not have died in vain---that this nation, **you know**, under God, **hmm**, shall have a new birth of freedom, **you know**, and that government of the people, by the people, for the people, **euh**, shall not perish, **hmm**, from the earth...**you know.**

This is certainly not the way the great Abraham Lincoln delivered his address. However, try to say it the way it is presented here with all of its hesitations and markedly aberrant extra words punctuated here and there. I know that it's a bit exaggerated, but you will better understand my irritation and cause to reflect seriously on such a matter. Read it out loud. Yes, read it so that you will get the full implication of meaningless and useless words that do not belong there. They aggravate rather than soothe the flow of words. CAUTION: do not get upset and do not reject this writer's cautionary measure of good, well-constructed and refined speech that well- intentioned and particularly self-respecting individuals have. It's a matter of living one's calling to the role of being the receiver of the power of speech. It's a power that can ennoble or corrupt. Choose wisely. That is what education is all about. The formation of the mind, heart and soul together as a whole. The power words and good speech are part of that wholeness... **YOU KNOW**.